A FESTIVAL FOR THE MOON

A J RICHARDS

First Edition

Book Cover Illustration by Akar Studio
Book Cover Design by oliviaprodesign

ISBN 978-1-0670632-5-2 (Paperback)
ISBN 978-1-0670632-3-8 (eBook)
ISBN 978-1-0670632-4-5 (Kindle)

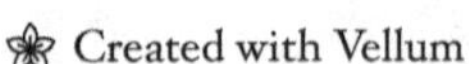 Created with Vellum

ALSO BY THIS AUTHOR:

Crown Your Head With Ivy

This novel is dedicated to Andy.
There's no one else I'd rather be with,
dancing in midnight fields beneath the moon.

CHAPTER ONE

"Watch out for that peacock!" yelped Leon. He yanked on the handle over the passenger seat so hard that I thought he would lift himself to the ceiling. I grinned and turned the wide steering wheel of our van, taking us on an easy loop to avoid the large brilliant-blue bird that had taken up residence in the long dusty grass on the left of the road.

"Calm down," I laughed at my husband as I continued guiding our small van down the winding dirt road to the campground. "I'm not trying to rally my way down here. The bird's going to be fine!"

Leon had the decency to blush as he lowered himself back into the seat.

"You could have fooled me, Ashleigh," he chuckled, before launching himself up again. "Watch out for that pothole!"

I laughed again. Leon was usually such a lovely and easygoing man. He was the sort of guy who took all manner of unexpected behaviour in his stride. But get him onto a winding road, and suddenly every one of his nerves started firing and all his panic and stress burst out of his pores. Despite his panicking, I did love him, and it was that love that meant I pressed on the brake a little harder, slowing the van as we twisted down the heavily rutted and worn dirt road.

"There you go," I smiled. "I hope that's better."

"It is, thank you," replied Leon. He lowered himself into his seat slightly.

Another sharp left and we were face to face with a car coming the other way.

"Whoops," I barked. I had to lurch the van to the left so that the other vehicle had enough room to squeeze by on the other side of the road. There was a soft thud from the large space behind the driver's seat.

"Whoops? Whoops? What if the stove came unhooked!? We could die in our sleep!" My husband's face was screwed up with anxiety.

I looked at the driver of the other car as he passed by, a thin man with long hair and a scraggly beard. He waved out the window of his low green station wagon. I raised two fingers off the steering wheel and lifted my chin in response.

"I don't think we are going to die in our sleep, Leon. For one thing, we aren't asleep. For another, we can always check that the stove has been reconnected properly once we get to our site."

Leon crossed his arms beside me. "I suppose that makes sense. But I don't want logic right now, I just want to be safe."

I reached over and squeezed his thigh. "Aw, my poor sweet baby."

"Bloody hell, hands on the wheel!" he squeaked. He grabbed my hand and threw it back towards the steering wheel. I shook my head and chuckled.

The dirt road curled around the steep hillside and wound lower and lower until it spilled into a green field. The deep ruts that we had been forced to follow split into a variety of tire tracks that spread apart like tree branches, leading off into unknown areas of the campground.

A temporary hut had been erected near the dirt road. A large hand-painted sign was wedged onto its side with the words

"Come Here firsT" splattered across it, so I drove the van over and parked next to it. The back of the van rattled as we bounced through the grass, and I knew Leon would be flinching at every sound.

"It's alright babe, we're nearly there," I said.

"Sometimes I just wish that these events could be set up somewhere that sealed roads lead to. A nice smooth and straight car ride is all I ask," he replied.

"Yes, I'm sure that would be enough to keep you satisfied your entire life, a smooth journey in a car for an hour. Then you'll never ask for anything else ever."

Leon laughed at himself again. "That's me! 'Never ask for anything' Leon!"

"Besides, you know that these events can't actually happen too close to civilisation. None of the right people would be there, all of the wrong people would come instead." I frowned. "Not to mention the noise control complaints and the light pollution." I wound down my window and looked out at the valley we had arrived in. "No, it has to be part of nature."

The valley was broad, a wide bowl set in the middle of a ring of low hills. I found it hard to imagine how far one would have to walk to reach those gentle peaks. They suggested deception, like a child with a secret, as though I might set out with the intent of climbing them for a morning hike but discover I still hadn't reached them by nightfall. The slopes were covered with dark green trees. At our end of the valley, where we sat in our van, the trees began to thin and gave way to an expanse of fields. At least two large creeks cut their way through the fields, and tents covered the ground in between the waters and the trees.

"I wonder where the stages are? You can't see anything from here," I thought out loud.

Leon leaned over to look out my window. Then he sniffed.

"In the trees I guess? More in the nature, like you said?"

"Come on, let's find out where we go next."

We climbed out of the van and walked over to the small hut.

Sitting on a rounded plastic chair outside the hut was a thin man wearing an unfastened denim vest and voluminous tie-dyed pants. His hair was greying and tangled and stretched down a little past his shoulders. He wore wraparound sunglasses and the short beard on his chin was beginning to show some of the grey that was already well-established elsewhere.

He gave us no sign that he had seen us as we approached. His slow breathing told me that he was probably asleep, and his feet twitched in small shuffling motions occasionally.

"Good morning," I said when we were standing next to him. He did not move. A fly landed on the hand resting on his lap, and he flicked it away. I leaned in a little closer.

"Excuse me? Good morning?" I said, louder this time.

"Huh, what?" he spluttered and sat upright. He lifted the glasses up from his eyes over his forehead and rested them on the top of his head. "Oh! Sorry, I was totally occupied with a dream there." He smiled and his green eyes sparkled. "It's always a pleasure to meet someone new!" He stood and I was shocked at how tall he was. The man was almost a head taller than Leon, and Leon was not a small man. The grey haired man stuck out his hand.

"My name's Roger and I'm the welcoming committee for Pandaea! Have you been here before?"

CHAPTER TWO

I took the tall man's hand and shook it. His hand felt bumpy. Heavy calluses scratched against my palm, while his fingers were surprisingly smooth. Then he turned and shook Leon's hand.

"I'm Ashleigh and this is my husband Leon. And no," I said, in reply to his question, "we've not been to this festival before."

"Virgins, fantastic!" Roger's smile was infectious. I found myself grinning in return. "Let me find your name on the list." He walked into the hut and came out carrying an old battered wooden clipboard with a thick wedge of paper tucked into the broad silver clip at the top. He flicked through the pages, flipping them over to hang precariously from the board. His eyebrows came together as he searched for our names. "Ashleigh, Ashleigh... Surname?"

"Murray," I answered.

Roger kept turning pages. "Ah ha, here you are! Yup, that's all good." He pulled a large green sticker out from the back of the clipboard and wrote the number one hundred and four on it with a thick black felt pen.

"There's not really a lot to let you know about, but everything important is here in this pamphlet." He turned around and leaned inside the hut to grab a folded piece of paper. I took it and opened it up, trying not to laugh.

The pamphlet had clearly been put together by someone who had very little familiarity with technology. At least fifteen fonts assaulted my eyes, and some information was explained in short bullet points, while at least one full page consisted of a single long rambling block of text. There was a map on the back that had the look of something official and so I would have to hope that it was as reliable as it seemed.

"You need to display your registration sticker in your vehicle," explained Roger. "That's how we know that no one got in unofficially."

"Is that really such a problem out here?" asked Leon as he took the green circular sticker with our number on it. It had a crescent moon on it, and a small artistic constellation of stars in the middle. My critical mind immediately noted that it's impossible to see such stars in the circle of the moon, even when it appears as a crescent. The shadowed side of the moon would block them out. *That's not the point,* I had to remind my critical brain. *It's just a lovely symbol of the festival.*

"After all, it took us almost two hours to get here, and a good chunk of that was along gravel roads through the bush," continued Leon. "Surely no one is going to accidentally wander into this festival?"

Roger's face grew stiff. It was only for a second, and then his smile returned. "Maybe some people didn't want to pay and register though. And although we are a welcoming crowd, there's still costs involved. Not fair on the others if we just let anyone in, is it?"

Leon nodded. I could see Roger's point. Even if the organisers were happy to just allow anyone and everyone to come along if they wanted to, there were costs involved in hiring acts and setting up equipment way out here. I could see why they would want to make sure attendees had contributed by buying a ticket.

"You can see on the map where the campgrounds are, where the stages are, where the bathrooms are." Roger bobbed his head in an apologetic way and grimaced. "Now, it's important that you know the toilets here are longdrops."

Leon blew a blast of air out his lips. "I hate longdrops."

I nodded and tucked an arm through his. "Me too babe, but you knew what we were getting into here. It's a festival way out in the middle of nowhere, did you think they'd have installed full plumbing?"

"No no, I know." Leon's mouth was set in a line.

Roger nodded. "I know how you feel, man. The smell isn't the best. You'll see that's why they're a long way from the stages and stalls. Not many people end up camping down that end either, at least not unless the rest of the site is packed."

"Speaking of that, where do we camp?" I asked.

Roger shrugged genially. "Go find yourself a space!"

We said our goodbyes and got back in the van.

"He seemed nice," said Leon as he clipped his seatbelt on.

"Yeah, I hope everyone here is that nice."

"Do you think Daphne and Dai are here already?"

"They left before we did, so I hope so. I was hoping we'd be able to find them in the campsite."

Leon picked up the pamphlet from between our seats and studied it briefly. "Babe. Finding one camp in all of this is probably about as likely as breaking your toe on a four leaf clover."

"Shush you pessimist!"

I drove the van over the fields between rows and rows of tents. Some were large domed things, looking like some sort of scientific exploration set up from a science fiction movie on another world. Others were little more than a tarpaulin hung over a rope that had been strung between a vehicle and a tree. People wandered through them all, wearing a riot of bright colours and flowers in their hair.

"It's even more of a hippie thing than I expected," said Leon as he watched three young men walk past wearing only long baggy cargo shorts and throwing a bright green flying disc from one to the other.

"Really? This is about what I expected," I answered, scanning the tents for Daphne and Dai. I knew they had a large green canvas tent, a solid room that could withstand all sorts of weather. Dai was hard enough to convince to come camping at the best of times, so Daphne had to invest in something that was as close to a cabin as possible if she wanted him to ever go with her.

"Not that I have any problem with hippies, I just want to get myself in the right headspace. I feel like this is going to be a bit trippier than some of the other festivals we've been to."

CHAPTER THREE

*L*eon's comment made me think of some of the other summer festivals we'd attended. Some of them had been little more than a group of people camping near the same beach and with a low key market set up in the middle. But others had certainly more focused on the all night dancing , to the extent that other revellers had looked at me like I had grown antlers when I suggested meeting up with one another during the next day. Sundown was time to rise for those people. Others had been all about public interactive performance art, and that brought its own terrors for my shy little husband. But I had to agree. From what I had seen in the advertising for the Pandaea, and from the type of people we could see sitting on fold-out chairs beside their tents and staring up at the clouds with mouths hung slightly open; or lounging around on blankets and chatting slowly but happily with their companions, this festival certainly might be more trippy.

"Wait, is that them?" Leon leaned over the steering wheel to point out my window. I swore and slammed my foot down on the brake.

"Hey, watch it," he complained as he bumped against the dashboard.

I lifted a knee quickly, giving him a bit of a shake up.

"It's quite difficult to see where I am driving the van when some great lummox throws himself in front of me Leon." It was amazing how clearly I was able to speak with my teeth gritted.

"Oh. Oh sure, yeah, sorry."

Now that my husband was suitably chagrined, I turned my head to see what he had been pointing at. A large green and brown tent was erected in the next row, tied down with what might have been the sort of monstrous ropes that tied cruise ships to dock. Yup, that was probably Dai's influence.

"I think you're right, I'll take us around."

"Wait wait wait, what was that you said?" Leon cupped a hand behind his ear.

"I said, I'll take us around, you don't expect me to drive through someone- Oh haha, very funny."

I reached over and squeezed my fingers on either side of his mouth so that his lips puckered out, a bit of revenge for his teasing. "Yes, alright, I understand. I said you were right. It's true, you can be correct sometimes."

I was surprised how long it took to drive along the lane of tents we were already between, get to the end where the field dipped away in a sudden slope to a creek beneath a bank covered in drooping dark trees, and then to get all the way back up the next lane. When we finally pulled in next to Daphne and Dai's giant canvas cabin, I had to assume that a full hour had passed.

"Funny how it can take ten minutes to get from right there to over there, huh?" laughed Leon. Okay, maybe it wasn't an hour.

"It's a pain in my opinion, but we're here now. Let's go say hi."

We climbed out of the van and went over to the entrance to our friend's tent.

"Hey guys, we made it!" I called as I approached, but there was no response. "Guys?

"If they're not here, can you spot anything of theirs?" Leon had pursed his lips. "I'd hate to find out we've parked on someone else's spot."

I leaned over to the cooler and some of the other equipment that was stacked near the door. Luckily, there was a very distinctive cap sitting on top of it.

"Yeah, it's them. Dai got that hat at the Stormweaver's gig, remember? And then immediately dropped it in the crowd, which is why it has that shoe stain on it?" I pointed out the dark smudge that traced the shape of a simple sneaker tread.

"Cool." Leon crossed his arms and looked around at the nearby tents. Despite it still being quite early in the morning, the tents were much quieter than I expected.

"Where is everyone?" I said out loud, not really expecting a response.

"It's the first day, right? Maybe they're all still on the way in to the site?"

"Some people set up last night."

"Why didn't we?"

"I didn't think you wanted to be here that long." I raised an eyebrow at my husband. "And I'm pretty sure you had to help set up the markets and toilets and stage and everything if you arrived yesterday."

"Good call babe, you know me well. Shall we have a cuppa then?" Leon walked back over to our van and opened the sliding door on the side.

Inside the back of the van was our home away from home. A mattress took up the vast majority of the space, but a series of cupboards and shelves had been built into every area that they could be fitted into.

I moved around to open the back of the van. The hatch was a broad panel that swung up and created its own small roof. In the back of the van, built under the foot of the mattress, was our water storage, a small gas cooker that we could pull out, and a few plastic tubs containing the plastic and tin cutlery and plates that constituted our travel essentials.

I pulled out the cooker and set it on the grass behind the van, then started rummaging through the tubs for the hob kettle. While I dug through purple plastic cups and surprisingly fragile forks, I spoke to Leon.

"Could you go and find out if there's any water taps? I figure there has to be, but we need to know if it's drinkable."

Leon didn't answer, so I looked up. He was lying on his stomach on the mattress in the van, with his hands hanging over the edge, propped up on his elbows above me.

"What are you doing?"

"Seducing you." He rolled over and away from me and tossed his head back, spreading his legs.

"You what?"

"Don't you find this all extremely seductive?" He tossed his head once again, pushing his fingers through his hair and hanging his mouth open like a duck.

"What is that expression?"

"It's what they all look like on the fashion shows, isn't that sexy?" He popped his lips open and shut a few times, making a popping sound.

"No. Now would you go check the water?"

"Seriously though, come on in here." Leon laughed. "We don't know how much alone time we're going to get, so let's take advantage of it now!"

I looked around the nearby tents. They were all quiet enough. I shrugged and climbed up from the ground. I pulled the boot closed and headed around to the sliding door and climbed onto the mattress next to Leon, whose mouth was grinning so wide he looked like a muppet.

"Alright, let's see what you've got," I said as I pulled the sliding door closed behind me.

CHAPTER FOUR

*L*eon reached out for my shoulders and pulled me towards him, laying my body along his. He stretched his face forward to kiss me. It was a familiar kiss, one that soothed me and sent flickers of electricity along my shoulders and arms. I pressed myself closer to him, seeking the closeness of his body.

I lay on top of him, my legs resting outside his, enjoying the feeling of holding him beneath me. His hands moved on my back, fingertips tracing around my shoulders before sliding up my neck to move through my hair. All the while he kissed me slowly and deeply. His lips felt soft and warm, his tongue dancing with mine.

Although we moved slowly together in the small space of the van, I could feel the tension beginning to build between my legs before I knew it. I began to move my hips against Leon, grinding forward, and I could tell by the way his lips flickered towards a smile and his breath gasped that he knew how I was feeling. My breath came faster now, and the space inside the van filled with the warmth of our bodies. The air pressed around me, its heat mixing with the warmth of my cheeks. He pushed a hand down between us, tucking it under my stomach, easing its way into my pants.

I sighed as his fingers found their way inside my underwear, tickling my hair, nudging the small hardness of my clit. He cupped the back of my head with his other hand, renewing the force of his kiss, as he began to roll his fingers in small circles over me, building up from a slow rhythm. I tried to stay with his kiss, but the tension was rising towards my chest, and it was hard to breathe. The air felt hot and humid. I looked down at my husband through heavy eyes. He stared back up at me, his eyes fierce and focussed. I moaned as his fingers continued to move over and over me.

He frowned as he tried to move his hand further inside my pants, but found that he couldn't move his arm the way he wanted. I reached down and undid the button, then started kicking my pants down until they were bunched at my ankles. Leon helped me get them the rest of the way off with his feet and then kicked them aside, never stopping the movement of his hand.

Now he rolled me over in the small space, one arm behind my shoulders. I could feel the muscles in his back shifting as he repositioned himself and then I gasped as he slipped his fingers inside me.

His shoulders moved like a machine now, with power and rhythm, as his fingers drove into me, reaching the places inside me that overwhelmed my mind. Electricity sparkled along my stomach, and I felt myself beginning to shiver and spasm in response to the feelings he was evoking in me.

"Yes," I panted as sparks burned their way to the ends of my fingers. I dug them into him, imagining that we were melting together as my fingers pressed deeper into the surface of his body.

Leon slid his fingers out of me, leaving a yearning space that begged to be filled. The low light in our van was still dimmer than before. There was a metallic clatter as he undid his belt and shoved his jeans down to his ankles.

Then he rolled on top of me and I felt the hot hardness of him pressing down. He reached down and moved himself against me, slipping between my lips, pressing against my entrance.

"Are you ready?" he whispered.

"Fuck me now," I growled, pulling at his hips.

He slammed into me in one solid movement, stretching me further than his fingers had, sending a torrent of golden electricity up my spine and erupting from my mouth. My eyes were on fire, and he began to pound against me. I was going to explode, blue lightning was going to run all across my skin, and sparks were going to tear the van apart.

The rhythm built, faster and faster, and I clutched at Leon's arms. His muscles were tensed and pressed against my sides, holding me pinned beneath and between him. He squeezed his arms around me tighter, holding himself closer to me. The movement made my breasts move, brushing against him through my tee shirt, sending zaps of sensation through my nipples.

I pulled my heels against the backs of his thighs, pressing him into me faster, harder. The crackling energy he was bringing to me leapt along my limbs and made my back arch, my head toss. Then, suddenly, the explosion happened deep in my core and every muscle grew tight. I wrapped onto Leon, binding myself around him. I felt him shudder and jerk and bury his face in my shoulder. Together we tried to meld ourselves into one creature as the pleasure spread and enfolded us.

Then, as the sensation subsided, we reluctantly released each other and rolled away. The air in the van was still as hot and heavy as a greenhouse, and I felt a sheen of sweat across my forehead and cheeks.

"Phew," panted Leon. "You felt really good today."

"You did too love," I smiled. Leon moved to roll into my arms and rubbed his chin against me. A moment later he rolled aside again.

"You know I love to cuddle up with you, but it is way too hot in here now."

"I agree. Let's get our clothes on so we can open this thing back up."

We pulled our pants back on, which is made much more difficult when lying on a mattress with shelves overhead in the back of a van. Then we slid open the side door and relished the burst of cool air that flowed inside, relaxing our hot skin.

"Nice to see you guys got here safe and sound," said a voice from a couple of metres away.

Daphne was sitting on a fold-out camp chair facing the van and sipping from a small green can of soft drink. She smacked her lips and smiled.

"Uh, hi Daph," I said. "How long have you been there?"

CHAPTER FIVE

"I've been sitting here long enough that I was about to knock on the door and let you guys know that we were back, but then the van started to rock," Daphne answered my question. She took another sip from her soft drink. "And we all know the saying. I figured I'd just wait for you out here."

Leon coughed to clear his throat. He was always a bit more awkward about things like this.

"It's so good to see you," I said as I walked over to hug Daphne. "How has it been? You got here last night, right?"

"We helped set up some stalls and mark out a few paths yesterday. It's been fine. Nice to meet some of the other people here, for sure." Daphne gestured to an empty chair beside her. "I can smell him on you, you know."

"Sorry," I laughed. "These things happen!"

She smiled. "They do. But maybe we should show you guys where the showers are, and then take a tour of the place?"

"The showers? I thought the toilets were long drops!"

"The toilets are, but some people apparently wanted showers, so they've done what they can. Dai will be back soon, then we can go."

"Where is your man anyway?" I asked.

"We met some cool people who are camping down that way a bit." She pointed back along the lane of tents in the direction we had driven up. There was a huge tree in the middle of the field, with a few tents clustered beneath its branches. I assumed that was where Daphne was gesturing. "He said he was going to go have a chat with them, then come back soon. We played cards with them over a few gins last night."

"Cool! Nice to already have met some of the locals. Shall we go over and say hi as well?"

Daphne shrugged. "Why not."

Walking between the tents in the midday sun felt wonderful. The sky was blue and bright and punctuated by puffs of white cloud. The breeze carried the scent of the bush on the hills that surrounded the campsite, and smelt like earth and leaves and grass. I twirled around with my hands outstretched. Leon laughed and grabbed me, planting a kiss on my cheek.

"Seriously you guys! You just finished, are you really ready to go again in the middle of the road as well?" chuckled Daphne.

Leon blushed and I laughed again.

We reached the campsite under the tree where Dai was supposed to be. It was quite an impressive encampment, more than I would have expected in a place like this. A few small one or two person tents were planted around the outside, clearly only used for sheltered sleeping by some of the group who had set up here. But in the middle of the space was a huge gazebo, and three massive tents were connected to it. There were almost no gaps in the structures, and I imagined a person would be able to walk through most of the site without leaving the large tents and the makeshift corridors.

"Dai! Are you in there?" Daphne called out.

A few heads poked out of door flaps in the tents, though none of them were Dai. All these heads were covered in long, thick hair. Some of them were even gathered into dreadlocks. Most of the men had scruffy beards, though others were more carefully groomed. Only one was fully clean shaven, but stubble was already making itself known on his chin.

"Hey Daphne!" called out a tall red haired man. He walked out of the canvas structures and strolled over to us with wide open arms. He was only wearing a pair of cargo shorts. He gathered Daphne into a huge hug that wrapped around her like a blanket and then softly shook her from side to side. "It's so good to see you guys have come back already! Who have you brought with you?" He released her and turned to look at me and Leon.

"These are some of my best friends, Ashleigh and her husband Leon."

"It is an absolute pleasure to meet you both!" Before I had a chance to reply, the tall man stepped over to us and took us both into a single large hug. His face was buried between ours as he breathed in deeply through his nose and then he stepped back but left his hands on ours shoulders.

"You smell like sex!"

"What?" spluttered Leon.

"You've just had sex, right?" The man's smile was just as pleasantly broad as it had been when he saw Daphne had arrived. His naked torso was only a foot or so away from me. I was suddenly very aware of the way his nipple had brushed against my shoulder in that hug. I stepped a little further away and cleared my throat.

"No need to feel self conscious, it's a great way to celebrate arriving at the festival! I had sex as soon as I finished setting up camp here as well."

"They totally did," Daphne said, nodding her head towards me and Leon. " I waited outside their campervan until they finished." Daphne's eyes shone with glee as she made the situation even more awkward.

"Leave them alone Chris," shushed another voice. A short curvy woman with thick dark hair clipped close to her head walked up alongside the tall man I had to assume was Chris. She smiled at me. "I'm Siobahn and Chris is my partner, unfortunately."

I smiled at her in return. This felt like some solid ground for me to reclaim my footing on after Chris had knocked me off balance with his direct observations. "I'm the one he had sex with," continued Siobahn. Maybe I just needed to get used to being off balance.

I snuck a peek at Leon. He looked as though he had just swallowed an entire cabbage and still thought he could get it down his throat.

"It's lovely to meet you all, our friends said you keep a cool camp here?" I was hoping that by skating right past the sex references, we could try to have a normal conversation quicker.

"Yes, these are all our best friends. We always attend the Pandaea together." The short woman grinned, and her teeth shone. "Unfortunately we can't all get to other events all at the same time, so we don't get to share our space much. The Pandaea is the one place where we can really let our hair down!"

"Whoo!" Chris whooped and jammed a fist in the air. He stood there with his arm held up and his smile wide as he looked around at our faces. "Am I right?"

We all looked at him for a moment, and then Siobahn ushered us into the gazebo. A moment later Chris lowered his hand and followed us in.

CHAPTER SIX

Inside the gazebo, Siobahn's group had laid a tattered mat spread across the ground, creating a rudimentary floor. Small aluminium camp tables were set up on either side of the mat, with a few heavy square containers of water, some snack food, and other useful camping items set on top. Sunscreen, bottle openers, a deck of cards. Siobahn pointed us to some folding canvas camp chairs and we all sat down.

"Would you like a drink?" she asked.

"Yeah, thanks, a drink would be lovely," I replied.

Siobahn turned to one of the tables and then returned with something dark in an orange plastic cup, like you might expect children to use at a picnic. After she gave me mine, she set about preparing one for Leon and Daphne. I took a sip and then coughed.

"What is this?"

"Just a little something I like to whip up while we're out of the house. It's mostly rum, but there's a few secret ingredients too."

"Mostly rum?" Leon coughed as well. I could see his eyes watering from where I was sitting, but he took another sip. "It's rocket fuel!"

"I just think of it as my special camping treat." Siobahn slugged back a half full plastic tumbler of the drink and then poured another and handed it to Chris. He knocked that one back in one gulp as well.

"Did Dai have one of those?" asked Daphne. "That would explain why he didn't reply when I called him."

"Might he be getting a massage?" asked Siobahn.

"A massage?"

"Didn't we tell you about the massages yesterday? We offer sensual massage to festival goers." Siobahn pointed through the corridors that led to one of the large tents connected to the gazebo.

I caught Leon's eye. They twinkled back at me and he winked.

"Sensual massage you say?" I asked, trying not to sound too excited by the idea. "And how exactly does someone sign up to get one of these?" I took another sip of the rocketfuel I was holding, and then shook my head until my vision returned. It had only taken mention of sensual massage for me to forget just how potent that stuff was.

"I'm so glad to hear you are interested!" Siobahn clapped her hands and grinned. "We're going to put a sign up this evening in case anyone is walking by and wants to come in. That's the way we usually get things going, but we are willing to work any time of the day!"

"I'm so glad to hear it. To be clear, what exactly does a sensual massage involve?"

"Lots of massage oils, incense, and your choice of masseuse, depending on who is around. We aim to take our time and really loosen all your muscles."

"That sounds good." And I wasn't lying, that did sound like a nice experience. I could feel the goosebumps on my arms settling down though.

"And then, if you want, we give you a happy ending."

My goosebumps returned with a vengeance.

"I see!" I caught Leon's eyes again. He had raised his eyebrows, but I could tell by the small tilt to his smile that he was very interested in what he had heard.

"We find that the massages are very popular," said Siobahn, grinning again. I suddenly had a vision of this curvy short-haired woman with oils dripping from her hands as she ran her fingers across my body. It made me squirm.

"Do you want one?" she asked me.

"Not at the moment," interrupted Daphne.

I could have killed her with one of the plastic tumblers

"Ashleigh and Leon haven't even caught up with Dai yet, so we are looking for him," continued Daphne, without a care for what she had done to my little fantasy.

"Of course! And you thought he might be getting a massage?"

"He better not be getting a massage!" Daphne's eyes flashed.

"Are you uncomfortable with sharing your sexuality?" asked Siobahn. There was no judgement in the way she spoke, just curiosity.

"It's not that," replied Daphne. The way she managed to keep her eyes on Siobahn as she answered that question without so much as a flicker towards Leon or myself was laudable. I almost applauded. "It's just that we haven't discussed this at all, and it seems like something that we should both be aware of."

"That makes a lot of sense." Siobahn leaned over and placed a hand on Daphne's knee. "You let me know when you have discussed it with him, and I'll be happy to take care of you."

Daphne blushed. It was delightful.

"But that doesn't answer the question of where Dai is?" asked my husband.

"Hold on while I double check," said Chris. The tall man stood up and walked over to the massage tent. He ducked his head inside and I could hear him muttering to someone inside. Then he came back over. "No, no one is getting a massage at the moment. Jenny and Tom are going at it though." He directed this last statement at his partner.

"You go ahead, I'll help these lovely people find their friend."

Chris nodded and leaned low to kiss Siobahn on the cheek and then walked back over towards the tent. He was already undoing his shorts as he stepped into the tent.

"Where else do you think your husband might have gone?" Siobahn asked Daphne.

"I don't know! He said he was going to come over and say hello to all of you here in this campsite, but that wasn't very long ago."

Another man came out of one of the other tents. He had long thick dreadlocks, and he was also only wearing a long pair of shorts with large pockets.

"Mati, have you seen this woman's husband?"

The man stopped and stared at us for a moment. Then he sucked in a deep breath through his nose and rubbed his stomach. The hair on his stomach and chest was blonde, which made it harder to notice, but very thick.

"Short guy. Glasses? I think he was wearing some sort of hawaiian shirt?"

"Yes, a dinosaur pattern," confirmed Daphne.

The man nodded slowly and rubbed his cheek.

"Yeah, I think Rania took him to the swimming hole."

CHAPTER SEVEN

*L*eon and I followed Siobahn and Daphne as the short woman led us through the campsite to the swimming hole.

"So the swimming hole is actually this really nice beach on the edge of this lake through the bush on the far side of the valley," she told us.

"I didn't know there was a lake in here," said Leon. "I was checking the online maps for the directions and I didn't see anything on there."

"Were the directions reliable?" asked Siobahn innocently.

"Mostly."

I had a sudden memory of Leon complaining that it turned out the roads in the map on his phone were actually paddocks full of cows. There had been one moment in our journey to the festival where we had agreed that the maps were clearly wrong and it would be correct to turn onto a narrow dusty gravel road on our left instead of continuing forward. After twenty minutes of bumpy driving we had stopped in front of a broad locked metal gate. An ancient piece of wood covered in white paint was tied onto the gate, with the word "No eNTrY" splashed across it.

We had turned back before there was any chance of banjos starting up.

"In any case, you can argue about the maps to your heart's content once you're swimming through the water."

"And you can show us the layout of the festival while you take us there," I added.

"Gladly! First things first, there's the water sheds."

Siobahn pointed off to the right past the last rows of tents. Some of these final tents looked much more comfortable than the rest of the campsite. They had thick wooden poles supporting them, and I was sure that the lanterns hanging in the corners of the huge structures were powered by electricity. I wondered whether there was a generator in the site, or if the lanterns used batteries.

Beyond the edge of the camping area, and set a fair way up a slope, was a large old tin shed. A couple of four wheeled farm bikes were parked alongside, watched over by a wide shouldered man with thick wavy brown hair that rolled all the way down to his backside. He wore a heavy ex-army jacket and jeans and I stared at him wondering whether he was hiding a layer of sweat beneath all that clothing, or if his glands had been overworked until they finally gave up.

A series of white plastic pipes protruded from the shed and led to a series of small one person huts that lined the slope in front of the shed.

"Those are the showers. Gravity fed, and the hot water doesn't last long, but when you really need to get clean, they're there."

"Surely they could have set up some flushing toilets with all that water," grumbled Leon.

"But flush it to where?" asked Daphne. "This is the middle of nowhere."

A narrow dirt track led between the water sheds and the camping grounds, clearly well used by some sort of vehicles judging by the twin tyre tracks that rutted the ground. The track led to a tall line of trees with a gap chopped in it, a shadow archway like a cartoon train tunnel. The passage reminded me of something from an old English fairy tale. It was lined by roughly shaped branches and trees opening to make a small path into shadows.

On the far side of the trees, we discovered the festival stalls, covered in streamers and colours and full of all sorts of people. I had to stop and admire them all, both stalls and people, because they overwhelmed my senses.

To the right was a long u-shaped area of food carts and old fashioned wooden stalls, selling all manner of food, hot and cold, vegan and meat based. Clusters of wooden benches and an assortment of odd-sized tables filled the space between the stalls, and at the far end was a caravan with a massive red cross painted on the side.

To the left were market stalls, gazebos, and a small stage with a tall pole in front of it. Stretched out from the pole were dozens of thin ropes, strewn with multi coloured triangular flags. It was like a tall thin circus tent, but with no walls. A young woman wearing a flowing white dress sat on the stage, strumming a large harp and singing softly into a microphone. The song was slow and light and sad, and the grass in front of the stage was peppered with people swaying in time with the music.

And the people! I was amazed at the styles and colours that they were wearing! Men wearing animal costumes in such extremes as pink fluffy unicorns, or more realistic half animal costumes with fur and horns. Men and women both with faces painted in bright yellows and reds and greens. Some of the body painting I could see was a costume of its own, adorning people whose skin was decorated in the scales and colours of dragons and so many other animals. Others had just painted themselves in patterns and rainbows. Bright wigs were common, and a cluster of people just outside the edge of the stage were spinning hula hoops around their waists and arms. One woman had at least five hoops going at once around various parts of her body. I was mesmerised as I watched her.

Seeing all these people dressed up made me wonder what they were like outside the festival, back in the "real world". I couldn't believe that this was how they presented themselves out there. So which version of them was the real one? Were they actually the person dressed in grey, catching a bus to their downtown office job, or was the pure version of them the colourful costumed version dancing in the summer sun here? Was the real world the diluted shadow of their real self?

"This way," said Siobahn cheerfully, and she led us past the stage and through the market.

"You helped set all this up yesterday?" Leon asked Daphne as we walked by.

"Yeah, it was actually really tricky to get all the vehicles pulling the caravans and food carts and stuff in through that path in the trees. If we got one in the wrong order there's not much room to turn around, so we'd have to back everyone up again and start again."

"You did a good job. It's all even more fascinating than I had expected when I signed us up!" I told her.

As we walked through the market, I investigated the goods for sale. There were a lot of clothes, light breezy things generally, in bright colours. But then there were also stalls full of crystals and carved wood and earrings. An older woman sat at the back of another stall, with a sign at the front advertising palm and card readings.

I stopped at one stall covered in dream catchers and woven wall hangings and necklaces. The table at the front of the stall was covered in a line of glass vases that looked as though they had been half melted onto blocks of wood that still bore the knots. I picked up one of the necklaces from the display to the side. It was a black cord, with a web of silver metal at the centre, shaped like outstretched wings with three deep blue crystals hanging from them.

I lifted the necklace and let it dangle from my fingers.

"Do you like it?" asked the thin older woman behind her display table.

CHAPTER EIGHT

"*I* do like it, it's stunning," I breathed in response to the woman. The necklace really was amazing. Something about the thin strands of metal that connected the points of the web made me think of the connections between all the people in the world. It was those connections that fired my curiosity in life. I was always talking to people about their relationships

"What are the stones?"

"They are all moonstone. Do you know anything about moonstone?"

"No. Is it special?"

"It's a stone that grounds its owner. Handling it connects you to your core, and keeps you from being led astray."

That does sound good, I thought. I undid the clasp and hung it around my neck, flattening the web against the skin of my chest. It felt cool and refreshing, like a gulp of icy water from a tall glass on a summer's day.

"It suits you babe," said Leon.

"It does!" agreed the stallholder. "It is also fifty dollars." She smiled.

"Fifty dollars!" I tried not to sound too shocked. "What's the metal made of?"

"True silver," she said. I raised an eyebrow. "Truly, it is! I'm afraid I don't have any documentation to prove it though. Would forty five be acceptable because of that minor deficiency?"

I ran a finger along the necklace again and then caught Leon's eye. He sighed and rolled his eyes and then dug into his pockets.

"Just cash I guess?' he said as he pulled out his wallet. The woman nodded and smiled. "Here you go then." He handed over a purple fifty dollar note and the woman pulled a small tin box out from under the table then handed him some change.

"Satisfied?" he asked me as we continued to walk through the market.

"Yes, very," I declared. Then I grabbed him and kissed him solidly on the cheek. "I have the best husband in the world!"

I fingered the thin chain as we left the stall. I wouldn't normally be worried about something needing to be pure silver, but it did make me feel as though the necklace was more special. Making something pure was so difficult. Everything in the world was made of mixtures, one thing blended with another, until it was hard to tell what the original even was. I was a mixture of so many different things. But when I was alone in the middle of a quiet night, sometimes I wondered what a pure version of me might be. I squeezed the chain.

Halfway through the market was a broad covered area, filled with tough outdoor beanbags. A long low wooden bar was set up in the shade, and a variety of drinks were being served. A dozen men and women were slumped across the beanbags or stretched out on the grass, dozing in the midday sun.

"They've been going hard already, it looks like."

"They've been to the Pandaea before. They know that it's worth resting during the day if you want to really enjoy the nights." Siobahn walked into the bar and ordered us each a vodka and lemonade. The glasses were dropped in front of us, clinking with ice and with beads of condensation welling on the sides.

"This looks pretty nice for a festival in the middle of the bush!" said Leon.

"I helped get the ice machine hooked up to a generator round the back," said Daphne as she took a sip then sighed. "It's not a big one."

"No, today is the best day for a drink like this." she continued. "By this evening they will be serving the odd ice cube in random drinks, and the mixers won't be cold anymore." She took a long sip. "Which is why we are having these now."

"It's got to be after five o'clock somewhere in the world," I said, then held out my glass towards Leon. He lifted his and tapped it against mine, nodding his head in a salute. "Cheers babe!"

We drank together.

At the far end of the market was a strange circular enclosure made out of tall wooden planks. It had a big gate in it.

"What is that?"

"I don't know, Dai helped get the thing up. Lots of swearing and yelling was involved, I can tell you that much," Daphne chuckled. "Siobahn, what is it? It looks like a big holding pen, for keeping animals in or something."

"No no, it's a rave."

"What?" I was curious how a ring of planks stuck vertically upright was a rave.

"Come and see." Siobahn took my hand and led the way through the meandering crowd to the enclosure. Once we reached the gate we found a DJ set up with his turntable, one hand clutching a headphone to the side of his head. Inside the enclosure, eyes closed, arms raised, spinning and swaying across the churned up grass, was a small crowd of people. They all had bright yellow headphones on.

"He's playing the music on their frequency, so they all hear the same music, but we don't."

"I'd feel so self conscious if I was doing that," said Daphne.

"It's almost like a performance art piece," I breathed. I was watching a woman in a long green and yellow dress spin sensuously near the entrance. "We observe them, and get to see all the magic of human rhythm. But they have volunteered to be a part of the display, and they get to express their own rhythm within it."

Siobahn walked up beside me and put an arm around my side, then leaned her head onto my shoulder.

"I could tell that I liked you," she said. Then she turned to Daphne. "I understand what you mean. It can be confronting to have your movements observed by others. Are they judging you, are you moving in a way that others appreciate, did you do something wrong?"

Daphne nodded. Siobahn smiled.

"I think you should come back here at night. When the lights are low, it can be much easier to forget about the rules and expectations that the world puts on us. When only the moonlight illuminates, your deepest self can be released."

Her eyes were wide and bright, and I felt slightly embarrassed to be watching the way she and Daphne were looking at each other. Daphne's lips had fallen slightly open.

"What's through here then?" asked Leon. He was walking towards another thick wall of trees with a broad entranceway carved into it. He was trying to keep a casual expression on his face, but I could see by the way the tips of his ears turned red that he was just as embarrassed by being an unnecessary witness to the connection between the two women as I was.

Siobahn turned to him with a wide grin. She bounced on her feet and clapped her hands. I pulled my eyes up and away from the motion of her tee shirt.

'That's the main stage! Come and see where we will hold our revelries!" She stepped forward and took Leon's hand, pulling him after her like a rowboat being towed by a large yacht.

Daphne shook her head.

"You doing alright there?" I asked.

"Mmm Hmm."

"And you were upset that Dai might have had a massage, huh? What's all this then?" I teased.

"Nothing!" Daphne snapped, her eyes widening in shock. She bobbed her head a little. "I mean, there was something there. But it hadn't happened before, I wasn't expecting it!"

"It's alright, I didn't mean anything by it." I reached over to give her a quick hug. "Come on, let's see what that young vixen is doing with my husband!"

CHAPTER NINE

Siobahn had led Leon under the heavy branches of the next row of trees and through an archway that appeared to have been slapped together with plywood and duct tape. In the daylight the wood looked fresh and rough cut, and the nails and bolts that were trying to keep it up had been punched into the wood haphazardly. The wood was so new and clean that it looked very out of place beneath the rough barks and twisted branches of the bush around it.

I could also see strings of wire were wrapped around most of the beams overhead. They looked like they were christmas lights.

Daphne and I followed the other two up a short rise, walking in the middle of a deep dusty trough. A soft cloud rose around our ankles. The dust was surprisingly thick, and with each step my feet sank into it like we were walking across dunes at the beach.

But then we reached the end of the wooden passage at the crest of the track and spilled out into a broad grassy basin, with a huge stage built to one side. Even though it was barely past midday, there was already a knot of people dancing in front of the stage. Thick slow deep bass thumped in the hollow basin.

"This place is great! How come we couldn't hear them in the bush just there?" I almost had to shout to be heard by Siobahn. I waved a hand at the track we had just emerged from. Around us, groups of people were settling down into the grass, rolling back and forward to really get comfortable and then laying back with arms behind their heads, or draping onto each other. It looked exquisite.

"The hollow is a wonderfully isolated area in the bush, it just swallows up the noise without a trace. That's part of why the festival was set up out here. We knew that it would be completely contained."

We wound around the back of the dancing crowd and studied over the stage as we walked by. It too looked as though it had been constructed by some enthusiastic dads over a weekend. It was made of lumber that was surprisingly clean to be holding up a wide metal structure for the lights that were rigged overhead, and a curving bank of speakers at either side of the stage.

In the middle of the metal structure overhead, a huge deer skull had been cut out of metal and attached somehow. Its antlers splintered away from the narrow eye sockets and jaw like lightning, stretching wider and higher than I would have expected in a natural deer skull.

"Is that skull so over the top on purpose?" I asked.

"What do you mean?"

"Those antlers seem like they have to be symbolic."

"Symbolic of what?" asked Leon.

"Maybe someone was compensating for something," shot Daphne, and he snorted.

"They are meant to carry some of that sort of symbolism," admitted Siobahn cheerfully. "But you should never overlook the fact that sometimes these things just look cool."

We all laughed as we began to walk up the far side of the basin and towards the edge of the bush on this side. I saw a peacock strutting up the slope behind the stage, heading for the trees. It had its huge tail up and spread, displaying bright glory to whatever it was facing. We were behind it however, exposed to the fuzzy grey-brown feathers of its backside, and I had to giggle. It was just like the rest of us, thinking that we displayed something spectacular to the world but keeping something so sad hidden behind.

The path through the bush on this side was much less obviously marked than either of the previous paths had been. There were no obvious archways cut into the branches, no wooden walls or decoration set up for attendees of the festival. Instead Siobahn wandered along the treeline for a minute, muttering to herself.

"Is something wrong?" asked Leon.

"Not wrong, I just can't remember where we go in…"

A young couple appeared in the bush, winding beneath the thick trees, moving around a trunk shockingly close to us. It was as though that had materialised behind a tree barely ten metres away from us, and then walked out and into our sight. They were holding hands and laughing.

The man was wearing loose jeans and leather sandals and a loose deep green button up shirt that helped him blend into the undergrowth around them. His hair was black and thick, bound into a number of short dreadlocks bouncing around his shoulders. He let go of the girl's hand and lifted it to drape over her shoulders. She was a broad shouldered woman with thick fiery hair that rolled like waves of fire down over his arm. Even from outside the bush, I could see that her eyes were a piercing blue.

The pair strolled towards us through the trees and waved to Siobahn when they saw her.

"I am so glad to see you two," she grinned. The short woman bounced up to the newcomers and gathered them into a huge hug. "I couldn't find the track to the swimming hole."

"What?" snorted the woman. She frowned and opened her mouth to say something to Siobahn but then she caught my eye. "Oh. Hi there." She turned and held a hand out to me. "My name's Sarah, what's yours?"

"I'm Ashleigh, it's nice to meet you," I replied and took her hand. Her palm felt rough and strong, and her grip was tight.

"Have you come to the Pandaea before?" She let go of my hand and stepped over to shake Leon's hand as well. The man with her stepped up and murmured that his name was Logan. His gaze stayed low, as though he couldn't meet my eyes.

"No, it's our first time here. So far it looks so amazing, all the people camping out in the fields, all these markets and stages." I gestured back across the wide basin behind us, the tall stage pounding distant rhythms, the small crowd that wound in front of it.

Sarah nodded.

"I'm so glad you're here." She touched Siobahn's shoulder. "You can see the path now. We'll catch up with you in the mellow tent, okay?"

"See you then."

Siobahn watched Sarah and Logan walk away for longer than I expected before turning back to the forest.

"Is something the matter?" I asked. "Did she say something wrong?"

"Not at all," came the chirpy response from our guide. "Nothing wrong at all!"

CHAPTER TEN

The path through the bush darkened quicker than I had expected. A shiver shot down my spine as cool air ran over my exposed skin. The sunlight that had warmed us in the campsite was hidden overhead now. Leon stepped up beside me and touched the small of my back with his hand, and even Daphne stepped closer. The track to the swimming hole turned out to be little more than a well beaten path between the tall thin trunks of the trees, and it could become hard to spot beneath the spreading leavers of hundreds of ferns. Creepers of some sort grew up most of the trunks, sprouting small off shoots of leaf and branch that flapped in our faces, and hid the way forward.

Birds fluttered overhead, and their calls bubbled up from time to time, but the walk was very quiet.

"It is so sheltered in here," said Leon. He squeezed my hip softly.

"That's why we're here!" said Siobahn from a few feet ahead. Sometimes she would turn a corner, or step around a tree, and suddenly be gone from my sight. I looked behind me at the path we were coming along. It was just as hard to see from that direction. I wondered if we would be able to find our way back to the campsite if we lost Siobahn.

To our left, the bush began to fall away down a steep bank. At the bottom, I could see a faint trickle of water that may have flooded into a creek at some points of the year. Rocks were exposed through the dirt, and clouds of tiny black insects were humming across the rivulets of water. A huge tree had slumped sideways without quite falling, lifting thick roots out of the dirt so that we were confronted with a gorgon's head of wood to our side, thick with spiderwebs and clods of black earth. The tree curled like a ram's horn where it lay across the meagre creek, trying to stretch back towards the very faint sunlight that cracked through the thick canopy overhead.

As we passed the tangle of roots, I saw Daphne lean in closer, placing a hand on one root which sank under her weight. She moved closer, eyes searching the darkness beneath the tree.

"Argh!" she shrieked and leapt away from the roots.

"What happened?" yelled Leon as he stepped past me. Daphne flapped her hands at her face and knocked a massive insect off. It must have jumped onto her cheek as she got too close.

I was right behind Leon, one hand on his shoulder as he crouched down next to where Daphne had dropped. He had a hand rubbing her back comfortingly, and he was telling her that she was okay, it was just a bug. But because I was standing back, I could see Siobahn on the path in front of us.

She was just standing there, one hand on her hip, watching us. She didn't come to see what had happened to Daphne. She didn't seem surprised. Her face was blank, unlike the smiling and happy person who had met us in the tents and led us through the festival site. She saw me looking at her and the smile eased back slowly, like a summer rain.

"All good?" she called as she began to walk towards us.

"Yes," said Daphne with a stuttering voice. "Just got surprised by a bug."

"It's a big fucker though, check it out!" said Leon, pointing down at the ground.

The bug sitting on the ground where it had fallen after being knocked off Daphne's face was an earthy orange colour, banded with dark muddy brown. Long thread-like antennae curved forward and then back over its thumb-like body. It was so large that I could see the big black bulbs of its eyes and I would have sworn it was looking at us. It began to crawl back towards the roots, thin spiky legs shifting one by one.

Siobahn looked down at it and then lifted a foot.

"Hey, it's just a wētā, leave it alone," I said, lifting a hand to stop her. "They're harmless, it just gave Daphne a shock. You'll be okay, right Daph?"

Daphne huffed but nodded.

Siobahn raised an eyebrow at me but shrugged.

"All right. Come on then, we're nearly there."

Around the next corner of the dark bush we found a wire fence leading through the trees and undergrowth.

"What's this?" asked Leon.

"It's the fence, don't worry about it." Siobahn followed the path as it turned to the left along the eight foot tall fence. It was held up by regular metal posts that were tarnished with rust. A wire mesh filled the space between each post and below a metal pole that passed along the top.

"Why is there a fence?" I asked. I thought it was odd that the fence would suddenly appear in the middle of the bush. There had been no sign of anything like this earlier. "When we were coming down the hill we didn't see any of this."

"It's fine! There's a deer farm or something like that in this valley, that's all."

"Oh." Her explanation would do, but it was strange that we hadn't noticed the farm on our way through the nearly empty dusty roads towards the festival.

A little further down the fence we came across was a section that had been damaged at some time in the past. Wire curled up from a corner of the fence, as though it had been peeled away by a giant hand. The gap created was extremely small, and tangled by the undergrowth, thin vines with thick green leaves and small white flowers weaving through its spaces.

"Shit, that's not good for the owner," said Daphne. She stepped up next to Siobahn and started pulling at the curl of mesh, trying to unroll it back towards the post. With her other hand she ran down the post, clearly trying to find how it was supposed to be attached.

"Do you think you can fix it?" I asked.

"Fix it?" Siobahn snorted. "This is the way to the lake." She motioned Daphne aside and then pulled the edge of the mesh open so that she could crouch down and duck through the gap. Once through to the other side she straightened up and shuffled a hand through her hair, flicking out a small twig that had become stuck there. Then she smiled and waved us forward.

Daphne frowned but followed.

Leon put a hand on my shoulder.

"Are you sure we should be doing this? It feels like trespassing."

"I know what you mean, but she seems so confident. All those others were talking about this swimming hole. I'm sure it's fine."

We followed, but there was a heavy feeling in my stomach as I dusted myself off on the far side of the fence. I looked back at the bush we had come from. Suddenly it felt as though it was another world, separated by a barrier thicker than the thin metal strands that made the fence.

CHAPTER ELEVEN

"Are you sure that we are allowed here?" I asked Siobahn as she led us along the new path.

"It's fine! The fence is really there for protection."

"What do you mean?"

"This farm lets people come in and do some deer hunting when the season is on, and they don't want people wandering through when someone with a rifle might accidentally shoot them."

"What?" snapped Leon. He grabbed me and pulled me close. His eyes started scanning the thick trees around us. "That's fucking dangerous!"

"And it's not how deer hunting works, at all!" added Daphne quietly, stepping closer to us. "I've never heard of any set up like that!"

Siobahn put her hands on her hips and laughed loudly.

"Relax! It's not the season, we're in no danger from the owner and his buddies!" She tilted her head. "We've been coming here for years and there's never been any whiff of trouble from him."

Timidly, we continued following her. I was becoming less enthused by our guide with every step.

We walked up a small slope where the trees began to thin, and then over a ridge. Beneath us the land fell away through scattered clumps of trees and long grass to the edge of a wide lake, so deep and blue that it was almost black.

Figures lay along the edge of the lake, soaking in the sunlight on grassy clay banks. A few were jumping into the water from rocky outcrops, and the surface of the water sparkled in the hot sun that had returned as soon as we left the shade beneath the trees. There was even a ramshackle corrugated iron shed at the bottom of the slope directly in front of us, one door hanging off its runners, revealing a shady storage space filled with kayaks.

"This looks lovely," I had to admit.

"I told you. It's fine. Come on, let's find your husband." Siobahn grinned, took Daphne's hand, and wound her way down through the scrub to the bank.

Three young men were playing some sort of game on the edge of the lake. A heavyset man in red shorts was standing on the edge, throwing a large ball out into the water. His hair hung down to his tattooed shoulders, and although he was a large man, his every movement revealed strong muscles that shifted beneath his skin.

The other two men, one small but broad shouldered, the other tall and thin as a nail, would dive into the water as easily as otters. They sped through the water, arms flailing and legs churning, until one reached the ball first and began to bring it back to the shore. Occasionally they reached the ball at the same time and began wrestling in the water, ducking each other beneath the surface of the lake and shouting and laughing together.

Dai was easy to spot. He was standing waist deep in the water, just off the clay bank to the right of us, water dripping from his chin. He was talking with a young woman in a bright multi-coloured bikini, occasionally dipping his hands into the water and splashing it up over his chest and shoulders.

"There you are!" cried Daphne from the water's edge. "Were you going to tell me that you were coming out here?"

"Daph!" shouted Dai. He glanced at the woman he was talking to, and then turned and began walking back to the bank. "Sorry, I didn't think about it! Rania was just showing me around the festival site. You remember everyone was talking about the swimming hole yesterday, right?"

"No, I don't remember that." Daphne had her arms crossed.

"Oh hey, hi guys! It's great you made it!" Dai waved at me and Leon, but I could see his eyes looked a little concerned.

"Hi man. Did you bring your togs?" Leon waved back at our friend. I wondered if he was trying to diffuse any situation between Dai and Daphne, or whether he just hadn't noticed. My husband was a sensitive soul ususally, but he could be obtuse sometimes.

"No, but I figured these shorts wouldn't get hurt by the lake. It's freshwater, you know?"

"Sounds good to me." Leon began pulling his tee shirt off and slipped his feet out of his jandals. Within a few moments he was ready to jump into the water himself. He went over to the ledge near the large man throwing the ball and jumped in where he had seen the other men jumping.

Dai clambered out of the water and walked over to hug Daphne, but she stuck out a hand on his chest.

"Not while you're still dripping wet! I don't want to get cold!"

"Sorry babe," he said, still smiling.

I decided to leave them to the conversation that they needed to have and walked over to where Leon was bobbing in the lake.

"How is it babe?" I called.

"Fucking cold!" he yelped back. I laughed and pulled my top over my head. I touched my new necklace for a moment, before I decided to lift it off and tuck it in with my clothes. Then I shucked down my pants and dove into the lake next to him, wearing only my underwear. He was right, it was bloody cold.

The water felt clean. I wondered if it was cleaning me of all the outside world that I had brought with me. Maybe when all the cares and concerns of the real world had been washed away, I would be left with the pure me, I thought hopefully.

After a short swim out into the deep and dark water, I began to feel nervous. Swimming in the lake was harder than swimming in the sea, like I was used to. The water didn't lift me up as well as salt water did, and I could already feel my arms and legs getting tired from the constant motion to keep me up. The darkness beneath my feet felt much deeper and unknown than it had looked while I was standing on the shore, watching people laugh and play.

"Come on babe, I think we should head back."

Leon's head was bobbing above the surface of the water nearby and he spun around to face me.

"Is everything alright love?" His eyes were concerned. "Are you too cold or something?"

"Sure," I said. The emptiness of the lake was getting to me, but it was cold too. I didn't want to make Leon feel weird just because I had a strange feeling in my stomach.

CHAPTER TWELVE

Once we were back on shore I scraped as much water off my skin as I could.

"You're looking good, in your soaked and skimpy underwear," growled Leon as he stepped up behind me and slipped a hand around to the front of my stomach.

"Oi, no!" I squealed. "You're cold and wet!"

"So are you!" and he bundled me into a slippery hug and lifted me off my feet while he kissed my neck. Then he popped me down again. "Are you just going to walk back like that?"

"I think I'll have to."

Daphne and Dai were still talking quietly, sitting together on a grassy lump further away from the lake. Dai had a hand on Daphne's knee, and she was smiling, so I hoped that they had worked through whatever the issue had been.

"Ready to go guys?" called Leon.

"Sure," said Daphne, and she pushed herself to her feet. Dai joined her. "Where's our guide?"

We looked around. The lakeside was covered in people talking, sun-bathing, reading, swimming. The quiet chatter of their voices was like a chorus of insects, and the effect was made stronger by the whistles and chirps of birds in the bush that covered the hills around the lake. Spotting Siobahn, with her short dark hair, amongst the crowd was almost impossible.

"We could probably find our own way back. It was basically just one well trod path the whole way, right?" I scratched at my wet hair.

"Yeah, the path Rania brought me along looked like one path. I reckon it'll be easy enough to follow." Daphne shot narrowed eyes at Dai when he spoke.

We decided to start walking back without Siobahn. The slope back up from the lake to the bush was clear and the path was easy to spot here. Together we slipped into the overhanging trees.

I nudged Leon softly and nodded to Dai. His brow wrinkled in an unspoken question, so I widened my eyes and looked at Daphne then back to Dai. My husband nodded and stepped up to Dai.

"So what did they get you guys to do yesterday? That stage looks pretty big. A lot of hammering and drilling, or what?"

The two men drew ahead of Daphne and I. I touched her elbow to slow her another step before I spoke.

"What's going on Daph?"

"What do you mean?"

"I mean, you clearly are annoyed at Dai. Is it about the bikini girl?"

Daphne rolled her eyes.

"I guess so, sort of."

"But I don't get it," I shook my arms, trying to remove more of the water than was making my skin so cold. I wondered how outrageous my nipples looked at the moment. "You guys have played with other people before. I mean, bloody hell Daph, we've played with you before!"

And the memories of those nights were some of my favourites. Nights spent rolling through the water of their spa pool, enjoying whatever skin I bumped into next. Nights where the four of us found ourselves together on a couch, nights where we moved into different rooms for private experiences.

Daphne smiled.

"Yes we certainly have!"

"Then why the hassle with him now? Surely it's no different if he's got a bit of a hard on for this woman?"

Daphne sighed and pursed her lips. She glanced at the men ahead of us on the path between the tall trees. The wind shook leaves above us, then she looked back at me.

"It's not that he might have the hots for her. I can cope with that. Hell, she looked like a pretty damn sexy woman, I get it. But he's been getting more distant lately."

"You think he'll leave you?" I was shocked at the implication. Dai's action showed that he was clearly obsessed with Daphne in my experience.

"No, not that he'd leave me. It's just..." Daphne cracked her knuckles. "He doesn't talk to me about anything. He just sort of lets things happen, and hopes that I don't mind. He was going out with some friends a few weeks ago, and I knew there was this woman going who he's played with before. I asked him whether he thought he might end up fooling around with her that night and he just shrugged."

"Did anything happen?"

"He says it didn't, but it's so hard to tell with him like this at the moment. He doesn't communicate and now I feel like maybe he's hiding something." She looked at me and I could see that she was twisted up inside. Her eyes were full of anguish and doubt. "We've been able to enjoy ourselves with other people because we communicated so well. How can I continue if he makes me feel this way? I'm not sure if I can trust him."

I put an arm across her shoulder.

"Oh sweetheart. It sucks to have this sort of thing bubbling up from inside you. But you can't let your feelings stay bottled up inside. It's when things are repressed and held in that they destroy you. They'll turn you into someone who you aren't, or at least someone you wish you weren't."

Daphne turned into me and we paused on the dusty track to have a proper hug. I squeezed her shoulders and she tucked her face into my shoulder. From the way she sank into me and held on longer and longer, I knew she must really need it. Eventually I pushed her away a little so that I could speak to her properly, looking at her.

"You need to tell him that you are feeling this way. Don't make it about how he makes you feel, blaming other people for your feelings always puts them on the defensive. But if you say what's going on for you, hopefully he'll understand, and you guys can get things sorted out."

Daphne snuffled and nodded. Her eyes were looking red with tears that hadn't quite come forth. I smirked and tilted her chin up a little.

"Who knows, maybe he could invite that hottie back to meet you both?" I winked at her.

She laughed, and then scrubbed at her nose with the back of her wrist.

"Yeah, that could be fun. Thanks Ash, I didn't realise how much I needed someone to talk to, who would understand."

"Hey, you know we love you guys!" I bundled her back into a hug again before we continued after the boys.

CHAPTER THIRTEEN

*J*ust before we got back to the gap in the tall wire fence, there was an open clearing in the trees like a much smaller version of the basin that the stage for the festival had been set up in. White trunks jabbed up from the slopes around the edges, stripped of leaves. I assumed that they must be dead trees, looking like strange fungus reaching up and out of the ground.

As we walked through the long grass, Dai lifted a hand and motioned for us all to be quiet. He and Leon slowly crept back to me and Daphne, without turning their heads to look at us.

"What is it?" she whispered for her husband as he got close. He flapped his hand at her and hissed softly.

"What?" she whispered again, even quieter.

"Can't you see them?" he breathed. Still facing away, he lifted a hand to point towards the edge of the trees, where the undergrowth filled with darkness. I followed his finger, trying to see what he had seen.

Then I spied three deer watching us from behind some low bushes. Two bright bodies, their fur such a pale cream that it was almost white. They were delicate and had no antlers, so I assumed they were female, though I had no experience with deer at all. Somehow the dappled shadow that fell across them enabled them to still hide effectively, despite the lightness of their fur.

Between the two does, a buck held his head high and stared directly at us. His fur was as shining and pale as the females, and the twisting pure white spikes of his antlers were something out of a dream.

"They're beautiful," breathed Daphne the moment I saw them.

"How did they get here?" asked Dai.

"Didn't your new friend tell you?" asked Leon. "Siobahn said that this place is a deer farm or something, and the owner sometimes lets his mates come in and go hunting for them."

"Hunting?" Dai jolted and began searching the trees. "Are there hunters in here?"

"No, she said that they don't come up when the festival is on," laughed Daphne. She stepped up and slid her hands around his waist, kissing him on the shoulder. He lifted a hand to cover hers. "No need to worry, you doofus."

"Glad to hear it!" he said.

We stood in the middle of the clearing, watching the deer for an eternity that was probably only a minute or two. They looked so serene, and unaffected by our presence. They were something from another world, creatures that had stepped out of a dream and had not yet succumbed to the mundane mixing with our own world. Then they shook their heads and walked stately back into the bush. The buck waited until last, watching us as his women left, and then bobbing his head in our direction before he went.

"Lovely, aren't they?" came an unexpected voice from behind us.

I turned, expecting to see that Siobahn might have caught up with us, but instead of our short bubbly dark-haired guide, it was another woman. She was no taller than Siobahn, but her hair was thick and curly and she wore a loose white blouse and fabulously loose and swishy green pants.

"Yes, beautiful animals," said Daphne. "It's so cool to see them as you walk through here."

"There's more around than you might think," said the newcomer. "My name's Mia. The deer are thick in this farm. It's almost a kindness to know that the hunters come up here."

"It sounds cruel to me," said Leon. I blinked and touched his elbow. I didn't realise that he would feel sorry for the deer here.

"What do you mean?" asked Mia.

"They're just trying to live their lives, but they've been trapped in this farm, fenced in, and then sometimes people come with the only purpose of killing them? Sound cruel."

Dai nodded. "I get it. When you describe it like that, it does sound a bit creepy."

Mia smiled. Her teeth were blazingly white. "I hadn't considered that point of view. But aren't we just as fenced in?"

"In the valley?" Dai's forehead wrinkled as he tried to follow the woman's point.

"I thought the fence was only around the lake, the deer farm?" I added, seeking clarification.

Mia's smile faltered and fell and she stared at us both in turn. She looked confused that we didn't understand her.

"No." She frowned. "I mean, in our real lives, we stayed fenced in just as badly as those deer. In our jobs, and our lives. You know what I mean."

The four of us nodded. Of course, we totally knew what she meant now. Wasn't it those same boring lives, following the usual paths that everybody else wanted to follow that had led us to jumping at the chance to come and attend this festival, the Pandaea?

"That's why we're here," I said, nodding. "We're getting outside the fences that we've been living in."

Mia smiled again, and her eyes sharpened.

"Now you're talking my language! Come on, let's go see who

else is ready to jump over the fences in their lives. Who is ready for some excitement!"

She tucked her arms into Leon and my elbow's and the five of us continued along the path towards the festival.

Before long we came out on the edge of the stage basin again. Extra stalls and covered areas had been set up at the back, far behind the crowd that danced in front of the stage. They were covered in striped material, red and white and green, and I could see big boxes being stacked inside them. The sound of the bass from the stage was thick in the air, soaking into our ears. I had to lean closer to Mia to make myself heard.

"What's in the boxes, do you know?"

"Water, quick and easy food. The sorts of things someone needs when they've been sweating and moving all night and need to replace some nutrients. It's a tiring workout having fun out here!" She grinned.

We paused for a moment to put our wet clothes back on, and I slipped my necklace under my shirt. We walked down the slope but curled around to our right, avoiding the thickest clusters of dancers. On the stage a woman in skintight silver clothes and a tall bush of dark brown hair was bouncing in time with the beats that she had chosen, one hand lifted to encourage the crowd to move in time with her.

CHAPTER FOURTEEN

We moved past the dancers and up the slope at the far side of the basin and back through the arched path under the trees to the stalls and markets beyond.

The crowd here was thicker now. I wasn't sure of the time, but I guessed it was almost two in the afternoon. I wondered what events would happen as the evening drew in. I was positive that a festival like this wouldn't leave its celebrations to chance!

Mia gave us a quick hug.

"I'm going to have to leave you. I want to find my friends before the parade."

"There's a parade?" I asked. I could feel my own eyes widening in anticipation. I bit my lip and smiled "What sort of a parade?"

"Look around you, what do you see?"

The four of us did as we were instructed. Milling around the silent disco and the other stalls we had walked past earlier were the crowd of festival goers. Body paint, fluorescent clothing, loose tie-dyed pants and vests.

"I see a bunch of people having a good time," I said, confused.

"No, I see it," said Leon. He leaned in next to me and pointed. "See, there's deer people everywhere."

I followed his finger and realised that he was right. More than half of the crowd had some sort of deer costume on. Most wore little headbands like kids would wear at christmas, with small brown antlers made out of some cheap soft fuzzy material. Some had facepaint on, to create the brown dappling of a deer across their cheeks, or the dark nose.

Others had gone much further. Artistically crafted sets of antlers that rose tall over their head in dominating displays. I couldn't imagine how those people weren't tottering left and right, tipping under the dramatic headpieces, or simply being squashed by the weight. Were there hidden support structures beneath their clothes that led down to their shoulders or backs?

A full deer costume walked by, clearly borrowed from a theatre. It was the sort of two person costume where the person in front got to walk upright, while the back half of the deer was walking bent over, clutching the waist of their partner.

"What's the deal with all the deer?" asked Daphne. She and Dai had their arms around each other, so I had to assume that they had got over whatever weird jealousy had caused them to be arguing earlier.

Mia turned to look at the couple, her tongue licking along her lip as she did. It slipped back inside her mouth and she scratched the back of her arm. Then she shrugged.

"This is a festival that takes place alongside a deer farm. I think this land used to be part of the farm too. I guess people thought it looked cool. Anyway, each year the festival begins with a parade before the real events begin in the evening. Enjoy the show!" She waved and walked away towards the tents at the market end of the campsite. Soon she had vanished between the canvas peaks and domes, thin black guy ropes criss crossing the scene like spiders' webs.

"I guess we should go find a good place to watch the parade then?" asked Leon. Daphne and Dai nodded.

"Come on, let's try out that stage we saw earlier. It would be a good place for someone to make announcements from." I said.

"Not the big stage in the hollow?" asked Leon, thumbing back in the direction we had just come.

"Can you imagine that lot stopping the music in order to hear someone talk when there could be listening to more beats? I think this will be some sort of speech-making occasion, and that lot just want to groove their brains away for hours still."

Leon smiled and he nodded.

At the far end of the stalls, next to the food carts and caravans, the stage with triangular flags hanging from a pole in front of it was now fronted by a large crowd. Most of the crowd were wearing the same deer headbands, and some were costumed more elaborately. A group of women were walking through the crowd and searching for anyone without a costume, and offering cardboard antlers to wear.

"No thank you," I told one woman with wavy grey hair as she looked at me. She smiled as she shrugged and moved on.

"What's the matter Ash, are you suddenly not cool with parties?" asked Dai. He was slipping a set of the crayon coloured antlers onto his head, pulling at the stapled-on rubberbands to settle them onto his head, and he looked absolutely ridiculous.

"Check out my mighty stag," laughed Daphne. "Isn't he a treasure?"

"He is!" I smiled at our friends, but then I moved closer to Leon and put an arm around his waist.

"Is something wrong?" asked my husband, leaning in protectively over me.

"I don't know," I said quietly. I was feeling disconnected from the crowd, and my stomach was tight. "There's something going on that makes me want to go back to the van. Maybe I just need some alone time."

"That's not like you." Leon squeezed me softly. "We can't go now, they're clearly just about to do this whole thing. Afterwards we can go back to the van for some quiet, alright?"

I nodded and dug my fingers into his arm.

"Welcome young and old! Welcome travellers! Welcome to the Pandaea!"

The voice that came crackling like thunder out of the huge speakers on the sides of the stage was deep and sonorous. It sounded like the sort of voice you might expect to hear rolling out of an animated walrus in a children's movie. And the figure emitting the voice looked exactly as I expected, with broad round shoulders and a thick bushy beard. Even from the back of the crowd that were gathered in front of the stage, I could see the man's eyes glittering.

"The Pandaea has come around again!"

The crowd cheered and whooped.

"And you all know exactly what that means!"

"Actually, I really don't," said Leon into my ear. I chuckled. "I mean it," he protested. "This was all your idea for a get away, I don't know what this Pandaea thing is at all!"

I realised that I didn't really know much about what the festival was for either. I had seen the website and the social media advertising, I had shared it with Daphne and we had talked about how it looked like such a fun idea, but I didn't know what Pandaea meant.

"There were a lot of moons and, like, spiritual geometry symbols in the advertising," I told my husband. He raised an eyebrow.

"Yeah, good, but what does that mean when it all comes down to it?"

I shrugged.

CHAPTER FIFTEEN

The crowd certainly acted as though they knew what the big man on stage meant, and there was a tension in the air over them. They were cheering and whooping, but it was contained. They wanted to hear what the round man had to say. And they were moving, heaving like fish schooling to the edge of a net, pushing up against the stage as though they wanted to take it over.

"That's right! It's time for the rangale to make itself seen!" The man lifted a thick arm and spread his fingers, making a crude antler shape in the air beside his head. Most of the crowd copied him, spreading their fingers in the air.

"What's a wrangle?" asked Daphne.

"I have absolutely no idea, but these crazy fuckers love it," said Leon.

And they really did. The crowd were partying and whirling like spinning tops, bouncing off each other as they careened around. There wasn't even any music coming through the speakers. However, the crowd stomped their feet into the dirt, they clapped and drummed against the wooden poles around them. A rhythm was definitely in the air.

"Is Dawn ready?" asked the man. He lifted a hand to shade his brow.

Down in front of the stage was a woman wearing taupe body paint and very little else. The shape of her body was very very clear, even from where we stood at the back. She didn't wear an antler headband, but instead her mousey brown hair had been lifted and twisted and teased into a set of small antlers extruding from either side of her head.

She tapped the ground with her feet and rolled her figure sinuously. Then she lifted a thumbs up to the man on stage.

"That's wonderful! Alright everyone, if this is going to beat the record from last year, then we need to track it properly! Follow Dawn through the rangale route and then when you come back to the stage, we'll have some cones set up. Walk through the cones one at a time so we can get a record of you. Let's see if this year's rangale is bigger than ever before!"

Without another word of explanation, the lithe woman in dappled paint spun and began jogging away in front of the crowd. The mass of people followed her like a swarm of insects, and once she had established herself in a leading position she slowed down. The swarm eddied away like thick mud, clumps swirling in place for a long time as the bulk slowly slowly moved away.

"Come on," said Daphne. "You were right that they were starting here, but who knows where they are parading now. let's see if we can watch the procession from somewhere else." She led us away from the stage in the opposite direction, moving us down between the market stalls towards the silent disco. Through the gazebos and customers we could see the parade of antler-wearing festival-goers on the far side of the market.

There were so many of them, matching along arm in arm, with huge smiles on their faces. Most of them only wore the small antlers that they had made earlier in the stalls, or had given to them by people wandering through the festival. Those partici-pants wore all sorts of clothes, from baggy shorts and loose tee shirts, to long flowing rainbow coloured dresses. Then there were those who had really done their best to dress as deer, to fully embrace the strange costume parade. They were bright and covered in fur, with elaborate constructions reaching over their heads. Children wove between the legs of the crowd, laughing and chasing one another. I hugged Leon's arm.

"We should have found some antlers ourselves," I said. I was feeling a strong desire to pretend that I was something different to myself. If I hid the version of myself that I presented to the world, I might happen upon the real me in the process.

"I did!" exclaimed Dai exasperatedly. "Look!" He pointed at the simple antlers on his head.

"You did," I admitted. "Maybe you should be in the parade."

Dai stuck his tongue out at me and then laughed.

"There's still time for the rest of us," said Daphne. "Look over there."

Walking through the market near us was a broad man with small glasses on and short blonde hair. He had a line of the simple antler headbands hooked over his arm and he was offering them to people as he walked by.

"Shall we then?" I asked the others. Leon shrugged, while Daphne nodded. Dai rolled his eyes exaggeratedly.

"Obviously!" he said.

"Come on!" I grinned.

I led the way to the man and eagerly snatched up the headband he offered, pulling it onto my head and tucking away the loose hairs that tried to escape. I turned to examine the others, as I helped Leon pull his high enough that it didn't try to fall down over his eyes. I had to cover my mouth not to laugh at the floppy pale blobs that were the hastily crafted antlers on his band. He raised an eyebrow.

"You look great!" I gasped and then I grabbed his hand and pulled him between the stalls over to the parade side of the market. The four of us dove into the crowd and were welcomed with high fives and happy shouts.

We followed the parade down past the high fence of the silent disco and wound almost to the archway through the trees that led to the huge dance stage. But instead of walking through and into that wide space, the parade turned sharply and followed the treeline for a while, leading past smaller stages and covered spaces. I tried to peek inside as we walked by, but it was hard to see between the bodies around us, and there was no chance to stop. The press of others around me kept me moving.

"Do you guys know what's in there?" I asked Dai and Daphne who were keeping pace with me.

Daphne shook her head, but Dai nodded.

"Yeah, there's a few small dance spaces, meditation tents, performance art, exhibits. It's all really interesting!"

"How do you know that?" asked Daphne.

"Rania showed me some of them on the way to the lake," he replied. I glanced at Daphne and saw the corners of her mouth stiffen.

"We'll all have to come back and have another look later," I said, trying to avoid any arguments right now in the middle of the parade. It was hardly the place for a careful unpacking of behaviours and preferences.

Dai jabbed a thumbs up and Daphne just sighed.

CHAPTER SIXTEEN

At the end of the large tents that we couldn't get a good look into the parade curled around in a small glade on the edge of the bush. As we followed the others through the tight circle, I looked out into the forest and noticed people standing there, watching us. There was something unpleasant about them, but I couldn't tell what made me think that. They sent a shiver up my spine.

"Who are they?" I asked.

"They look like creeps to me," muttered Leon. "Just standing there, staring at us."

He was right. The figures were spaced out between the trees at random distances, but never together with anyone else. They stood motionless in the shaded space between the tree trunks, arms crossed, empty faces watching us.

"I feel exposed," said Daphne. I could see her shoulders shrinking down as she tried to make herself less noticeable in the crowd.

"It's okay babe, we can see who they are." Dai put an arm over her shoulder. "If one of them comes around being weird, I'll protect you."

It was true, the figures all had quite distinctive faces. One man had a long narrow nose, and a thin goatee. One woman's face was round and full and her green eyes were shockingly bright even in the undergrowth. They weren't wearing masks or costumes or anything. I felt as though I would be able to draw any of their faces with perfect detail, even though I wasn't particularly skilled as an artist.

"Look, the parade is continuing. No one else seems worried," Dai added. "Let's get to the end of this, get the wrangle counted, and then we can go relax at the campsite. I think we need a break!"

The parade ended up winding back up through the market stalls it had missed on the way to the grove and finally led back into the space in front of the small stage where we found the man with the loud voice was waiting. As we approached the stage we were asked to take turns walking through a set of ropes that defined a path along the front of the stage. By the time it was our turn, at least half of the parade had already passed along the path and were now cheering and dancing next to it. I felt my chest swell as my walk through the ropes and cones was greeted by hoots and hollers and triumphant fists in the air.

"That felt great! I said once I had had my photo taken and joined the others at the other end.

"It really did!" grinned Daphne in reply.

"Are we ready for that break?" asked Dai again.

"Sure," said Leon. "But after this big parade, I'm curious to see how big they go this evening?"

"Just wait until you see how much these guys like to dance," said Dai.

The break at the campsite had been enough to rest, have a drink, eat a simple dinner, and then Dai and Daphne had led us back to the basin as the sun was setting.

We could feel the throb of the dance stage from outside the basin. The ground rumbled with the bass of the pounding music as we walked up the dusty path to the ridge and looked into the basin. Giant walls of speakers faced out from the stage, outlined by fluorescent lights, and I could see them vibrating with the effort of drowning out the silence of the hills. The basin was filled with dancers, a sweaty swirling throng that twisted and spun and bounced and lept in time with the beats.

As the blue of the sky drained down the horizon and stars had opened their eyes, the music had wormed its way under my skin. Somewhere far ahead of me, standing on the stage, a DJ lifted their hands, guiding the crowd in their exultations.

I didn't know how long we had been dancing. My hands were tucked above my head, with my elbows stretched out beside me as I twisted my waist and twirled my hips. I could feel small beads of sweat rolling down my spine, though the night air was icy. I was overwhelmed by the press of bodies around me, and I couldn't stop the movement in my body that echoed the shifting bodies around me.

Leon appeared in front of me and I clutched at him as he passed through the swirling throng of bodies around me. Above us the stars shone brighter and brighter out of the inky black-blue night sky. A brilliant moon was just lifting over the edge of the hills in the direction of the lake, like some bone-coloured eye. The light wound over our bodies as we danced.

I caught onto Leon's arm and was pulled through the crowd, like a dolphin playing in the wake of a speeding boat. I bumped gently into revellers, meeting some of their eyes, catching some of their smiles and reflecting my own back at them. Leon turned and gathered me into his arms, leaning into me, his hands pressing into my shoulders as he kissed me. Our lips moved and I felt his tongue touching me. A shock ran through me, relishing the sensation that he enabled in me.

I slid my own hands down his sides, feeling the way his muscles shifted as he swayed with the music, the music that pressed in on us from all sides. My fingers moved over the ridge of his shorts and then curled around his ass, digging into his body. I moaned against his mouth at the feel of him.

Leon pulled back and grinned.

"This is one hell of a party Ash!" His eyes were full of stars. "This was a very good idea of yours!"

"I know," I grinned.

His eyes passed across the crowd around us. "Actually, what do you think about keeping our options open this evening?"

I pecked his lips again and then spun away from him.

"I think that sounds like fun. You can thank me later," I winked as I clapped a hand to my own ass.

"Oh I will!"

For now we drifted apart through the dancers, holding onto the memories of each other and lost in the ever moving moment that was now.

CHAPTER SEVENTEEN

Another body moved up behind me in the dancing crowd, close enough that I could feel each twist and sway as they danced. I turned around to find it was a young man with short black hair and a wide smile. His eyes were bright and he winked at me.

"You look stunning," he shouted, barely audible over the music.

"Thank you," I allowed, turning more fully so that we could dance together. His hands lifted to my hips as I moved them in a low circle, pressing myself closer to his legs. I let my hands drop around his neck, resting on his shoulders.

We stayed like that for longer than I could follow. At least one neverending rhythm changed before I became aware of his fingers tracing along the top of my skirt, softly moving across my stomach. I opened my eyes and focused on his face, a breath away from my own.

"Can I kiss you?" he asked, the cheeky smile never faltering.

"Yes please," I replied and I pushed forward to taste his mouth.

The experience of kissing someone new is one that I always enjoy, and doing so while surrounded by people who were all dancing and waving only heightened the experience. His lips were strong on mine, and his hands gripped me harder now, making me shudder. An ache rose in my core. I pulled my hands back so that I could rest them on his chest. I could feel one of his nipples under my palm, and I rubbed my hand against him. I was pleased to feel it harden beneath my caress.

"What's your name?" asked the man, his voice soft in my ear. I sighed as his breath warmed my neck.

"Ashleigh. What's yours?"

"Finn."

"It's a pleasure to meet you," I said and then I leaned in to kiss him again. My tongue dove into his mouth, trying to search through him and find each part. His tongue traced over mine, exchanging positions as I felt his lips move. My hands curled up around his shoulders. His muscles felt strong and the hardness of his bones was pleasing to run my fingers along.

Other bodies dancing in the field banged into me, pushing me from behind and beside, pressing my body against his. Briefly I opened my eyes and looked beyond his shoulder, where I caught multiple smiles watching over us. I smiled in return and arched my neck as Finn's thumbs pressed above my hips as he held me tight, controlling the movement of my hips, the rhythm that met him. We existed against one another in pure now, with no before or after.

His breath moved across my collarbone and my exposed throat, and my spine shivered in response. I breathed deeply. The droning thump of the bass in the music rose up to meet my sensations through my feet. Together we danced and kissed and held each other close as the moon rose higher over the gathered people.

Finn and I danced our way across the field towards the edge of the crowd. The air was colder here, despite the residual heat of the summer day. The thickness of the bodies in the crowd and the smoke in the air between them had insulated me and driven my body temperature higher and higher. But now in the darker quieter air of the edge, I felt my skin rise into goosebumps.

Finn took me by the hand and drew me out across the grass, moving towards the inky darkness that flooded the space beneath the trees that circled the hollow. Our shadows shot into the distance, outlined by the bright neon and twirling chaos that erupted from the stage behind me. Finn's fingers felt soft but strong and I followed him willingly.

As we stepped into the dark, Finn moved closer again, pulling an arm around my waist. His kiss was strong and sure, and he moved his free hand to my stomach, working his fingers at the elastic of my long yellow and blue tye-died skirt. I shuddered as the tips of his fingers pressed against my stomach and slid lower, creating an expectant pressure as they sought out the intimacy between my legs. I shifted my feet, so that he could move between my thighs, and sighed as his fingers reached my centre.

The movement of his hand matched the movement of his kiss, a steady rhythm that worked to build up the sensation inside me. The fingers of the hand on the small of my back curled and dug into my flesh. I felt myself falling lower, my muscles weakening under the contact and trembling that Finn was drawing from me.

I held onto him, wrapping my arms around his shoulders to keep myself standing. My eyes opened.

I was sure that I could see someone standing under the trees nearby, a black shape by the tree trunks.

"Wait, stop!" I spluttered, stepping back from Finn. I stumbled as his hand was caught in my clothing, and he nearly fell over into me.

"What? What's wrong?" he answered as he caught his balance. He stepped slightly away from me and pushed a hand back through his hair.

"I saw someone." But as I pointed to where the shape had been standing, light from the moon spread down through the branches and illuminated a clearly open space. "I could have sworn..." I began to walk forward carefully, investigating the space.

Finn moved up beside me, placing a hand on the small of my back as he turned his head, searching the grass and twigs that filled the space between the trees. There was clearly no one here. He turned to me and shrugged.

"I can't find anyone now," he said. I could tell by the tone of his voice that he was trying not to make me feel like I was seeing things. He stepped closer, his hands lifting to my sides. "Shall we...?" he let the rest of his question be asked by the movement of his head closer to me.

"Not here." I placed a hand on his chest. It felt strong and broad, and I let my fingertips brush down towards his stomach. "I don't want some creep watching me from the shadows while I get it on. I know somewhere that will be properly private." I took his hand and began to lead him towards the van back in the tents.

CHAPTER EIGHTEEN

s Finn and I walked through the campsite towards the van, it was comforting to see more lights all around us. Although there were no campfires allowed at the festival, most of the sites had one large lantern lifted high over the clustered tents, which provided a thick yellow light for the people who were sitting and laughing and drinking amongst them. I wasn't sure of the time, but it was certainly late enough that I was surprised how active the campsites were. Plenty of people were still socialising, playing cards, and dancing slowly in their own spaces. Most of the dancers were playing their own music, as the music from the dance stage couldn't be clearly heard past the treelines and the market. Finn and I exchanged smiles and greetings with more than one couple walking along the rows as we went.

By the time we had arrived at the van, I was feeling as tightly wound as a spring. Walking with Finn's hand resting on my back, occasionally stopping to steal a kiss before continuing, had only raised the heat inside me and sharpened my desire to feel more of his skin against my own. I was thrilled that the van was so near.

However, as we drew closer, I realised that the side door was open.

"It's ready and waiting for us?" asked Finn, but I knew that Leon wasn't the sort to leave the van open when we weren't in it.

The curtains that could be drawn to create privacy in the back of the van were half pulled, and I saw a leg lying on our mattress.

"I think my husband might have beat us to it," I said.

My eyes began to grow used to the shadowy interior, able to discern more of what was going on inside.

Leon was the one laying on the mattress. It was his naked leg that I had seen. His muscles shifted as he moved his leg around another figure that was lying on their front between his legs, and I could see their arms hooked around his backside, holding on to his hips.

The figure's head lowered towards Leon's legs, though it was hard to see what was happening in the darkness. From the movement of muscles, and the groans that leaked out into the night, it was clear that the figure was sucking on Leon's cock.

The sight made me think of Leon's cock in my own mouth and the memory was enough to make my lips tingle. The feeling of his skin inside my mouth, the way it felt when I curled my tongue against his shaft. I stepped closer, wanting to see how this other person was enjoying Leon's pride.

Now I could see a thick beard on the figure. It was a man taking care of my husband closely and thoroughly. The man's arms flexed and pulled Leon closer to him, his chin lowering as he opened his mouth wide to accept more of the cock he was tending.

Finn stepped beside me. "Should we still be here?" he whispered.

I swallowed thickly, my head swimming at the overwhelming sight of my husband laying with a man between his legs. I nodded a little.

"You're right. We'll go find ourselves another spot." I ran my fingers down my front, pressing them against my pussy. "Just a moment longer."

In the van, Leon had placed a hand on the back of the other man's head, his fingers tangling in the tight dark curls of his hair. He pressed the man closer, the muscles over his hips shifting and pulsing as he thrusted. I watched his skin pull as the man clutched at him, dark lines appearing where the man scratched his fingernails along Leon's sides.

Leon gasped and bucked, his mouth hanging open and his head lolling backwards. The man held on tight, focusing his attention on Leon's orgasm, not relinquishing any pressure or sensation until the paroxysm had worked its way fully through my husband. Then he slid upwards, allowing Leon's cock to fall from his mouth, before shifting up on the mattress to kiss my husband on the mouth. Their chins moved together and my husband ran a finger along the man's face.

Leon shifted until he was laying underneath the man now and reached deeper into the darkness of the van. When his hand returned, he was holding a condom, and he offered it to the man, who smiled. His expression glowed within the shadowed interior of the van.

"Alright," I sighed as Finn pulled me aside.

Together we walked past the other tents and found a small copse of trees. The campsites around it were dark and I wondered whether the inhabitants were asleep or elsewhere. Finn drove my thoughts from my head with his lips, his fingers, the feeling of his body against mine. As he slid his hand towards my pussy, the fire that had been smouldering inside me flared into full life again and I pulled him to me, kissing him hungrily. I wanted to feel him touch me, I wanted his fingers to slip along me and inside me and I shuddered as he did exactly what I wanted. I rubbed my hand along the length of him through his shorts, then began fumbling at the fastenings, my eagerness to touch him overtaking my coordination.

His shorts fell to his ankles and I thrilled at the feeling of my fingers wrapped around him. I pulled at him, feeling the skin moving over his hardness, enjoying the moans that wallowed in his chest. As I squeezed and tugged at him, I melted from his fingers that pushed inside me, reaching the places that liquified my muscles. We hung from each other's shoulders, connected by our mouths, lost in the satisfaction of each other's bodies.

CHAPTER NINETEEN

Finn and I leaned against a small tree as our hands explored each other's bodies. I shuddered and gasped as his fingers explored me and drew shockwaves of pleasure from my core.

"Do you have a condom?" I murmured.

"Yes, thank god," he replied, and he bent down to retrieve it from his shorts pocket. I shivered as his fingers withdrew from me, but the fire in my body continued to rage.

I turned to the tree beside me and leaned forward to rest against it. The bark scratched my forearms and I flinched, but I rearranged my arms on the rough surface and then braced myself. I wasn't going to let a little discomfort stop me now.

I heard Finn preparing himself behind me, and raised myself a little to make it easier. He pulled up my light skirt, and then pulled aside my underwear. The breath of the cold night air against my wetness somehow only served to stoke my flame. Then I felt his hardness press against me, opening me, driving inside me. My breath caught and I hunched my shoulders as he slid inside. I felt every part of him pressing deeper, reaching into me and soothing the raging fire.

As he put his hands on my hips and used them to drive

himself into me, the feeling of the rough bark and the cold air withdrew. I felt as though I was becoming smaller, becoming just my body around him, and the heat that burned and ebbed with his movements.

He increased his rhythm quickly, his fingers digging into my flesh, and the slap of his skin on mine sounded louder than a thunderclap. All I could see were the orange flames that swirled and danced from inside me, lifting higher and higher until they erupted from every pore of my skin. I shuddered and wilted against the tree.

Behind me, I could feel Finn still moving, hear the breath caught in his throat as he approached his own climax. I tried to will my body to respond, to help him reach a plateau as satisfying as my own had been, but I was so emptied that it was difficult to move. A few moments later, he stiffened and gasped. He was able to reach his satisfaction on his own.

Finn slipped out of me and we tidied ourselves up and then leaned into each other's bodies to kiss once more.

"Now that was a great evening," he told me, his eyes wide and serious.

"It was!" I laughed. "Maybe I'll find you in the dancing tomorrow too."

"If I'm lucky!"

He walked back to the van with me. When we got there, the doors were closed. I hung my arms around Finn's neck and kissed him softly and slowly.

"Thank you," I said, and I meant it utterly. "That was a wonderful evening."

"You're welcome," he replied. We parted and he walked away, waving slightly.

I knocked on the door to the van. There was no reply, and so I counted to three, waiting in case Leon still had his guest with him. Then I opened the door. Inside I could see a figure lying on their side, with a tangle of sheets around their legs. The thick smell of sex filled the small space.

I crawled onto the mattress and lay down behind the figure, leaning in to feel them, see them, smell them. I recognized my husband and cuddled in closer behind him.

"Hrmm," he murmured. He reached behind himself with one arm, touching my shoulder. "Ash?"

"Yeah, it's me." I could tell that he was not really awake. I thought it was sweet that his dreamy brain was acknowledging me.

"Good night?" he asked.

"Extremely," I smiled at the back of his head in the darkness. "And yours was too I saw!"

"Mmmm," he agreed warmly. "Love you."

"I love you too babe."

The morning sun found us hiding in our van before I was ready for it, heating up the small space and making me feel sweaty and sticky. Leon was curled around behind me, one arm along my side. His closeness made me feel a safe warmness in my belly, which was at odds with the heated flush of my cheeks and forehead. I groaned and shifted his arm so that I could roll closer to the sliding door and pull it open. A wave of cool fresh air rolled in and cleared my head in a moment. Outside, the morning sun was halfway over the hills and its light swam across the valley, peeking between the tents and cars that littered the fields.

I heard Leon mumble something as I crept out of the van and slid the door halfway shut. I paused and leaned closer so that I could catch what he was saying, but he didn't repeat himself. I smiled. My husband was so cute. I left the door a hands width open so that some of the cooler morning air could drift inside and I hoped it made Leon more comfortable.

Then I turned and faced the world beyond our little van. I stretched my arms high above my head and twisted my back, hearing small pops and cracks as the bones resettled after my short night's sleep.

"Tea. There has to be tea," I said to myself, and I turned to the tent that we had parked next to.

Dai and Daphne's tent was large and square shaped. I often wonder why they still used it, with its heavy poles and thick canvas, when so many campsites were now full of light dome-shaped structures. Somewhere in there my friends must have a small portable gas cooker, a plastic box full of teabags, and a kettle. All I had to do was find them all.

However, as I shuffled through the ankle length grass towards the tent, I noticed that its sides were shivering slightly. A muffled gasp leaked from the fastened door facing me. I grinned. *Sounds like I need to give them a little bit longer.* Instead of searching their tent for a cup of tea, I grabbed one of the towels that hung over the guy ropes to the tent. A shower might be a good way to get the morning circulation going, and by the time I got back hopefully Dai and Daphne would be ready for company.

CHAPTER TWENTY

The showers were blessedly quiet at this hour of the morning although I was surprised to see plenty of people moving back and forth in the avenues between the tents in the fields. Lots of bleary faces that nodded in my direction as I passed them, or carrying bundles of clothing for some reason. I wondered if I looked the same to them, and tried to pat down my hair just in case.

The showers were close to the arch in the trees that led to the market, slightly up a slope from the track. I climbed up the grass and joined a short queue of people waiting to take a turn in the small wooden shed that held the makeshift shower. From this spot up the hill I fingered my necklace as I watched the thick crowd of people that were returning from the dance stage only now that the sun was rising.

They wore bright fluorescent clothing, and leaned on one another as though they were the best and oldest of friends. I wonder how many had met each other while dancing through the night, or even had only met moments before I saw them as they trudged on weary legs back towards their tents. They were silent as they walked, but even from this distance I could see the smiles and joy that blazed off them like steam.

"But how did she get away?"

The voice came from just behind me. The person was speaking quietly, in a hushed and worried tone, but they were standing close enough that I could make out most of what they were saying to the person beside them.

"I heard that she kneed him in the goolies."

"Amazing how the classics are still worthwhile."

"Actually, from the way she described the guy, I'm amazed that it even had an effect."

The conversation drained the heat from my stomach. It sounded as though something terrible had almost happened to someone last night. I hated that. The festival had looked like such a positive place, and I had enjoyed everything I had seen yesterday. The thought that reality could intrude even here was deeply disappointing. I pressed my lips together and sighed slowly. *I suppose there's nowhere that a person can truly escape from the real world*, I told myself.

I refocused on the discussion happening behind me. The person who had heard the story was now describing the attacker, and the details they were using sounded unlikely.

"... tall, like maybe more than seven feet, and mostly skinny, but broad shouldered and strong."

"At least we'll know him if we see him."

I nodded a little to myself. Someone over seven feet tall would stand out like a lone tree on a plain here.

"She said he was extremely hairy, a full beard, shaggy hair, and hairy all over his arms and chest too."

"Easy to spot."

"That's what I thought. If we keep our eyes open, we might be able to point him out and get him kicked out of the festival."

A little joy warmed my heart at the thought. I found myself hoping that these two would be successful in finding the culprit. If he was tracked down and identified, then the festival would be safer for everyone. But if they didn't find him, or if someone else didn't get rid of the guy, then I would spend the rest of my time here watching over my shoulder and feeling uncertain. I thought of my encounter with Finn the night before. I had met him and quickly led the way into the darkness alone with him, and if I had realised that the festival was just as dangerous as the real world, I might not have been quite so eager.

I looked out across the sea of tents that filled the fields, domes of lightly fluttering grey and blue and red material, occasionally punctuated by pyramids and cubes in more muted taupe and caramel tones. In the midst of the tents were irregular small copses of trees poking up and providing some shade for those who had claimed the sites beneath their branches early in the festival. I retraced my steps with my eyes, following the path I had woven to reach these small wooden sheds, with steam leaking from the haphazard boards nailed up to create walls. It wasn't difficult to find which way I had come, and then I could see my and Leon's van. As I watched, the door slid open and a figure climbed out, stretching his arms over his head and twisting his back. I was familiar enough with my husband's morning routine that I could imagine exactly the sound of the bones in his spine clattering back into place.

I wondered if he would see me if I waved. The queue around me shuffled forward, and I stopped paying attention to Leon as I stepped along. There were only two more people before me in the queue, though the number behind me had grown immensely.

I looked back over to the van and Leon. The conversation that was still muttering behind me reminded me of my tryst with Finn last night, and I sent my gaze searching along the campsite, looking for the tree that we had propped ourselves up against as we fucked. It took me a moment, longer than I had expected. I realised that I had been turned about and confused in the darkness of the middle of the night. There were two or three sets of trees that looked like they might have been close enough to the van to be the ones that we used. I had to think about the shape of the shadowy branches that hung over me in order to figure out which it was.

Eventually I was quite sure that a thickly twisted tree left of my van from where I stood was the tree where I had shagged the young man I had met last night. I also found the campsite of the massage group, where Siobahn and her friends were set up. Three thick trunked trees loomed over the cluster of tents there.

A hand jutted past my shoulder.

"There, "I'm pretty sure she said it was by those trees."

CHAPTER TWENTY-ONE

The couple conversing behind me had moved slightly closer, and one of the women was pointing out where the creep who had attacked her friend must have made his move. I shuddered at the thought, but then followed her finger so that I could see the location for myself. I wanted to make sure I wasn't anywhere near his known haunts. I wanted to make sure there was a whole festival between me and whoever it had been if at all possible.

But then I realised that the finger was pointing straight at the same gnarly tree I had just determined was my own location of interest.

"Hey!" I spun around. The two women behind me stepped back, and their eyes widened in shock.

"What?" barked one of them, a short woman with shoulder length red hair that was bundled to one side. She wore a loose blue floral summery dress. "Did I bump you or something?"

"No, I just-" I shook my head to refocus. I pointed out at the trees. "Were you just pointing at that twisty tree?"

"The twisty-" The woman leaned forward to look along my arm, glancing at me as though I was a strange animal that might snap at her if she let down her guard. She blinked and then straightened up again. "Yeah, that twisty one. Why?"

"So, you're saying that there was a horrible guy attacking a woman at that tree last night? Like, early in the night?"

"I don't know... I think she said it was later on. She was on her way back to the tents after some dancing when she bumped into him."

I stared at her and a cold feeling expanded in my stomach, as though I had swallowed a lump of ice. Some monster had been hanging out near the same tree I had fucked someone I barely knew, and possibly at around the same time. I wondered if he had been watching me and Finn as we explored each other, getting his rocks off to the sight. It made me feel sick.

"Are you okay?" asked the other woman. She reached over to touch my shoulder.

I nodded but rubbed my mouth and then shuddered again.

"I think I was out by that tree around that time of the morning."

"Shit!" the first woman pressed a hand to her face. "I'm glad you are okay!"

"I just hope someone finds the bastard and gets him out of here."

"Yeah, it's tainted my whole view of the festival at the moment. I'll be keeping my eyes open way more," said the second woman.

There was a creak as the door to the shower shed was pushed open and a skinny man with long dreadlocked hair stepped out, wrapped in a faded towel. He smiled at me and gestured towards the steamy space inside the shed.

"Hey, thanks for the information," I said to the women behind me as I moved forward, ready to clean myself. Suddenly I felt even more grimy than a night of dancing and outdoors sex would normally leave me feeling. I wondered how hot the water in this shower could go. I felt as though I would need to sluice myself in bleach.

"You're welcome," said the red haired woman. "We've all got to stick together."

When I got back to our van after scrubbing my skin as hard as I could, the other three were sitting around on their folding camp chairs, sipping at tin mugs of tea and coffee. The kettle sat on a small gas stove to one side, though it had been turned off. Leon smiled at me and hefted his mug.

"Need a cuppa babe?"

"Yeah, that'd be great, thanks," I said as I slipped into the remaining chair. Leon must have pulled both of ours out of the space under the mattress in the van, and I was grateful that he had. He got up and began rummaging in the supplies stored at the front of Dai's tent.

"I heard about something pretty horrible just now," I told the others, without looking at them.

"What do you mean?" asked Dai.

"Some guy attacked a woman not far from our camp last night."

"What? Holy shit!" yelped Daphne. "What happened?"

"I don't know a lot," I admitted. "Just what I picked up from a couple of women chatting behind me in the shower queue. It sounds like this tall skinny hairy guy tried to get some woman, but she managed to kick him in the nads and it stopped him enough that she was able to get away."

"Fuck," moaned Dai in a slow voice. "That's horrific. Was it near here?" He looked around as though he expected to spot the creep lurking at the edge of one of a nearby tent, fingers curled around the edge of the material, eyebrows waggling, and a leer smeared across his face.

"The women I overheard seemed to think that it happened over there." I pointed out the gnarly tree further down the line of tents. It was in the opposite direction to Siobahn's site.

"That's so gross," said Daphne. "I feel so exposed here all of a sudden. This festival was meant to be just happiness, pure love and celebration. Now it's been mixed with something awful."

"Like milk and lemon," suggested Dai. "Once you muddle them they react to each other. You can't get a nice drink of milk back out of it."

"Let's go see the others," suggested Leon, just before he tipped the last mouthful of his morning tea into his mouth. He swallowed and ran a tongue over his lips. "They've been here heaps of times before, so they might know some ways to enjoy the festival after hearing such shitty news."

Dai nodded, but turned to see what Daphne thought. She pursed her lips and then nodded too.

"Why not?" she said. "Even if they can't help with this, they clearly know the best ways to spend the days here."

When we arrived at the massage tents, we were welcomed by a pile of people lounging around in the gazebo. About eight people were hunched over in camping chairs or laying out on the multi-coloured mat that was spread out across the ground. Siobahn was one of the people laying on the ground, her head resting on the belly of a smiling woman with deep brown eyes and dark hair streaked with grey. The woman lifted a black plastic stick to her lips and then breathed out a large sweet smelling cloud of vape steam.

"Hey guys? What's going on?" Siobahn asked with a concerned face as we ducked into the gazebo. Even this early in the morning, the sun was beginning to pound down on the festival. Inside the gazebo was shaded but still scorchingly hot. I assumed that we must all look as shocked and unsettled as I felt, and I opened my mouth to answer, but Leon got there first.

"We've heard rumours of someone attacking a woman last night, near our campsite. It's left us pretty rattled, I can tell you!"

CHAPTER TWENTY-TWO

"What?" Siobahn sat up from where she lay. Her eyes widened. "An attack in the tents?" She looked around the space, meeting the eyes of a few of her friends and holding their gaze one at a time.

"Yeah, it's left us pretty shaken up," I said. I looked at the others around the tent who Siobahn was focussing on. There were two lanky men in chairs, wearing loose singlets and baggy shorts. One had a thick black beard with jewellery woven into it, while the other had long brown hair. They both had shocked expressions, eyebrows raised high into their foreheads. The other person Siobahn was looking at was a woman with straight shoulder length black hair with a layer of blue dye peeking out from underneath. She was frowning and her eyes had flicked to the ground as she started thinking deeply.

"Is everything alright?" I asked, watching these three.

"Yes, sort of," said Siobahn slowly. Her eyes stayed on her friends as she spoke. "Over the years, this festival has become bigger and bigger. It's been wonderful for sharing the celebration with more and more people, but we can't be as careful about who we let in anymore." She shook her head slightly.

"What do you mean 'anymore?'" Dai sounded incredulous.

"What did you used to do, background check every single person who showed up to dance in the forest?"

"Sort of."

"That must have taken forever!" Dai was fully disbelieving now. He clearly thought the idea was ludicrous and that Siobahn must be making it up.

"No, we didn't do things as formally as that," chuckled Siobhan as she lifted a hand in protest. "We all knew each other back in the early days, for the first few celebrations." She drew a deep breath and lifted her eyes, seeming to look at something we couldn't see somewhere in the roof of the gazebo. "Back then there were not nearly so many of us, and we all came here to show reverence to the moon and her guidance, her flux, and her stability. We knew each other, or knew someone who knew someone, and the connections were enough to feel safe with one another. And then it grew and grew, and we met new people, and it was good for the festival." She blinked and looked back down at us. "It really was good for the festival! Some people say that all of this is just turning into an excuse for one big party. But I think that even if only a small handful of people here pay attention to the reason we are here, then that's still more than the couple of dozen who came in the first years." It sounded to me as though Siobahn was trying to convince some of the others in the gazebo with this statement. Sure enough, I was certain that I caught more than one set of rolling eyes as I checked the reactions of her friends.

"You have to acknowledge that the growing popularity means we have to deal with the same problems that exist in the world outside the festival, back in the 'Real World'." The interjection came from a fat man with a scruffy beard and long hair, standing near the edge of the gazebo. He shuffled his shoulders, resettling the denim vest he wore unbuttoned.

"I do." Siobahn sighed and then lay back onto the woman below her. "There are negative sides to the popularity for sure."

"Hang on. I didn't realise that you were one of the organisers," said Daphne. She looked from Siobahn to the man who had spoken. "I mean, I knew that you were in the know of the whole event, but from what you're saying..."

"No, I never organised anything. We are all just eager participants."

This time the group grinned in reaction, and quiet chuckling broke out.

"With that in mind, do you know what can be done about this attacker?" asked Leon. "As Ashleigh said, we're feeling quite shocked and vulnerable after that news."

"Yes, I imagine you would be. Look, there is only so much that any individual can do, other than be careful. But rest assured that we know the people to know and we will do everything we can to search out the culprit and make sure that you don't have to worry about such rumours in future!"

The others nodded and sat down amongst the group in the gazebo, but I paused as I was looking for a spot to settle myself. I felt my forehead crease as I thought about what Siobahn had said. She hadn't actually said what would happen to the creep, just that we wouldn't have to worry about rumours. Would he get kicked out? Would the police be called? I glanced up, ready to ask a question, and met her eyes.

"What might be even better is a swim in the lake," she suggested, her storm blue eyes staring directly back into mine. "There's nothing that feels as rejuvenating as a clean and refreshing dip in that fresh water."

"It's like being baptised and born again," quipped one of the others around us. Laughter bubbled all around me.

"I just had a shower," I protested feebly. I could see Dai and Daphne looked enthusiastic about the idea. Leon reached over to touch my knee. "It does sound good though," I added. Leon squeezed my leg, which sent a flush of love through me. I felt as though, with my husband by my side and our friends with us, we would be able to take on whatever was thrown at us during the Pandaea Festival.

CHAPTER TWENTY-THREE

s she had the day before, Siobahn led us as we walked through the other tents and then past the market stalls. The stalls were busy with the festival-goers who had not spent their entire night dancing. The morning crowd were taking part in small activities or buying crystals and handmade clothing. I saw a family trying out sets of stilts and laughing as they tumbled to the grass.

"Before we head to the lake, you have to see some of the art that's here too!" Siobahn told us, her eyes sparkling with excitement. She led us past the archway in the trees and on to some more tents. "These art installations pepper the festival grounds. They're easy to miss when you are focused on heading from one place to another without pausing to take in your surroundings. Here, this is one of my favourites this year." She pointed out a low, wide tent with no sides. The curved material between the taut ropes and strong poles hid most of what was inside.

"What is it?" I asked.

Siobahn grinned and led me by the hand.

"I'll show you."

Inside the tent were five tables, the hard plastic sort that corporations use for picnics. They were covered in a light material that wafted around the edges of the tables, disturbed by the air that danced in response to our passage.

Each table was covered in small and elaborate masks. They were the sort of masks that someone might wear to a masquerade party, built up of thin and delicate wires that would only just cover the eyes and the bridge of a nose. They curled in silver and gold, and some held milky pastel crystals embedded in them. I walked past the tables slowly, allowing myself to absorb the beauty of the masks. My fingers trailed over the objects on the table as I walked by.

"They are gorgeous."

"Try one," smiled the older woman who stood behind the tables, watching us browse. She had long grey hair that tumbled in waves on top of the deep blue shawl that covered her shoulders. "There are other styles over here as well!"

I followed her past more tables, and noticed that the masks on each one were different. The next table was covered in masks that looked as though they had been shaped from porcelain, smooth and white and gently curved to follow the forehead and cheek of the wearer. The next table had masks that erupted with colour and feathers.

"Are they for sale?" I asked. Behind me I could hear Daphne and Dai talking quietly. They sounded just as impressed by the artistry as I felt.

"No, not at all," laughed the older woman. "I give them away."

"What?" I blinked and stepped back slightly. "Why would you do that?"

"That's the whole point of the project," explained the woman. "This is my art and where other artists create visual splendours that everyone can walk by and admire and hold in their memories, my art is designed to be used and worn."

"It's another way to celebrate her. The Pandaea is always looking to the artists and their creativity for new ways to celebrate her.' Siobahn said this from over my shoulder. I blinked in surprise and turned to look at her. She wore a very serious expression.

"Celebrate who?"

"The moon, of course." She smiled with her mouth, but the intensity in her eyes remained. "That's why we are all here in the first place. That's why the first small group of us started gathering in this valley at all! To sing and dance and be joyful in honour of her."

"Right right, I get it." I felt uncomfortable with Siobahn's intensity. I glanced around, hoping that Leon would be near enough to rescue me from this conversation, but he was talking to Dai and Daph on another table.

I moved along to look at the masks on the next table. Maybe Siobahn would let me focus on that instead. The table was covered in animal masks, made out of the same smooth white material as the ones on the other table had been. They were still only big enough to cover a person's eyes and nose, but the small extrusions that spread out from their edges suggested different creatures remarkably well. Tigers and rabbits mingled with bears and dogs. I reached out for a particularly fierce looking dog. The snout included a curl that exposed a long canine tooth, and the brow was twisted with anger.

"You like that one?" asked the woman.

"It is impressive. But I wouldn't wear it myself. It's a bit too intense for me." I heard Siobahn breath out sharply. "I didn't mean any offence, is this the sort of thing you would wear?" I asked her.

"I try not to wear any masks at all, if I can help myself," she said, frowning. "Especially here. For me, the Pandaea is about being more fully myself."

What an odd thing to say, I thought to myself. But the masks kept my attention. I enjoyed the way the masks felt when I touched them. I ran my fingertips along them, following the ridges and spikes, slipping across smooth cheeks. I picked up another one and looked at it. There was something strange about this one.

"More deers huh?" asked Leon as he stepped up behind me and slipped a hand around my waist.

"What do you mean?"

"You've found another deer." he pointed at the mask in my hands. I looked at the small jagged antlers that sprouted from the corners of the mask and turned it around to look at the black elastic band.

"So it is." I hadn't been able to figure out what the mask was until Leon pointed it out. The antlers looked more like a bolt of lightning, or wide spreading branches from a tree. The face of the mask was white, except for a small black spot that I assumed must be the nose. But it was only a circle, so it could have been anything. "It must have been for the parade yesterday then."

"That's what I'd say," he agreed.

"Why are so many left though?"

CHAPTER TWENTY-FOUR

"What was that love?" The woman who made the masks leaned closer to Leon and I. "So many what?"

"Deer masks." And now that Leon had pointed it out, I could see them all over the tables. Every third or fourth mask was some sort of deer. I looked back at the earlier tables, the ones covered in feathers, the smooth ones, the wire ones. Even though they weren't strictly deer masks, many of them had suggestions of antlers, made of multiple feathers stuck together, or zig-zagged corners of wire that jabbed out from behind the mask's eyes. "You have heaps and heaps of deer left. Didn't you give away heaps before the parade?"

The woman looked down at the tables in front of her. She looked as surprised as anyone else to see deer all through the masks.

"I did, indeed. There were plenty of my masks in the rangale, but there are always so many who want to be a part of the parade. I suppose I must have brought more along than I had realised." She smiled again when she looked up. "Would you like one?"

I rubbed the mask in my fingers a little harder. The material was solid but had a papery texture. I lifted the mask to my eyes. Just as it got close enough that I could see through the eye holes, I thought I caught a strange expression pass over the woman's face. For less than a heartbeat her eyes grew hungry, and the skin of her face pulled taut with eagerness. I stopped and moved the mask away from my face before it touched my skin. Her face was expectant but innocent now. Had I imagined something?

"I don't think I want to be a deer. Something about that makes me uneasy."

"Oh?" asked Siobahn. She was wearing a multi-coloured mask that looked like a bird whose wings cupped the sides of her face. A small black beak touched the top of her nose. "Nothing wrong with deer. Very traditionally associated with the moon. That's why we have the rangale."

"That's something I've been wondering," asked Leon as he looked between a wired mask with two glittering black stones at the outside corners of its eyes and a smooth mask that looked exactly like the prop from the Phantom of the Opera. "What's the deal with all the deer and the masks and the wrangle and the idea that this whole event is about the moon and all of it?"

"In ancient times there was a strong connection between the moon and deer," said Siobahn. "They were the sacred animal of the moon goddess. That's why we started making a bit of a competition of the rangale. It's a challenge, to have more people representing a deer come to the festival each year. The parade is just a way to manage the count in a fun way"

"Why is called a wrangle though?" asked Daphne. She and Dai had caught up to us now.

"R-a-n-g-a-l-e. It's an old word that refers to a group of deer."

"What about the masks?"

"Again, that's quite a traditional association with the moon. She changes all the time, passing from one face to another and back again, which is a reflection of our selves. We all present a changing face to the world around us, hiding our truth to varying degrees of success. By honouring her, we can learn to manage ourselves."

Leon made a grunting noise that I knew meant he vaguely understood what had just been said to him, but he wasn't interested enough to ask more questions about it to clarify. Unfortunately Siobahn must have thought that it was a grunt that meant he wanted to hear much more. And so she continued.

"That is part of what this whole celebration is about. The Pandaea is a festival that celebrates the hidden depths in our world, the layers that we all use to obscure the things that we would otherwise hide away. Just as the moon is always changing how she appears, we all change ourselves every day. We present the face that we think others will want to see. We might be scared of how they will react to us, or perhaps we are embarrassed to admit something about our true nature and we are trying to hide it from ourselves. In any case, the goddess knows all about the way we try to hide, and she is here to embrace us anyway, and to support us in shedding the masks. Somewhere beneath all the layers is our pure soul."

Siobahn's face was glowing and her eyes brighter than I would have thought reasonable in the dim tent. She was a real believer in all this stuff. I knew that she had been part of the festival for a long time, so she must have been into the ideas it was based on, but I was surprised at how fervent she was! This was exactly the conversation I had been hoping to avoid. *Thanks for bringing it up Leon!*

"This festival is a chance to embrace all the true aspects of one's self, to really let out the parts of you that you keep hidden in regular society. Sometimes the most freeing thing you can do for your inner self is to put on a mask like these. By hiding your face, you feel protected enough to act how you truly want to."

I nodded. It made sense to me. I had been to various costume parties in the past, and I had always felt much more licence to act silly or do something ridiculous while I was dressed up as a mediaeval princess or a pirate.

"I get it," said Leon. "But we don't really hide ourselves out in the real world." He took my hand behind my back and squeezed my fingers. I squeezed them back and smiled. He's right, I thought to myself. We have always prided ourselves on really allowing each other to be our authentic selves,and loving one another for it.

Siobahn raised an eyebrow.

"That sounds extremely lucky for you both. Forgive me if I seem somewhat doubtful though."

CHAPTER TWENTY-FIVE

I picked up another mask from the table next to me. It reflected the dull light in the tent from multiple shimmering surfaces beneath the main mask. Its outer layer was grey and roughly textured, like quickly made papier mache. But underneath there was a blue smooth surface, like polished metal or an oil slick that held a solid form. The inner surface peeked through multiple cracks that tore across the rougher outer surface. I could see glimpses of my own face in that inner surface as I looked over the mask, turning it in my hands. But the reflection was distorted by the shape of the mask. I even saw a flash of Siobahn there, swirling like she was made of smoke that someone had set it in motion.

Dai walked up to me wearing a multicoloured mask with a bulbous nose that made him look like a clown. It was red and yellow and blue and looked as though it was made out of handfuls of bubbles stuck together, with piles of curvy 'hair' falling down over his eyes, and big rounded cheeks.

"Look, Ashleigh, look!" He grinned. "They made a mask that looks just like me! Can you tell if I'm wearing it or not?" He lifted the mask up from his nose, holding it just above his head and then lowered it again, repeating the movement rapidly a half a dozen times. "Huh? Right?"

I rolled my eyes and laughed.

"Why no Dai, it is impossible to tell the difference between that mask and your silly face!" I reached over and grabbed his face softly, squeezing his cheeks a little as I shook it side to side. He pulled away and laughed.

"Easy! That's not the mask!"

"Come on," said Daphne. "Let's get to the lake."

We walked away from the art exhibits and through the trees towards the basin and the dancing stage. A peacock stood in the trees near the market, watching the crowds walk by, completely unperturbed by the swarms of people.

My mouth fell open when I saw that there were still some dancers going strong in front of the stage. There were far fewer than there had been during the night, but any at all stepping in rhythm with their hands in the air was a surprise. Instead of a throng that stretched back past the mixing deck and across the grass, the last dancers were clustered up near the front of the stage, squelching in mud. It wasn't even a wet field, and there had been no rain, but the number of feet pounding on the earth had broken it up and mixed it into a sludgy mass.

I had seen an exodus back to the tents not long after the sun had risen while I was waiting for a shower, and I had naturally assumed that the stage must have shut down, freeing the dancers from that endless feeling of "just one more song!" But no, about thirty people were still going, and by the looks of the DJ on stage, a man with thick brown hair and unfocused eyes gazing out across the remaining dancers, he wouldn't stop before they did. As we passed toward the other side of the hollow I wondered if any of the dancers would collapse rather than stop for sleep or food. We left them behind and ducked under the branches into the bush.

We had joined a small group of some of Siobahn's friends as we reached the dance stage, and we spread out along the path in twos and threes, chatting about our lives with each other. One of the broader women was walking with Leon and me, while Dai and Daphne were further ahead talking to another couple. I couldn't see Siobahn, though I assumed she was still at the front, leading the way. There was something about that woman that always wanted to be in charge.

"No, we haven't been to any other festivals before," Leon was saying to the woman, whose name I had been told but had forgotten almost immediately.

"We used to go to those big music festivals," I chipped in. I didn't want the woman to think we were totally useless.

"Music festivals?"

"You know, those all day events, with heaps of bands and artists?" We hadn't been in nearly four years, but I was always aware of the advertising each October, building up the hype for a day of sweltering sun and pounding music late in January.

The woman smiled a little and nodded. A little puffing sound came from her nose.

"Are you laughing at us?" I asked. I could feel my brow wrinkle.

"No, no, just a bit of pollen. It makes me want to sneeze." She wiped her face with the back of her hand. "Those sorts of days are a bit different to this though."

"Yes, of course," I replied quietly. I had a feeling that I had not done anything to endear myself to her.

"While we were travelling there was a new moon festival at one of the islands we stayed at in Asia. Was that when we were in Thailand babe?"

I remembered that festival. We had gathered on a beach alongside scores of other vacationing westerners, and bought over priced beer from local merchants. A series of bonfires had been lit on the beach and we had danced in between them until the early hours of the morning. I vaguely recalled that there had been a full moon that night.

"I'm not sure," I had to admit. "We visited a lot of places in a short time."

"Uh huh," said the woman. She smiled again. "I hope you find the Pandaea is worth coming back to then. It sounds like you guys know how to enjoy a party."

I squeezed Leon's hand. I was becoming quite sure that this woman was making fun of us. I peered down the trail ahead of us, trying to catch sight of Dai and Daphne, but the path curled around the trees so that their trunks and branches were in the way. I couldn't tell how far ahead they were. I looked back over my shoulder and saw two more of the people from the massage camp, but I had no idea if they were the last people in our group or if there were even more people stretched out along the trail.

There was a flicker of movement in the trees behind us, and I stopped to look at it more directly. Leon stopped with me, and then the woman. I felt her step up behind me.

"What is that?" I muttered as I looked closer. The movement was hard to catch, flickering from one trunk to another, or between bushes. It often seemed to jump invisibly between hiding spots and so I would only catch subsequent movement from the corner of my eye, even though I was looking directly at where it had just been.

CHAPTER TWENTY-SIX

"It's not more of the group," said Leon. "They wouldn't be that far out in the bush, would they? Off the path like that?" He turned to direct his question to the woman. She smiled widely with bright white teeth.

"I suppose they wouldn't," she allowed. Then she carried on "It is probably just more of the deer, or some birds. Come on, the lake isn't far."

I watched the movement in the trees longer, until the woman took my elbow and tugged me to follow her.

Walking through the shadowy trail through the trees made me feel cold. When we had woken up in our van, the world had felt hot already, and I had needed a shower to clean off the sweat that had built up on my skin after my activities in the night. The water had restored my energy levels. But now, despite walking beneath a searing sun through the markets of the festivals and across the broad open dance hollow, my shoulders shivered and I was rubbing goosebumps on my forearms.

We passed through the broken fence and kept walking. I glanced behind me often, trying to see if the movement in the trees was still there, but I saw nothing.

"Can you see the others?" I whispered to Leon as he straightened up after crawling through the gap in the face to join me on the lake side.

"No." His face was blank and then he blinked as he noticed my expression. "Are you okay babe?"

I shrugged.

"I think so. I just feel like something is wrong."

Leon put an arm around my shoulder and held me close. "I'm sorry love. Would a swim help you feel a bit more relaxed?"

I nodded. I hoped so. Thankfully we arrived at the ridge that led down to the lake before I could spiral too far into my own worries.

The panorama of the lake spread out below me was full of people enjoying the water and sun. Now that the trees thinned out, the sun's heat returned and I felt it warm and soothe my shoulders. I stood up straighter. Ahead of us I could see Dai and Daphne standing with their arms around one another near the edge of the lake, talking to a group of the others we had met at the massage campsite.

"See, they're fine," murmured Leon as he squeezed me again.

"Yup." I felt silly for even worrying, so I started jogging down the slope, eager to get into the water.

The water was full of people swimming out from the small sandy ledge that we had seen during our last visit, splashing out into the deep black water of the lake and then looping around and back. I would have almost said that they were racing one another, but they just seemed to enjoy swimming out and then back regardless of who might have been winning or losing. Others were throwing a ball into the water and diving in after it, throwing small striped balls back and forwards between each other, or standing in the shallows and talking or kicking small waves at each other.

I stopped on the edge of the bank, a spot where the dusty earth and thin grass simply dropped away into water that looked bottomless, and began pulling off my light summer dress. I dropped it to the ground and then removed my necklace and folded it under the material. I straightened up and as I checked that my bikini was straight, I heard a voice saying hello. I turned around and saw that Finn was standing nearby, his smile wide and his eyes trying to stay on my face, and mostly succeeding.

"Fancy seeing you here," he grinned.

"Hey, how are you!" I jumped over and gave him a tight hug. He kissed my cheek and then we stepped back. "Did you have a headache or anything this morning?"

"No," he replied. His smile was wide enough that I thought his head might split in two. "I felt really good this morning, thanks to you I'm sure."

"Stop it," I giggled.

"Who's this?" asked Leon, who had just caught up with us.

"This is Finn. He and I hooked up last night."

"Nice to meet you," said Leon. He held out a hand to shake Finn's. "How did you two bump into each last night? Just out dancing?"

"Yeah, we were getting our groove on and one thing led to another." Finn sniffed and rolled his shoulders. His eyes flicked from side to side nervously. "That's alright, yeah? I mean, I didn't want to cause any trouble here."

"No, of course it's fine," smiled Leon. "We trust and love each other. Just because we have connections with other people sometimes doesn't mean that we love each other any less."

I beamed as I heard my husband explaining this out loud. It had been something that we had worked out with each other early in our relationship, as we realised that the societal expectation to only ever desire each other was simply impossible to maintain. It first sprang from our desire to be open with each other, and truthful about our emotions. The first steps had been cautious and nerve wracking but we had soon managed to agree that we would still find other people attractive. After all, we weren't blind!

And then, over the years, we had found ways to explore that and reached the stage that we were at now. It made me so proud to hear him explaining our understanding to others. I saw it as another sign that we had worked hard to uncover who we really were inside, to reveal our deepest selves, not just to each other but to ourselves. We had helped one another to take off the layers that we hid ourselves in, and it meant that we were free to share that self with the world around us.

I thought about the low gazebo we had been exploring not long ago, and smirked. We had no need to find a physical mask that would help us find the confidence to take off the metaphorical mask we wore through the real world. We had no such masks!

On top of that, it was fun! I loved Leon, and I had loved him ever since we met at a house party in West Auckland. It made my heart bloom to see how wide his smile grew when he talked of an encounter he had had, and I know he loved to see me having a good time as well. After all, when you love someone, don't you want them to experience all the joy that they can?

Leon and Finn had kept talking while my thoughts rushed through my head. They were laughing, joking about the dancing and music from last night. Dai and Daphne wandered up and Daph touched my shoulder.

"Are you swimming or what? You had a shower this morning, but I didn't. I need to get rid of the grime from dancing in dust and mud all night." She shuddered and scrubbed at her bare arms with her hands. I had to admit, I could see the dark smears that she left on her skin. She really was pretty dirty right now.

"All right, let's get in there. You coming babe?"

Leon turned and nodded.

"It was nice to meet you Finn," he said. For a moment I thought he might ask Finn to come swimming with us. But before any of us could ask, Finn nodded to us all and walked off towards another group he seemed to know.

CHAPTER TWENTY-SEVEN

"Who was that?" asked Dai as Finn left.

"A lover Ash picked up last night," said Leon.

"Hah, nice work Ash!" said Dai as we moved down to the sandy ledge at the edge of the lake.

To our right, people were jumping off a grassy bank that jutted a metre or two above the water's surface. Dai watched them as we all stripped down to our togs.

"Any of you keen for a bomb or something?" he asked wistfully. It was clear from his tone that he had already resigned himself to easing into the cool water on the same sandy ledge as the rest of us.

"It could be dangerous," said Daphne. She was folding her t-shirt into neat quarters as she spoke, which she then laid on top of her shorts where they already sat in the grass. "You never know what's under the surface in water like this. If you jump into a rock or a log, you could kill yourself."

We all watched as an extremely large man took a short run up to the edge and then launched himself into the air, pulling one leg up as high as he could with his arms and tilting slightly backwards. The resulting cascade of water swamped his friends on the bank and nearly washed us off our feet. A whoop rose from the crowd watching on the slope above the lake.

"Yeah. He's probably cracked through a hollow log and got himself stuck. Or maybe he shattered his spine on a boulder," Dai nodded, with a concerned expression.

The man rose out of the water with both fists above his head, roaring in victory.

"It must be a fluke that he survived," sighed Dai.

We all walked down the sandy ledge and into the water. I could see that the other three found the fresh water invigorating, and they scooped handfuls up to clean themselves with as we reached waist depth. I had already cleaned myself that morning, so instead the water just felt cold to me, but a few more steps and we were all leaning forward to swim out deeper and I forgot my discomfort.

It was a beautiful moment as I swam out into the lake with my friends. The sun shone down on my back and the cold water made my skin tingle. A relaxed sense of joy crept through my muscles as we sculled away from the lake's edge. The sounds of conversation on the bank faded surprisingly quickly, as did the splashes of people playing. I rolled over to float on my back, staring up at the sky above us. It was blue and strong, painted with soft puffs of cloud. The heat from the morning sun baked my face while the cold from the dark depths of the lake plucked at me from below. The contrast made my breath catch and my heart race.

"Ash!" called a voice from nearby, muffled by the water in my ears. I rolled back to my front and looked around. Leon was waving at me nearby, while Dai and Daph were swimming away from us. I pulled over to my husband quickly.

"Is something wrong?"

"No, but Daphne wants to swim around that headland and explore the bush there. You coming?" He jerked his head in the direction that the others were swimming. The hills around the lake all flowed into a narrow headland of rock that stabbed out into the lake. A few tall trees stuck up from the ridge. The others were swimming past the tumbled boulders and crags that surrounded its base. I could see the white tips of ripples breaking and splitting between the rocks.

"Go on then, race you!"

I lunged past Leon and started pulling my arms over my shoulders in what I hoped was a decent crawl. I caught a glimpse of his shocked expression as I swam by, kicking as hard as I could. By the time I caught up with Dai and Daphne, Leon came crashing past. We both stopped near Dai and Daphne and treaded water. I was panting and Leon grinned at me.

"You cheated," I spluttered.

He raised an eyebrow. "Yup. I brought an outboard motor with me. I thought you wouldn't notice."

"Is that what you've been packing in those tiny speedos buddy?" asked Dai with a twinkle in his eye.

"Amongst other things."

Daphne rolled her eyes.

"Alright, settle down, you idiots. It looks like there's some space to get up between the rocks over this way."

Daphne was right, there was a passage between the rocks that had enough broad smooth surfaces for us to climb over, and less tiny spiky rocks to injure ourselves on. We gathered in the water at the edge of the rocks, pressed in close to each other as we tried to manoeuvre through the narrow way out. I reached out one hand to the rock and held myself up in the water. Daphne bobbed beneath my arm, and my skin rested across her shoulders, her skin smooth and slippery from the lake water.

Dai had been swimming alongside her, and so he bumped against me gently. I felt his fingers press into my waist as he caught his motion. The water around me swirled as he kicked to stay afloat. He smiled awkwardly at me.

"Whoops, sorry!"

"I don't mind," I told him, watching his cheerful eyes so close to mine.

Leon swam past, and the motion knocked the rest of us closer still. My breasts pressed against Daphne's side and a pulse of annoyance shot through me. I wished that the thin material of my bikini was gone, so my skin could enjoy the contact with hers. Dai's hand had to slip right around me now, and his fingertips made me shiver as they drew across the small of my back. I slung my other arm around his shoulders, and enjoyed the way he pressed in closer.

Leon pulled himself onto the rocks and then shook slightly, a little like a dog, flinging droplets of water off himself, before standing up. He turned back and chuckled as he saw the three of us clustered together.

"Come on, you reprobates."

CHAPTER TWENTY-EIGHT

*D*aphne slipped out from under my arm and moved to follow Leon. With more space, I drifted away from Dai, and he just smiled as I moved, letting his hand drift further across my skin as I went. Daphne reached up from the water and Leon knelt down to grab her arm and help lift her out of the water. His shoulder muscles tightened as he pulled her up, and then he put his other hand on her side to help her keep balance on the wet rocks. She stepped up next to him, one hand touching his chest for a moment, her face only millimetres from his, before she smiled and stepped past him. I saw the fleeting flush of blood in my husband's cheeks and I grinned.

Daphne began to walk along the trail leading away from the rocks and up along the ridge of the headland. I couldn't look away from her ass as she moved. Each step made the inviting curves of her hips and buttocks clench and move, and her bikini bottoms had tucked up, revealing a line of pale skin where she had not tanned. It was calling out for someone to run their fingernails down that pale crescent. I caught Leon's eyes and we both knew that the other had been admiring Daphne's figure at the same time. He grinned sheepishly, and I snorted then swam closer to the ledge.

"I'll help her out," said Dai from behind me. "You can start heading up."

I was fairly sure that I knew what sort of help Dai was thinking of offering. The idea started a familiar electric buzz between my legs.

Leon nodded and turned to follow Daphne up the slope. I placed both my hands on the rock and lowered myself in the water, ready to push myself up as quickly as I could, out of the water and onto the ledge. Dai's hand met my side as I moved, and then pushed with me as I rose, helping lift me high enough to get a secure purchase on the rocks. As I fell forward and reached up to get a new handhold, his hand shifted lower, helping steady my hips, then pressing against my bottom as I moved forward. I lifted one leg, using the knee to steady myself and climb further out of the water, but also knowing that the movement would open the space between my legs in his face, leaving only a thin strip of fabric between his face and the heat that was growing inside me.

Once I was high enough on the rocks I spun over and sat on the edge, facing Dai.

"Thanks for your help," I said, kicking a little water towards him.

"It was absolutely my pleasure," he replied.

"I thought it would be." I bit my lower lip and looked around. The rocks were high and hid us from the crowds still swimming by the lake's edge. "Can you show me how much of a pleasure it was for you?"

For a moment Dai looked confused. His smile remained, but his brow furrowed as he tried to think of a clever way to answer me. Then he shrugged in the water and lay back, floating and lifting his hips to the surface of the water. With difficulty, he managed to pull the top of his togs down far enough to allow his hard cock to rise. Then his face dipped below the water and he thrashed about as he pulled his togs back up and tried to cough and clear his throat of water.

I covered my mouth as I laughed, waiting for him to recover.

"Sexy," I said once he steadied himself and caught his breath.

"Hey, you asked how much I liked it!" he said with a rough voice, and then coughed again.

I tilted my head to one side and beckoned him closer to the ledge.

"That looked pretty disastrous. Is he still there?"

Dai pressed his mouth into a tight line.

"No, he vanished pretty quickly there."

"Come over here, let's see if we can get him back then." As I spoke, I spread my legs wider and leaned back where I was sitting on the edge of the water. I lowered a hand to my thigh and trailed my fingers up the soft skin towards my bikini bottoms. Dai's face brightened and he swam closer.

"You don't need to ask me twice!" he said as he arrived between my thighs. He must have found a rock to stand on, because I shuddered as I felt both of his hands reach out to my legs and move along them, rubbing the curves of my calves and thighs. I could feel the heat of his breath all along the wet surface of my inner thighs, and my stomach was quivering with the knowledge of his closeness to me.

Dai's lips touched my skin and I sighed. Then he began to kiss softly along my thighs, closer and closer to my bikini. His fingertips brushed closer and then across the wet fabric, pressing just enough to leave a fluttery feeling between my legs. I shifted my hips closer to him.

He pulled at the elastic along the sides of my togs, lifting them away from my pussy and exploring the soft skin at the edges. I shivered and water trickled down my spine. Dai's fingers moved closer, edging along my lips, tickling the small hairs. I closed my eyes and tilted my head back, enjoying the warmth of the sun that beat down on me.

He pulled at my bikini further, pulling it aside and exposing me to him. I felt his face moving closer, his nose pressing into the skin above me and then the warm welcome shock of his tongue slipping between my folds. I lifted a hand to the back of his head and pushed him closer, pressing him into me as the sensation spread through my body.

I gasped and moaned as he worked his tongue up and down, teasing my clit, and searching into my depths. The contrast of the heat from his tongue and the cold water of the lake sent a shudder up my spine. I couldn't tell if he was making me wet with desire, or if the lake water was still beading across me, but the slippery sensation made my hips squirm. His hand moved around my leg, holding onto my hip. His fingers pressed into my flesh and I wanted to envelop him.

His other hand came in beside his face, sliding one finger inside me. He pressed carefully, moving through me as he sought out the parts of me that elicited the best reaction, the best sounds. I trembled and lay further back on the rock, feeling the rough surface prick my lower back and my arms.

I wondered what could be seen of us by others. The thought made my skin warm. Were any of the crowd swimming by the lake's edge out far enough to see us? And what would they see anyway? A woman lounging on the edge of the rocks? I shifted my hips, pressing myself against Dai's tongue and fingers as he kept his rhythm, building the sensation. They would probably barely even see him.

Dai's fingers were building up speed, pounding into me harder and harder. I heard him splutter as a wave caught him by surprise.

"Get up here you idiot," I said, grabbing his head.

CHAPTER TWENTY-NINE

*D*ai pulled away from me and smiled, then hauled himself out of the water and lay alongside me on the rocks. I reached down to the solid tent that poked out of his togs and smiled as he moaned at my touch. I traced the outline of him with my fingers, curling tighter around the base as best as I could through the swimsuit. He leaned towards me.

"This is always a lot of fun," he murmured before he kissed me.

I leaned into the kiss, moving against his mouth, sending my tongue seeking his. We rolled against each other on the rock, carefully. His hand cupped my breast and tweaked my nipples through my bikini top before running over my stomach and seeking my pussy again. I broke off from the kiss as he pressed between my lips and the heel of his palm began to rub my clit. The fire from his earlier efforts still blazed, and soon he was building up his rhythm again.

I tucked my hand down inside his togs, gripping his shaft tightly, his rough hair scratching my hand as I began to pull, seeking to match his rhythm. One finger strayed to his balls, scratching them gently with its nail.

The fire inside me built until it was a roaring bonfire, pulsing in time with the rhythm that Dai was setting with his hand, and meeting the endless rays of hot sunlight that bore down on us from the sky. I felt as though my whole being was going to melt away beneath the heat from all sides, and the liquid that had once been me would drain away into the lake, to become one with nature. Then the bonfire exploded.

I shuddered and clenched my legs around his hand, my jaw locking in place and my stomach tensing. I felt the pulsing of my orgasm grip his hand and I tried to control myself, but it felt like an eternity before I regained control of my own muscles. I immediately leaned back into our kiss, and redoubled my efforts with my hand around his cock.

"Do you think I could fuck you?" he asked, shifting so that his hips were angled to fit between my own if I said the word. I leaned back from him and considered.

"Do you have a condom with you?" I asked.

"Tucked into my togs? No, I don't."

"Well... I don't think so then."

Dai looked disappointed but he nodded.

"I should have thought of that before I asked."

"It's alright, I like knowing that you wanted to." I smirked and squeezed him extra tight, just enough to make him gasp and his eyes pop. "Maybe we'll get another chance later on in the festival?"

He nodded rapidly, with wide eyes.

"That sounds like a brilliant idea!"

"In the meantime, I think I owe you something in return..."

I pressed his chest until he lay back down on the rock, and then I pulled his swimming shorts down to the tops of his thighs, leaving his manhood standing high. I started sliding both hands up it, beginning by encircling the base and cupping his balls, and then running my hand up the shaft and off the top. Each hand took a turn making the motion, slowly at first but then faster and fast. I could feel him swell and stiffen as the sensation must have been growing for him as well, until he slapped his hands down beside him onto the rock and he came, covering my hands and his stomach.

"Oh my god Ash, you're really good at that," he groaned as he lay back along the rock.

"Thank you," I accepted his compliment as I dipped my hands into the water and washed them clean. Dai waited until I was finished and then lowered himself back into the water for a minute to do his own cleaning.

"Alright, that was a nice way to pass some time on the lake. What do you think the others have been up to?" he asked after he pulled himself out of the water again. He looked at me with a studiously innocent expression and laughed when I winked.

We pulled our togs back into place and then walked up the ridgeline towards the trees. Before long, we found Leon and Daphne lying fully naked on the ground, with Leon's arm around her shoulder, and her hand on his stomach.

"Did you two have a good time?" asked Dai.

"Absolutely," said Leon happily, and he squeezed Daphne's shoulder. Then he disentangled himself from her and pulled his swimming shorts on. He stood up and walked over to me, grabbing me and kissing me.

"We could hear you two having a good time down by the water yourselves," he said as he kissed me. I kissed him back and dug my fingers into the skin of his sides.

"You know how it is, " I chuckled. "One thing leads to another."

"You know, I do know something about that actually!"

Over by the tree beside us, Daphne was blushing as she stood up to talk with her husband. She coughed and umm-ed, clearly unsure where to look.

"Is everything alright?" I asked. I was concerned that Daphne might be upset about what had just happened.

"Yes, it's fine," she muttered. Dai stepped up to hold her, and she hugged him back, but she still had downcast eyes.

"Are you sure?" I ducked my head lower, so that I could catch her eyes. "You seem like you might be having regrets?"

"No, it's not that."

"What is it? We've always enjoyed our time with you guys, you're our best and closest friends."

CHAPTER THIRTY

*D*ai was looking concerned as well. I knew that he would be worried that he had done something to upset his wife. He loved her more than anything else in the world. I knew that the prospect of a bit of extra fun, no matter how fun, would never be enough to make him do anything that might make her worried.

But we had spent many nights in the past sharing one another, whether it was all piled warmly on the couch together, or subtle fingers in a spa pool. This strange response hadn't happened before. Daphne had never been remotely bothered by our other intersections!

"It's always been fun," she agreed. "I'm not upset with anyone, especially not you babe." She finally lifted her head and kissed Dai. "But I have been feeling a bit off since I arrived at the festival, and I know that we all know each other so well, but I've wanted all of Dai's attention." She looked embarrassed.

I remembered how she had sounded worried about the attention that he had been paying to Rania when we had found him at the lake the other day.

"It's okay," I said. "We are all allowed to feel the way we feel.

If you feel like you want more of your husband's attention right now, I'm sure that can happen."

"You know it can love!" exclaimed Dai.

Daph smiled, and they kissed again, longer this time.

As we all kept walking up into the bush, I wondered what had made Daphne feel this way. Was she feeling more insecure than usual? Was there something she had noticed at the festival that she didn't think that she measured up to? I thought of the pretty young things that I had seen so far, swimming at the lake, dancing beneath the moon. Surely Daphne wasn't feeling fragile in that way?

I wondered if it was a sense of self security that had affected her. Perhaps she was feeling exposed in this new place, with all these unknown people. Maybe she wanted the attention and love of her husband because she was scared, and she wanted the safety of him around her more than usual. I hadn't thought my friend was the sort to be intimidated by a situation like this festival. But I remembered the conversation I had heard in the shower queue that morning, and the fact that some arsehole was still wandering around the Pandaea after trying to attack a poor woman. Maybe it was reasonable for Daphne to be feeling this way.

We explored the bush around the edge of the lake for nearly an hour, trying to find trails between the trunks, but being held back by the thick brush that wove in between.

"I never knew how difficult it could be to get through some bloody trees," grumbled Leon.

Eventually we made our way back down to the rocks beneath the ridge and swam back across the lake to where everyone else was playing. If anything, even more people had arrived now, and it was actually difficult to find enough room to climb out. The buzz of conversation was thick in the air, as though a swarm of flies were humming through the thin branches around us. Eventually we managed to clamber over the sandy shelf of shallow water, and squeeze between the people lounging in the water. On the grass we looked for our towels and then dried off. Dai kept slipping an arm around Daphne's waist, or dropping a hand to squeeze her bottom, until she was so annoyed that she flicked him away. She smiled as she did it though, and he laughed, so I hoped that they were feeling more comfortable with each other.

Leon rested his chin on my shoulder as I watched our friends.

"Are you doing alright babe?" he murmured softly into my ear. His breath tickled a little.

"Yeah, I just hope that those two are okay."

"Why wouldn't they be?"

"Daphne hasn't seemed so out of sorts before. I'd hate to have caused any sort of arguments between them."

Leon spun me around and drew me in close to him. I enjoyed the way my body pressed against his, and I was glad that he was still only wearing his togs. The skin of his chest still felt slightly damp against mine, and I enjoyed running my fingers up his shoulder. He leaned closer to me, his eyes watching mine.

"You're a treasure, Ash. You could never do anything that would be a problem for your friends." He leaned in closer and kissed me firmly, pressing his lips hard into mine. "And if they did have some issue, it wouldn't be your fault."

I sighed. "I hope you're right."

"I'm sure I am. Come on, let's get back to the festival." He let me go and reached down to pull on a loose grey tee shirt with an outline picture of a ruru on it. I smiled as I admired his body and then sighed as the shirt covered up that wonderful skin. Then I slipped my loose summer dress over the top of my bikini and the four of us made our way back into the bush above the lake.

The walk back through the bush and past the music stage was quick. My blood was still rushing and hot from our time on the rocks, and the feeling of Leon's fingers interlaced with mine as we walked made my head float. Then we emerged from the archway in the trees and were faced with the sprawling stalls and enclosures of the festival once more.

The crowds were thicker now than they had been in the morning. More people had woken from their hazy slumber after a night of dancing, and were now strolling through the stalls, seeking enlightenment of one form or another. A small cluster of thin men and women wearing skimpy leather outfits were passing a joint around and leaning back to allow the sunlight to wash over their skin.

CHAPTER THIRTY-ONE

The market itself was clogged with people crushing under each overhang out of the sun, and so the four of us decided not to go in there. Instead we turned right and followed a string of artists who had set up workshops under the treeline.

Large boards had been set up, like construction fences that only stretched a few metres in a run, and a man with a shaved head and swathes of multi-coloured tattoos was spray painting one of them. I thought that he would be doing some graffiti art, using strong edges and bold curves, making something powerful and awe-inspiring out of a few well chosen words; but it turned out that he was creating a fantasy landscape. It was something straight out of an eighties movie, broad rolling hills, lush forests, and tall ethereal glowing towers striking towards a starry sky over it all.

Beyond the spray painting we found some more traditional artists painting on easels, mostly portraits of passers-by who were stopping and then cooing over the results. A woman with a thick leather apron was hammering at a glowing orange piece of metal, twisting it and hooking it onto a structure that was developing next to her. A thin cord was set up as a fence to keep anyone from accidentally stumbling into her strikingly hot work.

As we reached the end of the artists, I thought that we were heading back into the campsite. Large tents were beginning to be more common, like mushrooms after a rainfall, but when we got closer I could see that a lot of these tents were open, at least on one side, and they had signs and tables implying that they were more than just a place to sleep for a tired reveller. Two older women sat on plastic chairs that stretched and shifted with every breath they took in front of the first tent. Spread across the heavy plastic camping table in front of them were a slew of tall thin cards, covered in exquisite drawings. I stood by the table and reached out for a card, but then glanced up at the nearest woman and nodded towards the cards in question. She nodded and so I picked up one of the cards to get a closer look at it.

The border of the card was made of a triple line in gold, that flashed as it caught the sunlight over my shoulder. The image covering the face of the card was of a tall mountain with thin spiky pines pricking up from its slope. Dark shapes crowded beneath the trees, somehow appearing to glare at me though none of the low silhouettes had eyes drawn on them. Glowing in the top third of the card, appearing as though it was stuck on the sharp peak of the mountain, a full moon was bright and round. Written in a scroll at the bottom of the card was "The Moon".

"It's beautiful," I said.

"Thank you my dear. Which one did you pick?" asked the lady who had allowed me to pick up the card.

"It says The Moon," I explained as I turned the card and showed her. Her eyebrows bounced higher on her face, but her smile stayed strong.

"The Moon! What a fascinating selection my dear!" The old woman took the card back in fingers that looked softer than tissue paper. She held it up as though she was comparing it to my face. "The Moon is a card that represents your unconscious mind, the fears and illusions that you cannot see in the waking world." She shifted her focus to my eyes and I was shocked by the clarity and strength in her eyes. They were green, deeper and darker than the lake we had been swimming in that morning. "What is hiding inside your mind that scares you my dear?"

I coughed and stuttered, but then Leon took me by the shoulder.

"Come on, the others have already moved on," he said, not unkindly.

"Did you hear what she said?" I asked him as he led me away from the tent. I glanced over my shoulder, but the sun had blinded me and now it was hard to see the women or their table inside the shaded tent.

"No. Oh, shit, sorry, I didn't check if you were busy!" Leon grimaced. "Should we go back?"

"No." I tried to gather my thoughts as we followed the distant shapes of Daph and Dai. "She scared me, but I don't really know why."

"Yeah?" Leon looked at me more closely, and then wrapped my shoulders with his arm and squeezed. "You do seem to be finding all the weirdos in this place. I think it'll be best if we stick with the people we know."

"Sounds good to me."

Daphne had stopped to look at a hand painted wooden sign propped up outside the next tent, while Dai had pulled open its flapping door to peek inside.

"Meditation," she said as we approached. "What do you think?"

"Sure," said Leon. "I've been unwinding ever since we got here, even though Ashleigh's had to put up with a few odd encounters. I think we should continue slowing thoughts, let's really settle into this place."

"I think I could use the anxiety break!" I laughed.

The four of us ducked inside the door.

Inside the large tent was a floor covered in blankets, and heavy cushions. A short woman with shoulder length blonde hair was sitting at the far end of the tent, and two other people were already cross-legged in front of her. The couple facing the woman were an older pair, one man wearing a cloth headband to keep his wavy grey hair out of his face, and a woman wearing a net-like tanktop.

"Good afternoon," said the blonde woman. "Welcome to my meditation space. My name is Holly. We were just about to begin a session, would you all like to join us?"

"Yes, we're all keen to lose ourselves a little," grinned Dai. He dropped to a cushion and mimicked the pose that the older couple were in. Daphne joined him, and then Leon and I sat down too.

"Fantastic, welcome. Would you mind closing the door? It's best if we don't have interruptions before we are done."

I was closest to the door, so I leaned over and zipped the door closed.

CHAPTER THIRTY-TWO

"Alright. Everybody place your hands together and rest them on your ankles. Lean your elbows on your knees, gently, don't push at your legs."

I watched as we all tried to get into the pose that the woman was instructing for us.

"Good, that's good," she smiled.

I felt a small flush of pride in my chest at her praise, and then snorted. I felt as though I was back at primary school, sitting on the mat and doing what the teacher told me.

"Let your head roll backwards, not too far, not too fast. Roll it across your shoulders and down your chest, then the other side. Move around and around. Around and around." Holly's voice was low and sweet, and I found that I was drifting away as she spoke.

"If you haven't closed your eyes yet, close them now."

I jerked as I noticed that I had closed my eyes without thinking about it. I was about to open them when I realised that Holly had just asked me to close them. I snorted again, surprised at how off kilter I was. Normally a little meditation or yoga was the sort of thing that I loved doing. I wondered if I was being put off because of the rumours and stories I had heard since I arrived.

Holly continued to quietly lead us through a series of mental exercises that were clearly intended to help the participants stop thinking about the past and planning for the future and to instead focus on the here and now. I found that it worked to a degree, but as I became more aware of my senses I was less able to pay attention to her instructions.

The rough material of the cushions poked into the skin of my calves and thighs. The air inside the tent was hot and still and full of the moisture of our breaths. Sweat pooled at the nape of my neck and dripped in slow tickling lines down my back. My silver necklace pulled softly at my neck, the stone cool on my chest. I breathed in hot heavy air and then pushed it back out again.

"Let the outside world fall away," whispered Holly from somewhere far away. My head drifted like a tree in the wind. "All the worries and concerns that exist outside of you and your self, let them go. Expose the inner you, the being that acts according to its true wishes. Remove the mask you wear everyday."

I heard a low rumble from one of the others, like they were growling softly. I feel the rhythmic thump of the bass from the dancing stage, all the way in this tent, past the trees. The faintest shimmer of the music finds its way to my ears, and I breathe with it, my heart beats with it.

"Stop reacting to the world as it finds you. Take charge of your world. Act in the world as though your mask is gone."

Again, I hear the growling sound, and I feel an answering rumble in my own throat. I can feel the short hair on the backs of my arms rising and my pulse is quickening. Before the feeling fills me up much more, Holly instructs us to open our eyes and lay on our backs. As I rearrange myself on the cushions, I catch the eye of the older woman.

Her eyes are golden in the shadows of the tent and there is a curl to her upper lip that I find threatening. Before I can react, the look is gone and the woman has lain down, placing her arms alongside her body. I pause and watch her.

"Is everything okay?" asks Holly from behind me. I flinch. I hadn't realised she was there. I turn and look up at her face as she stands over me. She is smiling, but her eyes seem intense, like diamonds. "Just lie down when you are ready," she encourages me.

I lie down, and allow my hand to slip over until it finds Leon lying nearby. His fingers hook onto mine, and the nearness of him calms me.

Holly leads us through another exercise, asking us to imagine we are in a deep cave, dark and quiet and still. We leave the emotions and baggage of the world outside the Pandaea here in the cave, and then we are allowed to sit up and speak to each other once again.

"Now that was a heck of an experience, don't you think?" said Dai immediately, while we were still all climbing to our feet. "I have never had to do a mental exercise like that before. It was amazing how much I felt as though I was there, you know? Like, this tent is quite hot and the air is humid, but I really felt as though I was in a cold cave, right? Did you feel like that babe?"

He helped Daphne to his feet, but she was more interested in getting out of the tent to where we could experience a bit of a cool breeze than in answering him immediately. Leon and I followed. The old couple were still lying on the ground as we left.

"Are you alright Ash? You grabbed my hand pretty tight there."

"I didn't grab your hand, I just... needed to hold your hand right then," I explained. Then I sniffed. "I just found something weird about those old people. They were kind of... threatening."

"The old people were threatening?" Leon raised his eyebrows.

"They weren't even that old," chipped in Dai, walking backwards in front of us. "I mean, sure they had grey hair, but they were so well preserved, did you see how tough that guy's skin looked? And the muscles, that was a man who's spent a lot of time being active in his life."

"Shhhh," I insisted, glancing over my shoulder. "Maybe they can hear us." The tent looked awfully close to me still.

"I'm sure they don't care!" declared Dai in a louder voice. "Come on. I reckon it's time for you to get your mind off these scary old people at the festival. Let's get a massage!"

CHAPTER THIRTY-THREE

Dai was practically skipping as he led us back through the festival grounds.

"Honestly, you will absolutely love the way they do their massages. The whole idea is that they give them away free to anyone who wants one. Siobahn said it's one way they give thanks to the moon goddess, by sharing calm with everyone."

After the strange rumours I had heard in the morning, and the odd looks from the couple in the meditation tent, I thought the idea of a massage sounded great. Maybe I would finally be able to get rid of the last remnants of stress that were keeping my shoulders tense.

"Hi, can we get four massages?" asked Dai as we ducked into the large gazebo where we had met Siobahn earlier that day. She wasn't there now. Instead a group of people who I absolutely did not recognise were smiling and laughing as we entered, and I felt a warm happy glow spread across my cheeks as a few of them rose to their feet.

"You totally can, my friend!" declared a tall man with a thick beard. "Come with me!"

We were all led out of the gazebo and into the tent next to it. It was one of those large multi-dome tents with a few rooms, each separated by a thin curtain that could be zipped into place. The man with the beard led Dai and Daphne to one side of the tent and a slender woman followed them. Two young men led the way for Leon and I to the other side.

Inside the room I saw they had set up a massage table that was made of a fuzzy brown material. It was the sort of table that can fold in half into a sort of suitcase. A makeshift shelf was lined with bottles at one side. The young man with short-cut hair smiled at Leon and led him through another curtain. I caught a glimpse of another massage table through there.

"It's a pleasure to have you here," said the man who had stayed in the room with me. He had dark hair shaved close to his scalp, and short stubble coloured his square jawline. He smiled. "My name is Lucas. Please remove as many clothes as you are comfortable with and then lie face down on the table."

He took a rolled up towel from one of the small shelves. "Anything you cover with the towel won't be massaged, and I'll keep asking you if you'd like it to be moved or adjusted as we go. It's totally fine to cover up an area later if you need to." He handed the towel to me and then moved away from the table and turned away.

I held onto the towel, rubbing my fingers through the textured material. How comfortable did I feel? I looked at the man. His shoulders were clearly strong and his jawline did intrigue me. It could be nice to have a strong pair of hands kneading my tensions away.

I took off all my clothes and then lay down on the table, leaving the towel on the floor within arms reach. I could hear rustling from the other rooms in the tent, although I couldn't see anything that was happening in them. I wondered if Leon was as naked as I was right now, and whether he was excited to feel the fingers of the young man who had led him away. I felt my skin rise in goosepimples as I waited for my masseuse to touch me. I could feel myself becoming slippery.

"All set? Excellent," said the man. I heard him step closer to the table. Then there was the sound of lotion being squeezed out of a bottle, and the soft noise of him spreading it across his hands. I breathed in deeply and smelt a strong woody scent.

"Did you light some incense?" I asked.

"Yes. The better to soothe your senses. I'm going to begin on your lower back."

I nodded against the crossed arms that I had laid beneath my head. Then, there was contact.

His hands felt broad, and the fingers strong. He moved slowly, pressing into my skin and moving the knots and stress consistently higher. The edges of his palms looped around my buttocks, and I felt my hips shift of their own accord in response.

He kept moving higher, working down to the sides of my waist, and curving up my ribs. The tips of his fingers brushed against the sides of my breasts, barely enough for me to even notice if I hadn't been straining to feel him. My skin was at once tingling like it was on fire, and soothed by the cool lotion that he was spreading over me.

As he pressed around my shoulder blades, I felt a click as parts of my spine shifted. The movement released a burst of satisfaction through me, and I felt the muscles in my limbs melt like butter.

He had been shifting the tension that he found higher as he moved, taking his time to sooth each part of my back. Somehow that moved the worries I had been holding in my shoulders up through my neck, until it felt like pressure all over my head. Lucas's hands worked their way across my shoulders, until he had fingers around my neck. I felt exposed to him, vulnerable to anything he might do now, and I couldn't stop a small gasp leaking from my throat.

I could tell that he laughed quietly at the noise, but I didn't feel silly for it. My senses were being overwhelmed, and it was wonderful. I thought I heard a moan from somewhere else in the tents and I hoped the others were feeling as good as I was.

Lucus then ran his fingernails up the base of my head, through my hair, brushing it into rows. He followed the pressure he had sent to my head, and squeezed just enough to release it, wrapping my head in his grip. He let his fingertips work along the rim of my ear and I had to bite my lip so that I didn't moan loud enough to distract him.

CHAPTER THIRTY-FOUR

He stepped down my body, allowing his fingers to drift along my skin, leaving a trail of sensation in their wake. Further he moved, until his hands were sliding across my ankles and around my feet. There was the sound of more lotion, and then his hands began to soothe my feet. I hadn't thought that my feet were sore, but as soon as he began working on me, the aches I had not acknowledged began disappearing. I groaned as he gripped my calves and pulled, sliding his hands down my legs and dragging the weariness out the ends of my toes.

He moved higher, and I relaxed more and more. His fingers pressed into my thighs, rhythmically massaging the muscle there, and I let my legs drift apart so that he could work his magic more easily. His hands continued higher, and then finally they brushed against my pussy.

It was a fleeting contact, but it felt like an electric shock after the relaxing massage, a bolt of light that shot straight into my heart and set it pounding.

"Would you like to adjust the towel yet?" asked Lucas. He had moved his hands back down my thighs so quickly that I wasn't sure if the touch had been accidental or not. "If you would like, we can offer a happy ending to the massage too." So probably not so accidental, I thought.

I didn't answer immediately, and Lucas spent the time rubbing my thighs and down around my knees. It was exceptionally pleasant. I lifted my head to turn and see his face. He was looking at me with a gentle smile on his strong jaw.

"I hope you're feeling more relaxed. If you'd like to get the towel, that's fine. I'd suggest an arm rub to finish."

I smiled at him. "No, I don't think I need a towel. I am interested in seeing how your happy ending works though."

His smile broadened. "With pleasure!"

I lowered my face back down and wriggled a little as his hands began to work their way higher once more. I relaxed into the feeling of his fingers on my soft skin, and then groaned as they reached the tops of my legs once more, the tips of his fingers grazing along either side of me.

He continued to work gently, with pressure and strength, but moving slowly so that I could relish the feelings he was drawing from me. He pressed the sides of me, which squeezed around my centre, and I gasped. He slid a fingertip from the top of my lips along them until he was running a finger up the curve of my bottom and then spreading a palm across it. He drew the hand away, scratching me gently with his nails.

I lifted my hips slightly. The heat inside me was growing, and I wanted to feel the soothing touch of his hands on me. I wanted to feel the release of tension that he had been so skilled at finding so far. He did not disappoint, rubbing softly at me and parting my lips until his fingers were rubbing on me, and teasing me, nearly entering me. As my breath began to come in small regular bursts, he worked on the small hardness of me, and I felt as though my senses were converging on me.

Sound receded from my awareness until all I could hear were my own rapturous pants. Sight was already reduced to the red darkness behind my eyelids. I could barely tell that I was lying on a fuzzy massage table any more, the only feeling left was his fingers, pressing on me, rubbing against me. I felt as though I wanted to explode.

Lucas knew what he was doing. He read the sounds of me, the motions of my body, and just when I was waiting on the edge of the explosion, he slid a finger inside me, seeking to draw out new sensations. I shuddered and groaned as my fire blossomed, and I felt myself gushing against him.

My muscles failed and I slumped further onto the table.

"There you are," he murmured. "I think you feel a lot better now, yes?"

I tried to nod, but it was hard to move my head. I stuck out my hand, trying to reach him. The fire had spread and dimmed, but there were still embers burning throughout me. I still needed something more. My fingers caught at his shirt.

"Are you okay?" he asked.

"Mmmm," I murmured. My fingers got a hold on him and pulled him closer. I felt the desire between my legs throbbing. "Finish the job properly."

"Are you sure?" he sounded uncertain. "We don't usually-"

I rolled over, enjoying the way his eyes flickered to my breasts and then back to my face. "I get that. And you don't have to do anything you aren't comfortable with either. But I would really like you to fuck me now."

I hoped my eyes were burning as brightly as they felt. Lucas looked into them seriously and then nodded and licked his lips.

"I would love to," he smiled. It took a moment for him to find a condom in the shelves by the lotion, and I turned back onto my stomach and waited for him to join me. I listened carefully to the sound of him removing his clothes, smiling at the sound of his zip lowering, and the rustle of his shirt hitting the ground. Then I felt his strong hands on me again, resting high on my thigh, supporting his weight as he climbed onto the massage table with me.

I felt his leg slip in between mine, and I adjusted so that he would find room. He straddled my leg, one of his powerful legs to either side of mine, and I shuddered as his cock rested on my skin. It felt large and hard, sliding across the top of my thigh and nudging at my buttock. I wriggled, and I enjoyed the way my motions nudged his length, setting it moving.

Lucas leaned forward, running his hands up the slippery skin of my waist and back again. As he continued to massage me, his hardness pressed further and further into me, and I bit my lip and tried to shuffle my hips against him.

His hands moved down my sides, gripping onto my hips and then lifted me higher. I adjusted my weight so that I could support myself as he lifted me higher. His cock slipped down past my bottom, and then brushed past my pussy. I felt a burst of wetness as I anticipated the feeling of that cock inside me. I hadn't even seen it, but the feeling of it was pleasing.

"Are you ready?" Lucas asked.

"Absolutely," I replied.

CHAPTER THIRTY-FIVE

There was a tearing sound as Lucas opened the condom and there was a moment of waiting as he put it on. I heard the slight crackle as the rubber was unrolled and then he leaned forward onto me. My hips were lifted into the air as I faced the massage table. I turned my head to one side, resting on my crossed arms. He pressed himself against me, finding my entrance quickly and then pausing and entering me slowly, deliberately. I purred with pleasure at the feeling of him filling me up. His fingers squeezed into my flesh and pulled me back towards him. I used my muscles to help, and soon the slow rhythm grew faster and faster.

A slapping sound began to fill the air, but I didn't care how loud we were being. The sound was caused by his balls swinging and hitting my clit, and each impact made bright white light flash across my eyes. The colour felt like a blanket of water, covering me and holding me closely as my body enjoyed the way Lucas was making me feel, but washing over me like a tide as well.

My fingers curled against the soft fuzz of the table, and I knew my mouth was hanging open, but I couldn't make myself act other way. Each thrust sent ripples up my body, flashes that blinded me and drove the air from my lungs.

"Yes," I yelped. "Keep going, don't stop!"

Lucas didn't reply, but his breathing was harsh and regular.

His finger dug into me deeper, the fingernails cutting into me. I gasped and flinched and then drove back against him harder. He began to pull at me more, striking into me with more and more force. Those fingers began to hurt.

"Too much," I panted, as I tried to twist my hips away from his clutch. "Back it off a bit."

Again, no reply from Lucas but his ragged breaths. His fingers did loosen a little though and I settled back into the rhythm of him fucking me.

I was aware of his legs rubbing against mine, of the hairiness of him against my own smooth skin. The air in the tent was close and hot and humid, and all I could hear were our breaths, out of time with one another but slowly creeping together. Thoughts of whether the others could hear us through the flimsy shetty walls of the tent entered my mind and were then forced aside as Lucas continued.

I tried to reach back and grab his hips so that he would press even further into me, but he was moving me so hard that I couldn't keep my balance on the massage table. For a moment I wondered if it might fall beneath our combined bodies but again, the feeling of this young strong man behind me drove the thoughts from my brain.

My breath came faster and faster, shallower, and I found my head beginning to swim. I was unable to process the world around me as Lucas began to sync up with me. Just as we both drew a deep guttering gasp he squeezed his fingers into my hips so hard that it hurt. I bit my lip and squealed as my muscles clenched around him, pulsing and squeezing him myself.

Slowly we pulled cold air into our lungs and held it there, giving our bodies time to relax from the heightened state they had driven to. Lucas ran his fingers across the small of my back and the sides of my bottom, before carefully pulling away. I gasped again as he left me, and then rolled onto my side, one hand on my belly.

Lucas stood next to the table, naked, and smiling. His muscles shone with a thin film of sweat, and his cock was still long and thick, though I could see it shrinking as I watched.

"Do you need that towel now?" he offered, reaching back to the shelves and putting a hand on an old pale green towel.

I laughed. "Yes, but I hope no one else is going to use it after me!"

He snorted as well and then threw the towel at me. "Consider it yours."

I used the towel to try and clean up the sweat and dampness that I was covered in. Now that we had completed our massage, I realised that I could still hear panting and squealing and slapping skin all around me.

"I suppose the others are enjoying their massages too."

Lucas only grinned.

"As long as you had a good time," he said. "I'll let you get dressed."

He gathered up his clothes and then left the room of the tent so that I could get dressed in private. As I pulled my panties up my legs and then shimmied into my top, I took stock of myself. The massage and its ecstatic ending had really done the trick. I didn't have the tension in my shoulders that had been there an hour or so earlier. Even when I thought about the horrible man who had tried to cause a problem last night, I didn't feel as directly threatened as I had before either. It was a concern, but I had spoken to plenty of people about it, and I felt more confident that we could take care of one another.

Leon's masseuse came out from the area they had gone to and caught my eye. He grinned sheepishly and then rushed on. Leon followed a few moments later.

"It was a good massage was it?" I asked with a raised eyebrow.

"You know it!" he agreed. Then he came over and put his arms around my waist. His eyes searched through mine. "You had an excellent time as well, yes?"

"Yes indeed." I leaned into him and kissed him, pulling his chest to me and hanging my arms on his shoulders. I breathed deeply through my nose, smelling his comfort and familiarity.

CHAPTER THIRTY-SIX

Outside the tent, Leon and I gathered in the gazebo where the other members of the site were still lounging. Dai and Daphne weren't done yet and so we chatted with some of the people laying out across the cushions. I snuggled down at one side of the gazebo with Leon, my arm around his waist and my head on his shoulder.

"How did your happy ending play out then," I asked softly beneath the murmuring conversation around us. I jabbed him playfully in the side with my fingertips.

"Very very nicely. I hadn't been expecting anything, you know, and then he made this offer, and I thought it sounded like a good idea."

"Go on then, what did he do to you?" I could feel myself growing warm and slippery just at the idea of my husband enjoying his masseuse.

"First, he rolled me over, and then he slid his hands along my hips. He moved them to my dick and pulled at me, just gently and encouraging me, and it felt really good. Then he lowered his lips to me and began to suck on me."

"Was he good at it?" I had one hand between my thighs, and I flexed my muscles slowly, enjoying the feeling of pressure.

"Yes, he was. He spent time moving up and down me, his fingers caressed my balls, and he just kept going." I could hear the timbre of his voice growling as he revisited the recent memory.

"Maybe I'll have to see if I can do what he did? Later on?"

"That sounds like an exquisite idea," said Leon, and his fingers trailed across my shoulder.

A sudden shout interrupted our reveries. Shrieks split the air.

"What the fuck is that?" yelped Leon, and he clambered to his feet from beside me. I tumbled onto the beanbag that he evacuated and then tried to shuffle myself up as well. There was a clattering noise, as though a pile of pots and pans had been knocked over in a kitchen.

"What's going on?" I asked him as I managed to pull myself up and cling to his arm.

"I can't tell."

The others in the gazebo were standing up as well, looking out along the campsite, trying to find the source of the noise. They stood with their hands across their foreheads, sheltering their eyes from the glare of the sun. One or two wore small frowns, but mostly they were more curious than anything else.

Then there was a burst of movement slightly to the left, out past the rows of tents opposite the massage site. A red dome was lifted like a bubble over the tents beside it before it spun sideways and vanished amongst the crowd. People were stepping out and looking around, trying to see what was going on. Another tent shook violently as something crashed past it and another voice rang out. There were shouts of anger amongst the crescendo now. Leon put a hand out across my chest and stepped forward.

I was expecting to see a wild animal come bursting from the tents when it reached our row and so I was surprised when a tall man wearing only a pair of ragged cut off jean shorts stepped through a gap between the tents. He was carrying a large leather drinking pouch and pulling deep mouthfuls from in as he strode forward, staggering sideways occasionally.

"Who's that?" asked Leon.

"Shit. Gunner's drunk." The comment came from a short man standing nearby. He had a thick mop of black hair tufting from his head, and loose tie dye vest on, fluttering in the breeze.

"Is he really causing all that mayhem?" I asked incredulously. It seemed impossible that a single man was causing so much chaos. How had he flipped an entire tent? He didn't look as though he would be able to hold a tent up in his hands long enough without falling over.

Then six more figures came out to join him. They were staggering as well, shoving each other while they grinned. Their teeth shone, even from this distance, and it made them seem even more dangerous.

A man in light blue shorts ran out from the tents after them, clearly angry with the way they had broken through his site, and he tried to grab the man at the back of the group, a figure in long hot denim jeans.

"What the fuck do you think-" I heard him snarl, before the man spun around and shoved him in the chest with both hands. The man in blue was sent careening into another tent, and I winced as I heard poles snap beneath him. A voice squealed as he fell on top of whoever was hiding in the tent.

The denim-clad man began to walk towards the mess he had made.

"Keep yourself to yourself, or you're going to get hurt, meatball" snarled the denim wearer.

Beneath him the other man began to try and stand from amongst the wreckage of the tent, but the denim man kicked him in the chest and he stayed down after that.

The rest of the group hadn't even looked around to see what had happened.

"What the fuck is going on?" I hissed. I reached up and clung onto Leon's arm in front of me, trying not to cut him with my fingernails. The man in the front, the one we had been told was Gunner, with his long face and shaved head, was walking directly towards us.

"He's just a bit of a shit," said the furry man who had spoken earlier. "You have to know how to deal with him."

Gunner walked up to the edge of the masseuse site and took another slug from the drinking pouch without looking away from us. Dark liquid spilled from the corner of his mouth. I was watching his eyes closely. They were large staring eyes. I was sure that he hadn't blinked since he had led his giggling hyenas out from amongst the tents. He sniffed as he jammed a stopper into his pouch and then wiped his face with the back of his arm.

CHAPTER THIRTY-SEVEN

"What are they doing?" The man asked. His voice was calmer than I had suspected. From the way he had stomped towards us, leaving a trail of destruction, I had expected his voice to sound like a chainsaw, like sandpaper wrapped around a cotton bud and then dragged through my ears. Instead it sounded like silk and whiskey.

He nodded at Leon and me, but kept his eyes on one of the others. His rabble kept giggling and repeating what he had said on the grass behind him, bouncing up and down on their feet and rubbing their hands. Some of them watched me with the same burning piercing gaze that a cat turns on a baby bird in the garden. I stepped further behind Leon.

"They just got a massage. Did you want one Gunner?" replied a man near the front of the gazebo.

Gunner's mob snarled and hissed and pulled the fingers at him, but the man simply stood and watched Gunner. The intruder stared back and then a smile cut across his face.

"Not at the moment. I'm already feeling very relaxed right now." He spread his arms wide, as though to take in all of the carnage he had left in his wake. "But maybe I'll come back later."

That sounded like a threat to me.

"You feel free to come back anytime Gunner. We'll be glad to see you." The man from the massage campsite smiled and turned his back on the angry man standing in the middle of the gap between tents. I couldn't imagine doing something like that. Wasn't he terrified that the arsehole would take a swing at the back of his head? Gunner seemed like the sort of person who could. Exactly the sort of dickhead who would take personal affront at such a snub, at the idea that someone wouldn't take their angry posturing seriously.

Gunnar's face twisted into a snarl but he waved away his gang of malcontents and they all started moving down the row. I could hear them still causing trouble in the tents, but thankfully they were not our problem anymore. I clutched Leon's arm tighter and he stepped back to envelop me in a hug. I felt a wave of relief wash over my skin like ice and I released the breath that had been trapped inside.

"Shit, what was all that about," asked Daphne. She and Dai were standing behind me. They must have only just come out from their massages.

"What did you see?" Leon asked.

"Just that big dickhead walking away and causing some shit down the line," said Dai. He scrubbed a hand through his short black hair.

"I did hear some noise before," added Daphne. "I assume that was them?"

"Yeah, that was them," I nodded.

Dai looked a little confused. He opened his mouth but then closed it again.

"Do you have a question Dai?" I asked.

"Noooo," he replied slowly. "I just..." His cheeks darkened a little and he coughed to clear his throat. "I didn't hear any noises."

Daphne rolled her eyes. "SOMEone was a little too preoccupied to notice those thugs coming up to the site."

Dai grinned sheepishly.

I laughed.

"Fair enough! I personally think these masseuse's are very very good at what they do here!"

We all laughed and then settled down into the chairs and beanbags in the gazebo. The members of the site didn't seem to mind us making ourselves comfortable.

"Do you think that was the guy you heard about this morning," asked Daphne.

"Oh shit," I flinched. "I hadn't even thought about that. He did seem like the right sort of shit to do something like that, didn't he?"

Daphne nodded. Her eyes were large and serious. I rubbed at the bridge of my nose and drew a long slow breath and then let it blow out from my mouth. I cast my thoughts back to earlier this morning, in the line for the showers.

"No," I finally said carefully. "They said that the guy was tall and hairy. They were very clear that he had a lot of hair." I could tell by the way everyone sat back and stared at nothing that we were all picturing Gunner in our minds. A bastard for sure, but a very bald bastard.

"What sort of place is this that has more than one absolute maniac wandering around it?" said Daphne. She was frowning. "Some people have kids here. This is pretty shit!"

Dai laid a hand on her leg to try and soothe her, but I noticed that he didn't have anything to say against her statement.

One of the women lounging in the gazebo near us was close enough to overhear our conversation and she leaned in a bit to contribute.

"You alright loves?" she asked.

"Yeah, I'm just a little shaken up by that guy. And we heard of a woman being attacked last night not far from our tents." I shook my head. "To be honest, I came here looking for a chance to really let my hair down and just have a good time, but I've encountered some scary things and I'm beginning to wonder if we should just leave."

"What? You are?" Leon sounded surprised.

"Yeah, just a bit." I felt as though my stomach was clenching in on itself as I spoke. I hadn't admitted that I was feeling this shaken up to myself yet. I had surprised myself by saying that maybe I should go. But as soon as the words had left my mouth, I felt my shoulders untense. Clearly it was something I had been hanging onto in the back of my mind, where I always didn't notice it. The pure happiness I had expected from the Pandaea had been degraded by the presence of these men. They were the lemons in the milk, and the festival was curdling. It was what always happened when diluted things spoiled pure ones. The pure thing was tainted and no good any more.

"I totally understand that," said the woman. "I can see how all of that would feel scary and overwhelming, especially when you're in a new place like this. But I can promise you, Gunner is all bark and no bite. He's an arsehole but he's never caused any real damage."

"What about all those tents that he and his idiots just crashed through?" I said.

"Okay yes, but not real damage. No one was hurt. And the Pandaea is an inclusive festival, those people will be taken care of. Look."

I had to admit, it did look as though she was right. Already small groups of people had gone over to check on the people who had been stomped on by the group of thugs. Repairs and hugs were already underway.

"Their belongings will be fixed or replaced, and now that Gunnar has stepped out of line, the organisers have good reason to get him out of the site. It will be taken care of, and you can be safe to dance and meditate and enjoy this place away from the trials of the regular world again."

"What about the attack last night? Did Siobahn tell you about that?"

The woman nodded. "I'm sure it was Gunnar or one of his goons. Don't worry, it will be fine once he's kicked out, and you can be sure he will be escorted out of the valley before you know it."

CHAPTER THIRTY-EIGHT

I felt better listening to the women in the gazebo. She spoke with authority, and she sounded very cheerful, despite the events of the last day or so. She smiled at me, and I thought about the good times I had experienced at the festival so far. The stalls, the parade, the swimming, the sex, the dancing, the art, the meditation. There was so much here that filled me up with positive feelings. So much of it had left me exhilarated and excited. Was I overreacting for what was a horrible and unfortunate coincidence? After all, with so many people in one space, it was inevitable, if depressing, that some of them would be gross and presumptive, wasn't it. I nodded at the woman.

"Yes, I think you're right. It will be okay."

Leon and I returned to our van for most of the afternoon. After such a big night, and a full morning, I needed the chance to lay down on our mattress with the doors open, letting my mind wander as my body relaxed, allowing the breeze to soothe me. Before long I was fast asleep, with my husband's arms around my waist.

"Hey. Hey guys." Daphne's voice was quiet but insistent. I yawned and stretched and tried to push myself up a little. The light outside was dim and streaked with gold and orange. Leon made a strange warbling noise behind me as he surfaced from the depths of whatever dream he was having.

"Whassit. Huh?" I managed to express as I blinked. My friend was standing next to the van, her hands over her head on it as she leaned in.

"Do you guys want some of our dinner? We just had some bacon that we fried up, and a bunch of rolls and bagged salad and stuff."

"Oh my god, fooooood," moaned Leon. He began to roll out of the van, not bothering to get his legs underneath him until he was beyond its metal confines. He looked like some sort of bug as he crawled out and collapsed on the grass before getting to his feet.

"Yeah, sounds good," I added. "What time is it?"

Daphne shrugged. "Dunno. But the important thing is that it's getting late, so the dancing is about to go off. I figured I should wake you guys up to get some fuel in your bellies and then we can all get out to the hollow!"

I loved Daphne in that moment.

We made ourselves some simple rolls and ate our fill, and then Dai handed out plastic camping cups with a deep serving of rum and coke in each. I took a long sip and sighed in pleasure. The drink warmed my stomach immediately, and I felt fully relaxed.

"You look happy Ash," Dai said after handing out the drinks.

"I feel good! Today had so many highs and lows, but clearly all I needed was a bit of sleep and a good drink."

"And good friends," said Leon, lifting his cup up in a toast to Dai and Daphne.

"Good friends," we all joined in. Somewhere out beyond the tent I heard the shrill call of a peacock.

After eating we dressed in something to dance in. I shook my head at Leon and Dai, who were wearing baggy shorts and loose button-up shirts. At least Dai went to the effort of sticking a crown made out of glow sticks on his head before declaring that he was ready.

Daphne took much more pride in her outfit. She dug out a pair of thigh high red boots and a sheer black bodysuit. Then she wrapped her waist and arms in red leather straps. Her face was made up with a thick black straight line that covered her like a mask, from the tip of her nose to just above her eyebrows. I couldn't help but search along the sheer bodysuit with my eyes. The high cut hips outlined her thighs so finely, the curves of her stomach and breasts so temptingly shaded.

"You look amazing," I breathed.

Daphne winked at me. "I should have brought more outfits. I didn't have enough energy to bother last night, but now I feel like I should have something else to put on tomorrow for the final night!"

I nodded. For my own dancing outfit, now that Daphne had inspired me, I pulled a light pink set of lingerie from the drawers in the van. The outfit lifted my breasts a little and gave me a bit of extra cleavage that I enjoyed, but actually covered me down to the top of my thighs. Little suspenders hooked onto the fishnet stockings I found, although the effect was a bit spoiled by the sneakers I had to wear. Then I gave myself some strong blue eyes and pinned a huge pink dahlia headpiece to the side of my hair.

Daphne reached over to help me tidy up my lipstick.

"You look like a dessert, ready to eat."

"Perfect!" I laughed. She and I linked arms and led our men, sipping from their bottles of beer, across the festival site towards the hollow, where steady deep rhythms were already pounding into the twilight.

The hollow was thicker than I had seen it before. The crowd swirled like a swarm of ants, tumbling around the grassy slopes. Knots of people pulled away and stumbled up the sides of the hollow until they were able to puff from their vapes, or sip at drinks. Couple were laying on the grass, kissing and running hands over one another's bodies.

Glowsticks and LEDs shone in the crowd, and a haze of stage mist or smoke hung over their heads. Lasers from the stage stabbed through it all, and the result was a scene of never ending chaos. It reminded me of mediaeval paintings of hell, but the sound and sensations were all positive and exciting instead of terrifying.

CHAPTER THIRTY-NINE

"Look!" whooped Dai, pointing towards the main archway through the trees.

A pair of gigantic men were escorting a smaller figure away from the crowd. I saw the figure between them had a bald head, but I wasn't sure who it was until he turned to glance around the hollow just before they moved under the trees.

"It's that Gunnar arsehole," I said in surprise.

"They really meant what they said," grinned Dai. "He crossed a line and it's time for him to go!"

The angry man made a small movement as though he was going to turn around and rejoin the dancers, but the giant on his left shoved him in the shoulder and sent him stumbling through the archway.

"I wonder if his buddies are still hanging around?" I frowned in worry.

"Maybe. But I've seen toadies like that so many times. Without their big bad boss to egg them on, they'll probably go hide somewhere with their tail between their legs." Dai grabbed me by both shoulders. "Ignore those pricks. The festival can only get better from here!"

"Let's get in there!" announced Leon and he took my hand and plunged us both into the maelstrom.

The crowd of dancers opened up before us and surrounded us like a living wall, enveloping us in hot sweaty skin and rumbling bass. Eyes were closed around me as hands reached into the flashing lights and mist overhead. I felt a layer of moisture cover me almost instantly, but it didn't feel as gross as I might have expected. It cooled me and helped me feel comfortable as I followed Leon through the figures, weaving past people who were pounding the dirt beneath their feet, or spinning wildly.

The rhythm was insistent, and I had to respond to the music myself, bouncing on the balls of my feet, wiggling my hips from side to side as I stepped through the people. I bumped into their sides, and bounced from body to body, but through it all I kept a hand clutched tightly to Leon. He stopped.

We were deep in the crowd. From the view of the stage, I could tell that we were near the front. Blinding lights glared down at the knot of people here, shoulder to shoulder, but I didn't feel irritated by the light. It encouraged me to lean back and close my eyes, surrendering to the sounds and sensations all around. Leon stepped behind me and laid a hand on my waist, bobbing and weaving to the music himself.

I was enjoying the dance and I looked around for Daphne and Dai. Surely they weren't far behind us. But I could't find them anywhere in the swirling mass of people. Instead I began to notice the seeking faces around me. Not all of them, but some, enough. Faces that contained eyes full of hunger, faces that were looking intently through the dancers instead of upturned towards the moon and the music. I saw a man wearing that expression step up behind a short woman with long dark hair. She was smiling, arms raised as she swung her hips in time with the music. The man began to weave in time with her, following the movement of her body with his own, edging closer and closer to her.

I wondered if I should say something, or call her attention to the man. I was too far away to move through the crush of bodies. But then she turned in her dance, hips swivelling, and saw the man. She smiled and laid a hand on his shoulder and continued to spin her hips, resting against him. He grinned and put an arm around her waist, pulling her even closer.

I blinked and looked back to the stage, with its DJ whose hair was shaved short on the sides of their head, beneath a brilliantly yellow flap of hair falling to one side. They held a headphone to one ear, and manipulated the switches and dials of the music in front of them. It was hard to think as the music pounded into me and echoed up into the night sky. I must have been wrong about that man's face. He wasn't a threat, that woman welcomed him.

There was something liberating about dancing in the night with my husband. The music was louder than anything I had experienced ever before, and the sound flowed around me like a physical presence. It was as though I could feel the waves of the music wash across my skin, driving a vibration of sensation as it went, sending a tingle across the surface of my body and then out to my extremities.

My mind retreated from the intensity of the sound, and I stopped thinking about what was going on at the festival. I stopped worrying about Daphne and Dai's relationship or what any of the strangers I might have accidentally offended might be thinking of me. I let go of the strange glances that I had noticed from the people who were such a strong part of this festival, the ones who had been coming for years.

Instead, I allowed my senses to admit their experiences in this moment, and I relished each sight and sound and scent. My eyes followed the beaming lasers overhead, swirled with the wheels of light that were mounted alongside the stage. I met the eyes of fellow dancers, outlined in neon, covered in bright makeup, their irises reflecting the chaos that engulfed us.

I could smell the weed that drifted in clouds through the

crowd. I could smell the thick richness of the earth beneath our feet that had been stomped and soaked and churned into a muddy paste. The heavy musk of sweat made me feel sleepy.

My muscles sent throbs of ache from my thighs, but then the cool night air would gust against my skin and I would feel re-energised. The thump of bodies around me sent me stumbling, but Leon's reassuring hand on my waist kept me upright. I smiled at him and slung my arms around his shoulders, behind his neck. He kissed me, and I kissed him, pulling each other closer and closer, pressing my face against him so hard that I felt as though I would meld us into one form. The taste of his tongue and the warmth of him made my breath quicken. I wanted to feel every inch of him alongside my body. My feelings spread through me, taking me over with pure lust.

CHAPTER FORTY

*L*eon and I danced together, close, as the bass pounded through the night and the crowd. I turned so that he was pressed against my back, his hands resting on my hips as I sucked in cold air. I opened my eyes to the colours around me, the figures dancing in their tight and shining outfits, the moon watching down over us all. A tall man with long dark hair and trimmed black beard was dancing nearby, his eyes closed. The man was wearing only a pair of heavy denim shorts that clung to his powerful legs, and the skin of his well defined arm muscles glistened. At first I thought it was sweat, or water that he might have poured over himself to help cool off, but then I realised that the shimmery sparkles on his skin were patches of glitter. His eyes wore some of the same shimmer in an eye shadow.

He opened his eyes and caught my gaze immediately. He glanced over me, with Leon's hands stretching around to me. Then he smiled.

I loved that smile. It dug into my stomach through my chest, and he felt strong and warm. I smiled back, hoping that my face looked excited and flushed with anticipation, though I was concerned I may have looked overheated and manic instead. The man stepped towards us, continuing to sway with the insistent rhythm from the stage.

"Well hello there," he said, nearly shouting in order to be heard. He leaned in close to me as well, and I became aware of the size of him. He was much taller than me, his powerful arms thick and strong.

"Hi," I replied. "Enjoying yourself?"

"Very much, and even more now," the man's eyes flickered over my shoulder to Leon. "My name is Lochie. Who are you two?"

"I'm Leon and this is my wife Ashleigh."

"It's a pleasure to meet you. Do you mind if I dance with you both?"

"I would love that," I said. Leon's fingers squeezed me slightly.

"Me too," he added.

The three of us danced together in the crowd, our own small knot of tactile pleasure beneath the moon and stars. The music around me faded as my mind became aware of the two men dancing beside me. Leon's hands still lingered on my sides, stroking up and down my back, dipping to my bottom once in a while, but now Lochie's touch joined him.

The man's fingers felt solid and firm and his touch was certain, not the tentative cautious contact that I had experienced in many other men. He placed his hands on my upper arms, touched my stomach as he danced beside me, moved in close so that I could place my hands on his waist. His skin felt smooth, but the muscles beneath the surface were pleasingly firm.

Soon my senses only spoke to me of the two men, Leon and Lochie. The only thing I could feel was their hands, their skin beneath my own. I was barely aware of my feet on the ground beneath me. It was as though we had begun to float away from the earth entirely, and now we spun around and over each other, like birds in the sky, or fish in the sea. I let my head fall back to lay against Leon's chest, and his lips lowered to my cheek, running along my jaw, drifting over the curve of my neck. His breath warmed my skin, and I pulled a hand behind his head, wishing that he would follow further. I wanted to feel his lips move over my breasts until my hard nipple caught between them.

At the same time Lochie had moved closer, hands holding hips firmly and pulling me closer to him, a slow movement that made me aware of his position between my legs. I knew I wanted to feel more of him in that position, to feel the heat of his skin as I pressed my thighs to his sides. I held out a hand to him as well, pulling his shoulder closer to me.

I could see nothing but I didn't know if my eyes were open or closed. It wasn't a darkness that surrounded me, but a comforting glow that I could barely describe. I caught a flash of Lochie's face, his eyes burning above his beard, as he moved closer, and then I moaned as his lips lowered to my neck. His beard scratched against my skin, but his fingers caught at the edge of my clothing, pulling it lower. I was concealed by his face, but the tiny stabs of his beard on my nipples made me gasp and then sigh as the soothing warmth of his mouth wrapped around me, his tongue flicking at me. I pulled him closer.

Leon's mouth opened, and his teeth nipped at the soft skin of my shoulder. I dropped my hand from behind his head, slipping it between our bodies below my hips. I writhed as I ran my hand across his hardness, thrilled by how strong it felt even through his heavy shorts. A tension was building in me and the muscles in my legs were beginning to quiver.

Just when I felt as though I was going to collapse between these men, Lochie shifted his hand, moving it between my legs. The pressure through my underwear sent a shock of relief through me and I moaned again. The feeling of his large strong hand over me, pressing against me, was so pleasurable that I felt as though my body was about to melt off my bones. He shifted slightly, allowing one finger to press between me, adding to the sensation in my centre. I fell, and he caught me in that hand, holding me up with desire. I squeezed Leon harder, rubbing my hand against the material of his clothes and wishing that it would disappear.

"I think we're a little exposed here," murmured Leon into my ear, his teeth nibbling at it as he did. "Perhaps we should take our new friend somewhere else?"

As he spoke, I felt my awareness return to the physicality of my body. The sound from the stage returned and I felt the solidity of the world lying beneath my feet. I glanced around over the broad shoulder of Lochie who was still hunched in front of me, licking at my breasts. I could see people in the crowd looking at the three of us, and it made me feel more self conscious. None of the spectators looked offended, or prurient, but I pulled my top up over my breasts anyway.

"Would you like to come back to our site with us?" Leon asked Lochie. The broad shouldered man straightened and smiled.

"Absolutely!"

CHAPTER FORTY-ONE

*L*ochie put an arm around my waist as we made our way out of the dancers, disentangling ourselves from the throng as calmly as we could while the fire of skin on skin still burned beneath the surface. I put an arm around his waist too, and felt the presence of Leon on the other side of Lochie. As we moved into the darker slopes around the hollow, I glanced past Lochie to my husband. Just as I did, Leon leaned over as well, and he kissed Lochie. The kiss started softly but then Lochie pulled Leon closer and they began to devour one another. I shifted so that Lochie could bring his other arm around and hold Leon close, and laid my own hand over Leon's as he squeezed Lochie's arse.

"I hope you aren't making me walk too far," muttered Lochie when he and Leon finally pulled away from each other. "I don't know how much further I can go without grabbing you both and tumbling us all to the ground." His voice rattled with desire.

"Our van is just back among the tents, past the market," I explained.

"We'll have to see if we can make it that far," he said.

We passed through the archway of trees, still struggling to walk as we touched one another in ceaselessly moving hands. We walked past the high walls of the silent rave, outlined in neon glowing uv paint and purple lights. The sight of the silent dancers contained within it made me giggle, and the men chuckled with me.

Lochie turned and lifted me up against the edge of the enclosure, pressing my back against the wood and tucking his arms around my thighs to hold me up. I was spread open in front of him, with his body in between my legs, and he pressed in towards me. I wrapped my arms around his broad shoulders and pressed my lips to his. We kissed hard, and deep, our tongues searching each other as though a secret was contained inside us.

I could feel every single finger that he had clutching my thighs, keeping me lifted high against the wooden wall. I could also feel his insistence, pressing his hips in towards me, forcing himself closer. I wanted to reach down and discover how hard he was, how strong was his desire for me.

I allowed my eyelids to flicker open briefly, and saw that Leon had stepped up behind Lochie. He had his arms around the other man's sides, and his lips lowered to Lochie's bare shoulder. I could tell from his movements that he was pressing himself close to Lochie from the other side. I wriggled my hips, hoping to feel where my husband's hands were.

I nudged against them and realised that he had both of his hands tucked into Lochie's shorts, slipped down between his legs. The rhythm of his own hips matched his arms, and I could tell that Leon was pulling and stroking Lochie's cock.

That bastard, I thought happily. *I want to be doing that!*

"We have to find a better spot," I managed to say around Lochie's persistent tongue.

"Okay," he breathed, and he let me down. Then he reached around his back and grabbed Leon's head, pulling him close to kiss him. The two men stood in front of me, Leon squeezing and pressing, Lochie groaning under Leon's attention. I pressed my hand over myself, trying to assuage the desperate need to be touched that was consuming me.

After an eternity, the men broke apart from one another.

"Come on, our van isn't far! We just have to focus on walking, and not grabbing each other every few metres." Leon's hair was ruffled and his eyes shone in the darkness. I wondered how pink his cheeks would be if I could see them properly.

"I'm sure I don't know what you mean," I declared, lifting my chin. "I'm very in control of myself." I turned to begin walking through the market to the campsites.

"Pity that I'm not," growled Lochie, who reached out and slapped my arse.

The three of us laughed and scampered back through the tents, hands slapping other hands aside, laughs turning into moans as one or the other of us would kiss someone else. Eventually, somehow, we arrived at our van and climbed inside.

CHAPTER FORTY-TWO

nce we were in the van, none of us wasted any time on pretended shyness. We all knew what we wanted, and we had been forced to wait already for longer than we had anticipated. I took a moment to unbuckle the fastenings of my outfit but soon kicked it to the end of the van, leaving me lying naked near the wall on my side of the bed. Leon hunched over to pull off his shirt and then rolled into a sort of ball to remove his shorts. Lochie lay back on our mattress and tugged his shorts off in one motion, revealing a long hard cock that turned to the side a little. I couldn't stop myself moaning as I saw it, and then I reached out and took it in my hand.

Lochie's skin felt so smooth in my palm. I felt him pulse and thicken as I held him. I squeezed, feeling the firmness of him, watching as his head swelled. I lowered my head and licked my lips as they opened, then took him into me. He groaned and I felt Leon shifting his position.

I let Lochie further inside my mouth, stretching my lips a little further to envelope him fully. My hand was around his shaft, and it moved lower, cupping his balls. The musk from his hair filled my senses, but it just made my stomach tense as I wished for one of these men to touch me. My tongue pressed up against the shape of Lochie in my mouth and he twisted to one side.

Then I felt Leon's hands on my hips and the thrill of finally being touched made a shiver fly up my spine. I felt Lochie jerk as the shiver moved my jaw around him. Immediately, the heat of Leon's breath on my lower back made my muscles melt. That warmth was heightened as Leon's lips met my skin, and then his tongue.

I tried to focus on Lochie but Leon made it difficult to keep my attention on the cock that I was tending to. His tongue slid across the curve of my buttocks, and slowly edged further and further to the centre of me, teasing me with its proximity. I tensed up but then accepted his tongue as it delved into me. I could feel my lips pull apart, wet and dripping, and then Leon moved a hand to run fingers along me. I came all at once, in an explosion of tension suddenly snapping. My arms and legs clenched and it took all of my will to keep myself from biting down on Lochie.

I had to lift my head and lay back next to his legs, trying to catch my breath and get control of my body. Leon smiled and crawled up Lochie's legs, smoothly taking my place. I managed to reach out and touch his shoulder as he lowered his mouth around Lochie's cock, taking exactly the same position that I had vacated only a few moments earlier.

Leon kept his tongue and lips entertaining Lochie long enough for me to renew my strength, reach between my legs, and bring myself to another orgasm. This time I stared into Lochie's eyes as I came, and he placed both of his hands on my husband's head, holding his cock deep in Leon's mouth.

"Do you have any condoms?" he asked after I had burst over the mattress.

Leon lifted his face higher and then nodded.

"I want you," Lochie growled, his voice rumbling in the small space within our van. Leon moved over to rummage in a small plastic tub near the end of the mattress. In a moment he was moving back up the mattress with a condom between his fingers. I saw that he had thought ahead, grabbing our small tube of lube as well.

Lochie rose to meet Leon, kissing him fiercely and grabbing the back of Leon's head. I could see the way his muscles tensed and how his fingers were grasping at Leon. It looked as though Lochie was trying to consume my husband, and I had to press a hand to my pussy as though I could quell the urge that was rising again.

Lochie pushed Leon backwards until my husband was lying underneath him. I watched as their cocks, both of which were as solid and stiff as I could imagine, bumped against one another. Their stiffness rubbed along each other's lengths as they shifted their hips, the tip of Leon's penis pressing into the hair above Lochie's. Lochie still had Leon's head in his hands, pulled against his lips. Leon was running his hands over Lochie's chest and down his sides, pulling him closer.

Without pulling away, Lochie unwrapped the condom and slid it over his cock. Leon squirted some of the lube into his hand and then threw the lube to one side. He moved his hand down between them, rubbing it around his arse, and then sliding the slippery gel along Lochie's dick. He squeezed and rubbed, drawing another growl from the big man.

Lochie positioned himself between Leon's legs and then began to press forward. My husband gasped and moaned, wrapping an arm around Lochie's shoulders and gripping the sheets in a fist with his other hand. I crawled closer, lowering my face to Leon's. He moaned again as I nuzzled his cheek and kissed his face.

"You can do it babe," I whispered in his ear. He barely moved, but I felt his nudge me. He knew that I was with him.

I placed a hand on his chest as Lochie moved further. It was as though I was lying on the mattress beneath him, right there with Leon. Lochie's eyes burned above us both, his hot breath panted down on us. His chest was taut and his arms looked as strong as trees as he pushed further and further.

Leon's legs were lifted up by Lochie's sides, hooked around his waist. Lochie began to thrust, pulling away and then forward again, slowly at first and then faster and faster. His face was serious and stern as he worked on my husband, who gasped and twisted beneath him. Lochie reached out a hand and clawed his way down Leon's chest, making him yelp. Then he grabbed onto Leon's shoulder, pushing his fingers deeply into the flesh.

As Leon's head arched back, I leaned in to kiss him, seeking in his mouth with my tongue, trying to ground him here in this moment. He returned the kiss with as much passion as he could spare, so overwhelmed was he by Lochie. I slid a hand down his stomach, seeking his cock as it bounced against his stomach. I knew this organ so well, I could recognise every twitch as it sought release.

Lochie came, hunching further over my husband as his muscles spasmed. At the same time I stroked and coaxed Leon to orgasm, his come flowing from him and up his stomach, before running down my fingers and dripping onto him.

Leon lay back on the mattress in the dark and I ran my fingers up his stomach to his chest and then snuggled into the crook of his shoulder. I kissed his cheek.

Lochie moved backwards, breathing heavily.

CHAPTER FORTY-THREE

"Thank you," I said with a smile, and I meant it. That was one of the most satisfying and powerful sexual experiences I had ever had.

"Hrrmmm," Leon agreed from where he lay.

Lochie nodded and smiled. In the shadowy interior of the van, it was hard to make out his face clearly. He pulled the condom off and dropped it to the side of the mattress.

"Hey, man, gross!" I reached over and picked it up carefully, and then dropped it into a bag we kept by the driver's seat for rubbish.

Lochie reached out and pulled my shoulder so that I ended up back next to him, lying on his thigh. I could see his face more clearly now, and he was still smiling, still with the burning desire in his eyes.

"What next?" he grinned.

"What do you mean?"

"Give me five minutes," he said as his eyes flicked to his softening erection. "I'll be ready to go again soon."

"Oh." I was nonplussed. I had thought that the final climax of our time had happened already. Leon was completely shattered, and although I could still feel the urge to be touched, I knew that the fires within were fading . "I suppose I thought we were finished now, " I said, wondering whether I sounded as confused as I felt.

"Finished?" Lochie's smile slipped. "I thought you two were going to be a good time. We've barely had a chance to start exploring!" He leaned in to kiss me.

I leaned away sharply. "No, I'm not feeling it now."

"Not feeling it? Oh, I'll have you feeling everything. You won't feel anything else!" I could see that his dick was already beginning to grow thicker again, but the desire to reach out and stroke it had gone. It just was like an invasive presence now. I shook my head.

"No, I think that's enough."

Leon sat up as well. "Hey man, don't ruin a good night."

"Shut up," snapped Lochie. He wasn't smiling anymore. "I was expecting to fuck you both, this is bullshit." The light in his eyes was darker now, and I felt scared. I was suddenly very aware of this man's strength, the broadness of his figure, the size of the muscles that I had previously been so enamoured with.

I pulled a deep breath. The air I drew into my lungs felt hot and thick. I reached over and slid the van door open. Cool night air flooded in and covered my bare skin in goose pimples. "I think you should go."

Lochie stared at me for long seconds. I held my breath, sure that he was about to get violent, and hoping that my husband would be able to get in between us. From the corner of my eyes, I saw Leon's face grow hard and his shoulder tense.

Finally Lochie shook his head and sneered.

"You two teases aren't worth the trouble." He grabbed his shorts from beside him on the mattress and shoved past me to the door. I scampered aside as quickly as I could, not wanting to touch him by mistake.

Lochie stood naked outside our van, bathed in moonlight. I shuffled closer to Leon, clutching his leg. Leon grabbed the door, ready to slide it closed.

"Fuck you both," snarled Lochie, his shorts dangling from his hand.

"Just go man," said Leon as he pulled the door shut.

The door squealed closed and slammed with a bang. Leon flicked the locks and they snapped shut. Almost instantly, there was another bang and I could see that Lochie had hit the side of the van. He pulled the finger at us through the window and then stormed off into the night, still naked. I watched his figure as he left, tall and strong, with thick long hair falling down his shoulders. I felt my stomach grow cold as I recognised that description.

"Oh my god."

"It's alright babe," said Leon. He reached around my shoulders and drew me into a hug. "I didn't know he'd be such an arsehole, but he's gone now."

"It's not just that. I just realised that he sort of looks like the description of that bastard who attacked someone last night."

"Oh shit!" Leon flinched as though stung. His hands stayed on me though, comforting and familiar. "Fuck, that's not cool at all."

We sat in silence in the shadows of our van, not looking at each other, but holding each other close.

"I suppose there's not much more we can do right now," I ventured eventually. My brain felt as though it was swaddled and slow. I wasn't sure if it was my shock or just the lateness of the night that was slowing me down.

"Probably not right now," agreed Leon. "But we can go and talk to Siobahn first thing in the morning. I think she'll know how we can report him and get him kicked out of here." He kissed my shoulder. "After all, we saw how they got rid of Gunnar really quickly."

I nodded. Gunnar. For a moment I had wondered if he had been responsible for the earlier attack, but he didn't really match the description that the woman in the shower queue had given. Lochie was much more likely to have been involved. Two different violent men. Was this festival worth that risk? I already knew it had been sullied by them.

Sleep was hard to find that night. I lay on the mattress in the back of our van, tossing and turning, always feeling either too hot or too cold. The only thing that helped soothe me as I felt the anxiety spreading out from the base of my head was the awareness of Leon lying next to me. I would roll to one side and then my leg would fall over the top of his, and he would shift his arm so that his hand was laying on my skin. Just the presence of those fingers drifting along my calf would settle my nerves and allow me to sink back into some semblance of sleep. But even so, dawn began spiking bright rays through our windows before I felt rested.

CHAPTER FORTY-FOUR

ogether Leon and I groaned and struggled to rouse ourselves enough to clamber out of the van. We managed to do so at great effort, and relocated ourselves into the small front room of Dai and Daphne's tent. Leon began setting up the gas cooker and kettle, while I tried to ignore the muffled noises coming from further inside the tent.

Dai and Daphne sounded as though they were enjoying waking up together. Every movement and gasping breath was clear through the thin fabric that separated us from them. I was tempted to press a hand into the material and find out how far from it they were. I wondered if I would be able to tell what body parts I was encountering if I tried.

Instead I focused on gathering four cups and helping Leon get hot morning drinks ready. He and I had settled back with our own drinks when Daphne poked a head through the hanging door and blinked when she saw us.

"How long have you two been sitting there?" she asked.

"Long enough to get you guys a tea and a coffee," grinned Leon, lifting his own mug as evidence.

Daphne blushed and retreated through the door again. I met

Leon's wide smile with my own and then we both had to hold our mugs carefully as we were overtaken by a fit of giggles.

"Coffee!" The ecstatic voice of Dai burst from the other room and his almost-naked body followed immediately after. He had managed to pull on a pair of dark blue silky boxer shorts, and I caught a glimpse of Daphne behind him, trying to pull a tee shirt over her head. Her breasts were lifted up by the movement of her arms, full and tempting. Then the tent door flapped shut again.

"You don't know how badly I want this coffee right now," said Dai as he settled down cross-legged beside Leon. "Thank you so much!"

"Any time man," laughed my husband.

Daphne joined us and added her own thanks for the tea. She rolled her eyes in appreciation of the drink.

"How was the rest of your night?" I asked her after she had swallowed a few mouthfuls of the hot liquid.

"Really good," she said. "I don't know how long we were dancing, but my legs are really sore right now."

"I think we came back to the tent just before dawn," said Dai.

"Did you guys get any sleep?" I asked. It was barely past dawn now! I wondered if they had simply stayed awake all the way through.

"Maybe it was earlier than that," Dai admitted.

"But it was definitely after three a.m." added Daphne. "The DJs kept calling out different times and talking about how awesome it was that so many people were still dancing with them."

"So maybe it was four?" wondered Dai.

"You two must be exhausted," said Leon.

"Not too exhausted," Dai declared, with a sly smile. "I had plenty of energy for a bit of morning exercise!"

"Shut up Dai!" laughed Daphne. Her cheeks flushed red, but she was smiling happily as they did.

It was amazing. The presence of my friends and the sound of their happy voices, meant that all feelings of fear and tension were driven from my body within seconds. I should have known that it would not last however.

"How was the rest of your night then?" asked Dai, with an arched eyebrow and a gleam in his eye. "I saw the two of you leading that hunk away from the dancers. Decided you wanted to do some private gyrating did you?" He wiggled his eyebrows up and down.

I coughed and drew a deep breath. Thankfully, Leon answered before I had to.

"Yes. He was..." Leon paused and frowned as he searched for the right words. He glanced towards me, meeting my eyes. "He was more trouble than he looked."

"Oh?" Dai's face smoothed towards seriousness. "Not a good time?"

"We ended up having to kick him out of the van, and then he got really angry," I murmured. I wrapped my fingers in the collar of my tee shirt and squeezed. The tight material pulling across my shoulders made me feel a bit better as I spoke.

Daphne reached over and laid a hand on my knee. Her eyes looked concerned. "Are you okay? Did he do anything you didn't want him to?"

"No, not in the moment." I put my own hand on top of hers. "Of course, in hindsight, I wouldn't have done any of it with him, but in the moment I was keen."

She nodded. We all sat silently in the tent for a few more moments. Then she spoke again.

"Did he..." She swallowed and then cleared her throat, making room for something that she clearly didn't want to say. "Did he look like the description of that other guy?"

My blood ran cold.

"The guy who attacked that woman the other night?" asked Leon.

Daphne nodded.

"Wasn't that asshole Gunnar responsible for that?" added Dai.

Daphne shrugged. "He was an asshole, but that doesn't necessarily mean he was that particular asshole, right?"

I thought back to what the women in the shower queue had told us about the attack.

"No, I don't think it was Gunnar," I said slowly. "That guy was supposed to be tall and lanky." I paused and thought carefully about Lochie.

"Our hunky dickhead was broad and muscular, not fuzzy and lanky. That's totally different." I looked over at Leon, who shrugged. "Isn't it?"

Daphne sighed. "Maybe."

We finished our drinks with less laughter than we had begun them, and then cleaned the mugs out and stepped out of the tent. All around us the campsite was bustling with quiet morning activity. Early risers were quietly drifting along the rows and talking with their friends, and small clusters of people drifted towards the shower block with towels over their shoulders.

One of those knots of people was walking along the row right in front of us. I could see that their faces were serious. I stood up and moved forward to lean on the front of our van, hoping to overhear the passers-by.

"... got some video of the guy when he ran away."

"This sucks so much! There's too many incidents this year, I don't know if I can stay."

"I know what you mean. I suppose it's just got to be such a big event, and there's so many people coming to it now."

"Excuse me," I said as they walked by a few feet from me. "What are you talking about?"

The people exchanged knowing looks with each other and then one of the women stepped closer to talk to me. She was short, with thickly curled chestnut hair and dark glasses.

"There was an incident last night. Some guy tried to chase a woman who was heading back to her tent."

CHAPTER FORTY-FIVE

"Oh no! Is the woman okay?" My thoughts started racing. I was sure that my panic would show on my face, making me appear guilty even though I had nothing to feel guilty about. I thought of the way Lochie had raged when Leon and I kicked him out of our van the night before. He had been so furious, and he had stormed away into the darkness. *Could he have decided to take out his anger on someone else after he left us?*

I tried to stop my hand shaking. *No one could say that Lochie chasing someone in the night after getting pissed off with me was my fault. Right? Surely they couldn't?*

"Yeah, she seems to be, I think." The woman answered my question, interrupting the buzzing thoughts in my head. "All I've heard is that he chased her through the trees, not that he caught her. Here, someone got some of it on video."

She held out her phone and turned the screen to face me.

The video she played was hard to follow. The deep black shadows of the night filled the screen, while branches and trunks created strange illuminated lines as the camera spun through the landscape. Eventually I was able to see a figure, slightly lighter than the blackness around them, running in the distance. Light from the market or torches from the tents must have made them visible enough for the phone camera.

Then something followed the figure.

Daphne's breath gasped from next to me. She must have leaned over my shoulder to see the screen as well. I reached backwards without looking and found her hand clasping for mine as well, and we squeezed each other's fingers tightly.

The thing that had slunk into view on the small phone screen was dark and pixelated. It was hard to really see what it was. But it was large, long-limbed, and it looked like it was furry.

"Is that thing even human?" was all I could bring myself to say. The shape of the figure, and the way its legs moved in long strides made me unsure. But relief was flooding through my veins as I spoke, because there was no way that Lochie was that lanky, or hairy. He might have been an asshole, but it didn't seem like he was this asshole.

"I know right? It's pretty bloody monstrous looking," agreed the woman whose phone I was watching. "But the story I heard was that the woman said it was a guy chasing her, and what sort of animal that looks like that even lives in New Zealand?"

Daphne's hand squeezed mine again. I turned to her, and took in the seriousness of her eyes.

"Hey, are you okay hun?"

She nodded quickly. "It just seems so scary. There's no bears or anything like that here, and I haven't seen anyone at the festival that looks so unusual. How am I supposed to even keep my wits about me to keep safe?"

The woman who had shared the story with us nodded and placed a hand on Daphne's shoulder.

"It's shit, I know, but I hope you enjoy the rest of the Pandaea anyway. It's normally such a great event, don't let this one incident ruin it." She smiled in a way that she clearly thought was comforting, and then walked on along the road between the tents with her friends.

"It's not the only incident though, is it?" muttered Daphne.

"You told us about some other woman being attacked the other night. And that guy Gunner was running amok through the tents." She shook her head. "I feel like it might be a good idea to let this all ruin the festival for me."

I didn't know what to say to her, so I gathered her into a hug. To tell the truth, I wasn't even sure that I disagreed with her. Like I thought before, once something pure was tainted, it was never pure again.

Leon and Dai had moved beyond our campsite and were walking down towards Siobahn and the massage campsite. Daphne and I jogged up to them.

"Hey boys, I take it that rumours of dickheads running around at night terrorising women is not interesting enough for you, huh?"

"No, that sounds really shitty," said Leon as he draped an arm around my shoulders. He frowned and looked at my face. "Do you guys think we need to leave?"

Dai sighed as he watched his wife for her reaction.

"You don't want to go?" she asked him.

"Hey, I've had some fun here, but if it feels unsafe, then we go." He shrugged. "I feel safe, but I'm not in the same position as you two, and I don't want you to feel compelled to hang around if you don't want to."

Daphne looked at me. "What about you Ashleigh?"

"I'm not sure," I admitted. Daphne looked a little surprised. "I mean, it does sound scary, but if we hang around with each other I think we'll probably be alright. And there is still a lot to explore here."

Leon squeezed my shoulders a little tighter. "I'm keen to see what else this place has to offer, but if you or Daphne want to leave, then let's leave." The strength of his arm around me made me feel good. It was as though he was letting his energy flood into me, to power me. I smiled at Daphne.

"What do you think?"

"Alright, we'll stay for a bit longer. But if anything else goes weird, I'm going to pull the plug on the whole festival."

We all agreed that her comment was reasonable and we would indeed bail if she called time.

As we walked into the large pavilion at the massage campsite, we were all discussing what parts of the festival we were interested in exploring next. Dai was keen to go swimming again, while Leon surprised me by saying that he really wanted to spend some time at the quiet contemplative meditation tents.

"There's a new event on today, and just for today," said Siobahn from where she was laying with her head on Chris's stomach. Her friends were all stretched out on piles of blankets and cushions, as they always were when we saw them. They peered at us with their lazy eyes.

"What is it?" I asked.

"Blind Naked Slip and Slide."

CHAPTER FORTY-SIX

"What?" I asked in shock, as Dai exclaimed "Oh, I think I'm very in for that!"

Siobahn laughed and grinned. "There's a big tent being set up, and if you are keen then they get a bunch of people naked, blindfold them, and let them loose on a slip and slide. It's great fun!"

"Oh Daph, we have to, right?" Dai grabbed his wife's hands in both of his own and clutched them up to his chin. "Come on, please?"

"I suppose we could," she eventually allowed.

Siobahn tilted her head and narrowed her eyes in curiosity. "You don't seem as sure as you would have been yesterday. Is everything alright?"

Daphne explained about the video that we had been shown, and how we had now had run-ins with a series of violent men that was making us feel uneasy about staying at the festival at all.

Siobahn looked horrified, and angry. Her cheeks flushed and her eyes glowed. "This is terrible! You do know that we got rid of Gunner from the festival, right?"

"Yes."

She pushed herself to her feet and came over to rest a hand

briefly on Daphne's shoulder, and then she looked at me as well as she continued. "Well, hopefully that is one source of concern dealt with." She drew a deep breath through her nose. "I'll spread the word about last night. We'll soon track down whoever that asshole is, and we will sort things out. Stories like this should not be spreading around the Pandaea! If you have any other concerns, you come and talk to me, alright?"

"Yes, absolutely." I personally felt a lot more confident that the remainder of the festival would pass safely now. Siobahn had shown she was a powerful personality, and the friends she had gathered around her all acted in exactly the same vein. I tried to read Daphne's face, to see if she felt better as well, but it was hard to tell. I would have to try and catch her later.

"Good. Look, that slip and slide won't be ready until just after lunch, would you like to join us at the lake for the morning?"

We all agreed that the lake would be a wonderful way to spend the morning, and before long we were all diving into the cleansing water, the dust and sweat of the day before sluicing off our skin beneath a warm sun. Leon and I spent some time lying together in the shallows, my head resting back on his chest, his hand curled over my shoulder. The morning was a breath held deeply, waiting to exhale slowly, as laughter and people chatting drifted through the air around us.

I watched as groups of festival goers swam, threw balls to each other, and jumped off rocks. Dai and Daphne ran past, holding hands and grinning. They waved to us, but scurried off into the bushes behind the clearing. Leon chuckled and pressed me a little closer.

The sun reached its zenith and Siobahn came looking for us.

"We were thinking we would grab something to eat from a stall on the way back to the tents. Are you guys ready to come with us? The slip and slide should be ready too."

"You bet," replied Leon enthusiastically, lifting himself up from the water's edge. A cascade of water droplets burst against my warm skin, making me shriek.

"You bastard, what was that about?" I laughed as I climbed to my feet.

"Oh shit, sorry love!" Leon laughed and grabbed me in a tight hug, sharing the cold water with his own skin. "Come on, let's go fill our bellies and see what this slip and slide thing is all about."

We gathered up Daphne and Dai, who were both grinning widely, along with a few of Siobahn's friends and strolled back through the woods to the festival grounds. The dance hollow was still thumping, as it always was, with a crowd of about thirty people swaying gently in front of the stage. A peacock strutted away from the crowd towards the trees at the far end. Ethereal music underlined by slow bass leaked into us as we walked by, guiding us all to step in time with the beat. I smiled at the others.

"I think I'm looking forward to coming back out here tonight for a good boogie."

"You know, I am too," said Daphne, stepping with an exaggerated sway in her hips. "I enjoy getting some good vibrations to go with my good gyrations right now."

Dai slapped her backside as he walked alongside her, and they leaned in to kiss each other deeply.

After some delicious filled wraps from the food vans, we followed Siobahn to a new part of the tents. Instead of following the usual path, past the hill with the showers and toilets, she led us along a small copse of trees to the right, circling around the edge between the tents and the market stalls.

A large grey canvas tent was set up on the edge of the camping ground, next to a small ditch that marked the beginning of the markets and art stalls. A small queue was lined up outside.

"It doesn't look very exciting from out here," I said, wondering if Siobahn might have hyped it up too much.

"It doesn't need to." She grinned over her shoulder at me, her teeth glowing bright white.

When we reached the tent, we saw that the queue had formed in front of a large woman with a serious expression on her face. She motioned us up to her. I was a little concerned that the people standing in the queue might think that we were pushing in front of them, but they continued to chat happily to one another and showed no sign that they even noticed us.

"How can I help?" said the woman once we reached her. Her face retained its serious glower, but the tone of her voice was friendly.

"I've brought these four newbies to experience the slip and slide Jackie," said Siobahn.

CHAPTER FORTY-SEVEN

"Oh Siobahn, I didn't see you were with them," replied Jackie. There was a faint twitch at the side of the woman's lips and I wondered if that was as much of a smile as I could expect from her. "Will you give them the rules, or should I?"

"You go ahead." Our host waved the woman on.

"It's very simple. We will allow in a limited number of people at any one time. Once you are inside, we will allow you to look around the tent and get your bearings and provide you with a blindfold. After you are blindfolded, we will invite you to remove your clothes. Then, you will be free to move about the sheeting and explore. We will use a loud but not unpleasant sound to warn you that time is up, and then you may remove your blindfolds. We ask you to gather your things and leave quickly, so that we can let a new group in."

"How limited is limited exactly?" asked Dai. "Can we expect to be in the next group that goes in, or will we have to wait longer?"

The woman looked along the queue and wobbled her hand from side to side. "It's not an exact science. We just don't want a huge mob in there. I think this group looks a good size right now."

"So, we're all moving around inside, blindfolded and naked?" asked Daphne. "What happens if we are uncomfortable?"

"Lift your hand straight up in the air, just the same as if you were in trouble in the ocean and needed a lifeguard. We have some big bouncers who will come and make sure you are kept safe and secure. They watch who is near who, and if you say someone needs to be removed they should be able to grab them."

"Does that mean the bouncers are just watching us in there?" I asked.

"Yes. But you will get to be introduced to them before we begin, and we will give you a chance to leave before it starts if you feel uncomfortable."

I nodded and looked at Leon and our friends. They all looked as satisfied as I was.

"Alright, when does it start?" I said.

We didn't have to wait outside with the queue for long before Jackie waved us in. She stayed at her spot though, and didn't even lift the tent flap out of our way.

As we walked in, I was intrigued by what I found. The space inside the huge canvas tent was way bigger than I would have thought possible. There were heavy support struts around the side, and they made me think of the thick ropes I had seen outside, pulling the tent firmly down against the ground.

The ground was covered in a layer of blue tarpaulin, and I could see where the edges of each one had been tied to the next. It was a bit like looking at a quilt of fading blue plastic. Two small women were upending big white plastic bottles in the middle of the tarpaulins, and they grinned at us when they saw us coming in. Clear liquid glopped out of the bottles and made slow melting piles by the women's feet.

"Come in, come in," one of them called to us, and I realised that I wasn't the only one who had paused in the entrance, and now we were blocking the way for more people. "There's plenty of room around the sides."

She was right too. Although the tent was mostly taken up by the tarpaulins, the blue sheets were surrounded by a small inflatable wall, like the edge of a children's blow-up swimming pool. Beyond the soft walls was enough room for about ten people to stand next to each other with plenty of space. I moved around to the far side of the tent and was glad to see that Leon came with me. Once we reached the far side and chose a spot to stand, I reached out for his hand. He took it and squeezed my hand warmly.

I watched the others lining up along the edges of the square in between us. Everyone was doing the same, and more than once I caught someone's eye before blushing and sending my gaze further along the group.

Quickly the sides were filled. Jackie must have told the queue outside to wait once more, because no one else came into the tent. Two large men with heavy rounded shoulders stepped up at either side of the square, before crossing their hands and resting them in front of their stomachs. They both had bald heads, though I couldn't tell if they were shaved or natural. One had a short cropped dark beard, while the other had a smooth chin. They were both very stern.

A woman I had never seen before stepped out from behind one of the men.

"Good afternoon my lovelies! I hope you are here for some delightful connection!"

There was a positive murmur from the crowd. Some of us nodded slightly.

"I'm so thrilled to hear it! But can we get a little more enthusiasm perhaps?"

This time there were some sheepish smiles and a slightly louder "yeah" from us all.

"A bit better, a little better," she allowed. She held her hands palms together, fingers pointing towards the top of the large tent. "Alright, we need to go over a few rules for this." As she spoke, another woman came in carrying a large bottle of oil. The thick liquid clung to the sides of the bottle as it sloshed inside. The second woman spun the plastic cap off the bottle and began pouring thick glugs of oil onto the plastic surface inside the inflatable walls.

"We are here together to experience something unusual, something wonderful," continued the first woman. "This is about sharing something beautiful with a selection of humanity. This is about the joy of pure connection. However, this is not about taking advantage." Her face was strict. "We are going to hand you out some eye covering that will do a good job of blocking out your vision completely. Part of this experience is about the lack of inhibition that will take you over, and you need to know that you are not being judged for that to work. You will then remove your clothes, while blindfolded, and climb over the walls. This experience is about physical sensation, and we don't want anything to come between your nerves and the feelings that you are about to explore."

CHAPTER FORTY-EIGHT

"Now," the woman paused, and pointed around the room at us all. "Whatever occurs between consenting adults is totally fine with us. We are all aware of that going in." Her eyes stared at us, willing understanding into our heads. "If you are not consenting to something that is happening, then you only need to raise your hand straight up in the air, just as though you needed a lifeguard at a swimming pool, or to call out. I will be watching over you all, with my accomplices here -" she motioned to the two large men. "- and we will not shrink from ejecting anyone who has caused someone to feel unsafe. Obviously, that does mean we will be watching. Some people have raised concerns about health before as well, so this is a good time to leave if you are uncomfortable with any of that."

The woman motioned to a flap at the other side of the tent, where we would be able to leave without being seen by the queue out the front. It made me realise that I hadn't seen anyone leave the tent while we were waiting. They all must have used that far exit. But she hadn't paused in her speech.

Two young women met each other's eyes and nodded at each other before they walked out. As they walked through the tent flap a slightly older man wearing a leather waistcoat sighed and then followed.

I squeezed Leon's hand and enjoyed the feeling of his thumb pressing into the corner of my hand. I looked up at him, to see whether or not he was comfortable with things so far. He returned my glance and grinned. Then he gave me a thumbs up with his free hand. I laughed. Alright then, Leon was still keen.

"No one else? Excellent! Now, here are your blindfolds."

The woman pulled up a sack full of broad black cloth that she began handing out. I took mine and pressed it across my eyes. I was impressed at how well the cloth was able to block out light! The edges tucked low over my nose, and high on my forehead, and tying a knot behind my head was easier than I had expected. I shook my head and nodded. The material barely shifted.

"These are good!" I exclaimed. A voice spoke up from almost directly in front of me, and I squawked in surprise.

"Thank you lovely," said the happy voice of the woman organising us. "We had to search for a long time to find something so effective. Now, everyone is blindfolded, you may remove your clothes!"

I had noticed that the crowd around the oily pool was made up of a broad assortment of people. Some were tall, some skinny, some had broadly curving hips beneath their mutli-coloured clothes, and some wore thick dark beards. It was fascinating to try and imagine what they each looked like as I heard the sound of clothes being removed and tucked away to the edges of the tent. I was careful to wrap my necklace into my clothes as I clumsily tried to put them aside.

"When you are ready, climb in. We will let you know as the time is running out."

I stepped forward slowly, feeling my way to the edge of the pool and then over the yielding inflatable wall. The tarpaulin surface felt strange. The material was slightly rough, but the layer of oil that covered it made it extremely slick and I nearly fell down. Around me I heard thuds and yelps and splashes as some of my companions must have fallen as well.

I grinned below my blindfold. Already I could feel my heart pounding in my chest and my skin tingled with the anticipation of sensations that I could not predict. I lowered myself so that if I fell it would not be far to the ground and then began sliding forward, one foot at a time.

Almost immediately I came into contact with someone else. The press of their skin against mine came as a shock, sending a current through me that made me gasp. My first impulse was to back away from them, to give them space. I stumbled along sideways on my hands and knees, slipping through the oil.

But then I stopped and reminded myself that this was part of why I had decided to climb into the pool in the first place. I chuckled and began crawling forward again.

This time when I bumped into someone I leaned into the contact. I was crawling but they must have managed to mostly keep their feet, because I was quite sure I had gone face first into their thigh. Their skin felt smooth. Before I could do anything else, they swung a hand towards me, connecting to my head with a soft clunk. Their fingers moved across my hair, and then patted on the top of my head. It made me smile.

The other person moved away from me though, and so I continued forward. I quickly found a pile of people who were all rolling along each other in such a way that I was unable to keep a count of how many of them there were. At first I thought it was two or three people, sliding over each others bodies and then letting the others tumble over in their turn, but I had no way to be sure. At times the pile felt too tall to be made up of less than five people, and I wondered if the pile spread out wider and made it hard to estimate.

Someone slid off the pile and onto my arm, so I lay down as they continued over me, slipping along the skin of my back. Someone else lay down over my arm, and so I waited as the pile moved over me like a slippery cloud.

It was warm under the pile, and somehow the darkness of my blindfold became even darker. Every part of my skin was tingling, either from the pressure of unknown bodies touching me and pressing me down, or from the anticipation that raced just ahead of the bodies that moved over.

Fear made my heart pound, fear that the pile would grow too heavy for me, or that I would be hurt. But everyone must have had the same fear, because the people passing over my skin were supporting their weight as much as they could, and the pressure never became unbearable. Instead there was a comforting presence, as though I had been tucked into a warm bed with a thick heavy blanket covering me. It was as though this pile of people were hugging me, and sheltering me, all at the same time.

CHAPTER FORTY-NINE

I had to admit that the throbbing in my blood was not all fear. I could feel a small firm pair of breasts against my shoulders, and I was keenly aware of the nipples poking into me. At one point a semi-hard penis drifted past my forearm where it lay on the ground. I could feel my own warmth growing in response, a tension between my legs that had my breath catching.

As the pile slid past me, I decided that I wanted to see if I could indulge that tension. I felt sure that the release of it would be a crescendo beyond anything I had experienced before. I reached out to feel who was nearby, wondering if they would be feeling something similar.

My fingers found slim curved shoulders, hunched alongside the pile. I ran my fingers forward over their collarbone, my thumb brushing against the soft skin of their neck, and then down the front of their chest. My hand slid over the rising slope of their breast and I tweaked their nipple gently as I reached still lower. The tips of my fingers clung around the breast and then drew back until I was holding their shoulder again.

I moved closer, pressing my own breasts into the person's naked back. Carefully, I lifted my mouth to their head, moving my lips along long hair that felt strong and damp until I found the delicateness of their ear.

"Is this okay?" I asked in a whisper.

"Oh yes," came the cheerful reply.

The woman turned her body beneath my hands, and the shape of her breasts moved against my own. I shifted my hands as she turned, letting them run down her sides, fitting her waist into the crook of my arm. I felt the warmth of her breath as she sought my face, and then her lips met mine.

The kiss this woman gave me sent a shudder through my body that was just like the time I grabbed an electric fence, tensing all my muscles at once, then leaving them loose and weak. Her hand cupped my jaw and her kiss drove into me harder. I opened my mouth and received her tongue, questing into me, as her fingertips dug a little deeper. My own fingers pressed into the softness of her waist. I lifted a leg over hers, but it almost immediately slipped off her because of the layer of oil that covered us both. She giggled against my mouth and then kissed me again.

We lay side by side in the oil. I was surprised at how warm it was, naked and covered in liquid. But the oil felt as though it had picked up the body heat of the people sliding through it, and was spreading that feeling of life out amongst us all.

I reached up with my spare hand and followed the curve of her breast. Now I was able to feel the weight of it in my palm, and the feeling made me twist my hips from side to side. Her nipple pressed into my palm, and then I shifted so that I could pull on it gently. Now my tongue was seeking its way into her mouth.

Her fingernails scratched softly along my stomach, heading from my navel down further until they caught against the short dark hair between my legs. I moaned and felt her smile. Her fingers moved along the softness of my lips, the vulnerable skin between my pussy and my thighs, and then pressed in between as they drew back up. She brushed over my small hardness, sending a shiver up my spine, and then pressed down against me.

I moaned again, and could not hold my face to hers properly. I broke from our kiss and my head hung back as I groaned and sighed while she moved her fingers in a firm circle around me. I let my legs fall further apart, willing her to dive back down, to slip inside me. The heat that my centre was creating felt as though it would erupt from my cheeks at any moment. Each breath felt as though it was billowing from a furnace deep in my chest, boiling my throat and mouth.

Instead, she kept moving around and around, her fingers soft and yet firm. At times she let her fingers come apart, holding me between her thumb and forefinger, squeezing and pulling in time with the thump of my heartbeat. It was as though, with eyes covered, she could see deeper into my body, finding the rhythms that drove it and timing her own movement to them. I knew she was leaning over me now, no longer kissing me. I could feel the breeze of her breath against my breasts, I could hear the rasp of her own desire in her throat. She leaned lower.

Now her hand could reach lower, and she separated me and sought my depths with one finger. My stomach clenched as I willed her inside me, whimpering with relief as she slid in, first one finger, then another. I could feel myself tightening around her fingers, and her shoulders moved against mine as she found a rhythm. She was rubbing inside me, and kept pressure outside with the heel of her palm. Her angle shifted occasionally, seeking new places to pull my pleasure from.

In the darkness lying under this woman, I felt as though I was falling from a thick night sky, with the rush of air blasting past my ears, pressure squeezing against me and pulling at my toes, fingers and skin. It was as though the sky was caressing me, through her fingers, passing along my hips and swirling through my body, centred on her fingers. I wanted to yell out loud, laughter tucking the corners of my mouth wide. Instead I gasped and then bit my lower lip gently, trying to hold the cry that wanted to burst from me inside.

I felt it grow at the bottom of my lungs, growing with each movement of her fingers inside me. Her thumb pressed to the small hardness at the top of my pussy and I sucked a mouthful of cool air deep into my lungs. My chest lifted as I did, and my back arched away from the thin layer of warm oil at the bottom of the pool.

With a rush like a hurricane, my orgasm exploded around her hand and I felt myself gripping her fingers tight enough to stop her moving. My skin tingled as though I had been dunked into a pool of icy water, and I could feel a wave of goose pimples spread along my back, my arms, my legs.

CHAPTER FIFTY

I panted and lay on the woman's lap as I tried to catch my breath enough to think clearly again. I could feel the woman leaning over the top of me as I willed my muscles to move me once again. As the blood returned to my mind, I lifted my hands and tried to pull myself up the front of this woman I didn't know. She lifted my shoulders, and her lips met mine. Her kiss was soft, and gentle.

"Wow," I stuttered.

"I'm glad you liked it," she giggled.

"You took my breath away completely! I hope you are going to let me return the favour?"

"I'd be delighted to see what you can do."

Her lips returned to mine, kissing me harder this time. I allowed the sensation of her lips to pass through me, but before I sank back into the feelings she had wrung out of me before, I fought my impulses down so that I could stay in control.

For a moment my stomach fluttered as I wondered whether I was having the same effect on her. I couldn't let those worries take over though.

With a clear mind, I pressed up from beneath her, placing a hand on her shoulder and moving her aside. I rolled so that I was able to lean over her this time, and then renewed myself to the task of kissing her as thoroughly as she had kissed me. I could feel my breasts lift away from my body and press into hers, nipples standing hard to attention as they brushed over each other. The feeling nearly derailed me from my mission. I had to pause and squeeze her upper arms before I felt in control again, ready to continue.

I let my hands slip along her arms, holding them and moving them so that they extended above her head. Once her wrists were crossed, I released her and ran my fingernails down the undersides of her arms, enjoying the feeling of them scraping across her delicate skin.

I scratched at the sides of her ribcage, and through the dip of her waist. As I passed lower, I nipped at her nipple with my teeth, and I grinned when I was rewarded with a gasp of surprise. My hands settled comfortably on the softness of her hips and I slid my body between her legs, gliding across the slippery mat beneath us and along her skin, until my face was pressed to the top of her thigh.

"I'd love to taste you," I murmured.

"Please," she moaned gently.

I breathed in deeply, enjoying the warmth and scent of her, before I leaned down and ran my tongue along her.

I moved slowly, not wanting to overwhelm her all at once. I teased the sides of her with my tongue, nuzzling at her with my nose. I leaned closer, and stretched my tongue out, parting her and then licking up to the tip of her, which I sucked on gently. The sighs and moans that followed helped me find a pace and rhythm that satisfied my mystery woman. I explored her with my tongue, returning often to the rhythmic attention that she enjoyed, and soon slid my finger inside her as well.

The rhythm of my movement gained pace, as my fingers pressed more and more insistently inside her, and my tongue kept its own pressure building. She grabbed the back of my head with both hands, holding me closer, pulling me into the warmth between her legs. An ache began to spread out in my shoulder and bicep, and my jaw felt stiff. Still, I had to keep going. My own will to succeed took the place of energy, and I kept moving longer than I thought I would be able to.

My efforts were rewarded when she explosively came across my face, soaking me. Her thighs crushed the sides of my head, and for a moment my arm was twisted awkwardly beneath me. I wondered if this was how I was going to go, smothered by a sexy woman in the throes of her pleasure, in a tent full of oil, at a dance festival.

Thankfully, she released me, and then helped me slide up so that our faces were near one another again.

"That was exquisite," she breathed into my ear before kissing my cheek.

"You started it," I said. She laughed, and the sound of her rang like clear bells on a bright morning.

"Go on, go and enjoy your connections," she said eventually, and we separated in the oil filled pool. As I slid and slipped along in another direction, I realised that it was entirely likely that I would never really know who it was that I had spent such a wonderful moment together with. When we got dressed and removed our blindfolds, how would I know who this woman was? What if I never heard her voice?

That was what made the experience so special, I realised. It was the way that only this moment was available to us, only this moment was truly alive and able to be shared and experienced. Neither of us had any past that we were bringing with us, blinded and hyper aware of the sensations on our skin as we were. Neither could we look ahead to the future. Instead, we had to sink into the feelings as they happened, and enjoy what pleasure and happiness there was between us in that one pure moment.

It was just like the rest of our lives, really, I thought to myself. In our real lives, the temptation was to spend too long digging up old skeletons and allowing them to walk around us, to threaten us, to remind us of demons that should have been buried and forgotten. Or even in good times, we look outside the experience into the future, hoping to relive it or remember it, without enjoying it while we can.

Even now, I was wondering where Leon was. I wanted to share this moment with him now, but wasn't that really my past associations putting their hand up and asking for attention? If I ended up slipping over his body, then that was fine, but I didn't have to seek it out.

I spent a lot of the remaining time moving around, trying to find as many bodies as I could. I found I wanted to make some sort of connection with as many of the people in the pool as possible. Some I held in tight hugs, shifting my body in tiny twitches that helped me sense the way they were touching me in return, a press of bellies together, a hard penis pressing on my thigh. Others I kissed or fondled, but I did not feel the burning desire to play any further than that with any of the other people I found in my movements. My encounter with the mystery woman had been perfection.

CHAPTER FIFTY-ONE

The end of the sessions was called out far too soon. Each of us was directed back to the side of the pool and told that we were back where we started. I wondered how they could be so sure that our dripping figures were now standing in the correct location. How closely were they watching us when we came in, I wondered. Did they have to make some sort of cheat sheet? With our descriptions? I felt my cheeks warm as I blushed. Did they make a note about the birthmark on my bottom?

Before we were allowed to remove our blindfolds, sticky as they were with oil, someone walked around us and pressed a strange object into our hands.

"This is a strigil," said a voice from the world I couldn't see. I recognised that it was the woman who had introduced us earlier. "It is a tool for removing oil from your body. If you feel along the shape of it, you will find that it is thin and curved. Press the strigil to your skin and scrape the oil from you. You can simply flick it outside the pool."

Carefully, I experimented with the tool and felt my skin clearing as I worked along my arms, then shoulders, stomach and legs. In moments I was ready to get dressed, though I was very conscious that there was a pool of oil dripping down the small of my back, and the soles of my feet were thick with it.

"Please, when you remove your blindfold, simply step forward and out of the pool to find your clothes. Then get dressed and wait for us to tell you to turn around."

I followed the instructions. I was pleased to discover that they had been exactly correct, and my clothes were waiting only a few feet away from me. I dressed, grimacing slightly as my top stuck to the dampness on my back. I didn't have to wait long before the woman spoke again, allowing us to turn around.

I turned and felt a huge smile breaking across my face. I looked around the faces of the others who had been slipping through the oil with me, and I saw a range of emotions reflected back at me.

Most of the faces looked as happy as I was. Broad smiles met mine, and many of the eyes that I could see sparkled with glee. I wondered which of these people I had made a connection with. Was this short woman with long black hair the one who had made me feel as though I was falling from the sky? Or was it this one, with marvellous wide eyes, and soft lips?

Many of the men seemed just as happy, and I could only imagine what they might have experienced during the session. I blushed a little, but smiled harder as I looked at them. From the raised eyebrows and sheepish smirks, I could tell many of them were wondering if I had been someone to have connected with them.

And perhaps I had! After all, I had rolled and tumbled by so many humans in that pool, it was very possible.

But there were other expressions in the ring. Some looked very embarrassed, and were clearly finding it difficult to look at the others around them. Some were looking at their feet, or the roof of the tent. I hoped that they hadn't done anything that they would come to regret.

It's a shame that the world makes people feel this way, I found myself pondering. When we come together to share such a vulnerable and sensational moment and we are held alongside each other in this space by people who have taken care of us, none of us should fear being exposed or judged.

And yet still, the real world of life beyond this festival comes creeping into our minds. The voices of those who we know would disapprove ring in our ears. The shame that they wield, to keep us in line, inches it's cold grip up our spine.

There was a movement next to me and I looked sideways. Leon had stepped beside me. He smiled at me and reached out to take my hand. Our hands were slick and mine nearly slipped out from between his fingers immediately. I laughed and he smiled.

"It's good to see you laughing! You looked so serious for a moment. What was going on in that pretty head of yours?"

"Oh nothing really."

"Come on Ash," Leon squeezed my hand as he encouraged me. "If your experience was anything like mine, you'd have a grin from ear to ear. Why such a stern face?"

"I just realised that some of the people here might be feeling shame or regret already," I replied, lowering my voice to try and avoid being overheard. A flash of concern sped across his face. "No, not me." I reassured him quickly. "But it made me sad that such a wonderful thing could still be tainted by the world outside the festival."

"This place is hardly some sort of magical wonderland, with no problems in it," said Leon with a smirk. "After all, we've already had plenty of assholes make our time here shittier."

I nodded. It couldn't be argued that our experiences had been all sunshine so far. But I was glad to have stuck around to be a part of this one. My reservations from earlier were definitely muted now. I felt refreshed and revived. My blood felt fiery again and I wanted to get out of the tent and re-engage with all the wonderful colourful people that were here to celebrate as well.

"Nothing is truly all one way, purely good or purely bad" I

said, agreeing with Leon. "We have to accept that some things have a little of the opposite to them."

"Life exists on spectrums, I've always said that. Everyone is just a little different to everyone else."

"And this festival is no different." I stood straighter and slipped my arm around my husband's back. "We've seen some of the shitty parts, but the whole thing has been beautiful." I squeezed him and felt his t-shirt squelch against the oil that was remaining in the small of his back.

"Come on," he said. "I think we're ready to see some more!"

CHAPTER FIFTY-TWO

It was already late in the day as we emerged from the tent. Leon led me towards the market, declaring that he was hungry after his exertions in the blindfold pool.

"Oh yes," I teased, elbowing him in the side. "And exactly how much exerting did you do?"

He grinned and pushed a hand through his hair. "Enough! I rolled around a lot, and I am sure you can imagine that I got aroused by all the bodies that were everywhere. Eventually someone put their hand around me, and we got together."

"Was it a guy or a girl?"

"I think it was a woman actually, from her voice."

"Oh, so you didn't actually have sex?" I was surprised. From the way he was talking, I had assumed that he had.

"No, they gave me a fantastic handjob and then left before I could do anything in return."

"So long as you were thinking about what you could do in return," I grumped. "I don't want my husband to get a reputation for being stingy!"

We wandered through the market, looking at the brightly coloured tie-dye clothing for sale, and some exquisite pale milky crystals that the stall holder had managed to wrap in thin metal wire. She had created bracelets, headbands, necklaces, candle-sticks, and all sorts of other shining objects. At the far end of the stalls, Leon bought two long skewers of spiral-cut potato that had been deep fried. The cook rolled the springy looking food in a white dust before giving it to us.

"What is that?" I asked.

"Flavour, miss," he replied with a wink. He wasn't kidding either. The burst of flavour that erupted on my tongue when I bit into the skewered potato nearly made my eyes roll back in my head.

"Oh my god, this is incredible!"

"It really is!" agreed Leon. "This is why we are here, you know? To give ourselves some new experiences and feelings that we didn't even know we were missing out on!"

We wandered out of the market, and headed towards the low archway of trees that led to the dancing hollow. Streamers were woven through the branches now, multicoloured lines of fabric that twisted in the breeze. Walking underneath them felt as though I was walking through a wicker basket full of bright yarn. It made me think of my grandmother's house on a Sunday after-noon, watching tv on the floor by her feet while she knitted dolls and blankets and jumpers.

"It is beautiful here," I said and I stepped away from Leon while I held on to the tips of his fingers. He spun me at the end of his arm and then drew me back, and small puffs of light dust rose from my feet. I whirled back into his embrace and leaned in to kiss him. His lips lit a fire in my chest that made me gasp, and I dug my fingers into the small of his back again.

"I love you," he murmured as our faces separated.

"I love you too," I said, squeezing him once at the waist. I giggled as I felt a damp squish under my fingers again, and he grimaced.

"Still quite oily under there huh?" I asked.

"Yeah, and the dust is sticking to my feet." I glanced down and realised that he was right. Both of our feet had a thick dark layer of oily grit under the sole. I wrinkled my toes and then my nose.

"Ewww, that's gross," I laughed.

"Come on gorgeous," Leon declared. "Let's wash this icky dust away!"

The hollow was full of people, just like usual, even though it was still a long wait until sunset, and it took time for us to wind our way through the energetically dancing crowd. Thick bass rolled through the ground and up our spines. I was nearly drawn into the dance myself, the rhythm was hypnotic. I saw faces turn towards me, tall figures with scraggly beards below piercing blue eyes, women with knitted rainbow shawls who twisted their hips like serpents to the tune. A wave of smoke drifted past and I was tempted to breathe deep.

"Come on you," said Leon, tugging me by the hand. "We'll come back and get our groove on after we take a quick swim."

I sighed wistfully as I followed him away from the pulsing swirl of people that I just wanted to dive into. "Yes, I suppose. I just want to dance now!"

"Sometimes good things take time!"

We walked up the gentle slope on the far side of the hollow and moved towards the familiar path through the bush. We had walked along this track often enough now that we knew exactly where to go. A shiver passed down my spine as we moved through the trees. Their shadows fell across my shoulder like cold blankets, and I felt myself hunching over beneath them

"Are you okay?" asked Leon.

"Sure," I nodded, but I hugged myself with my arms, trying to hold onto some heat. "Is it just me, or is it always really cold in here?"

"You're not wrong actually," sniffed Leon before blowing a strong puff of air through his lips. "It's probably the oil on our skin cooling us down."

We continued on, following the trodden dirt between the tree trunks. I looked around the trees, trying to cheer myself up.

It felt like there was something wrong with them. My stomach rumbled.

"Can you hear any birds?"

Leon stopped on the track and looked into the branches. He frowned and scratched his chin. "No, I can't see any." He paused, and then frowned. "And there's no song at all."

Together we stood still, holding our breaths so that we could focus on any sound coming from the trees around us. My ears must have been flicking around like a cat's. The muscles of my neck tensed as I tried to will sounds to make it into my ears.

"Nothing," I had to admit eventually.

"It's weirder than that," muttered Leon. "I can't hear the dance stage any more either."

We both stood silently again. I sought out a hint of the booming dance music and Leon held still to allow me as much concentration as possible. I shook my head.

"I don't hear it either. Did we usually hear it this far into the bush?"

"I can't remember, but it seems way quieter than it should be in here." Leon was beginning to look concerned. "Come on," he continued, taking my hand and stepping briskly down the trail. "I think we should get to the lake as soon as we can."

CHAPTER FIFTY-THREE

Our feet crunched against the loose dirt and dried leaves under our feet like fireworks. We had just been trying to be as silent as possible, so I flinched every time a twig snapped, certain that the sound was the indication that some unknown thing was about to career out of the trees into me.

It took longer than I expected to reach the bent and broken section of fence that we had to crawl through in order to make our way to the lake. I felt certain that we had somehow gone around in circles in the bush. But there had been no intersections, no paths for us to turn the wrong way on. The shade from the boughs overhead still set my skin to shivering.

A wild yell burst from the bush ahead of us, long and loud. It carried a mix of fear and anger with it, and was immediately followed by the crashing of a body through branches. Leon and I both lept to the side of the path, clinging to the tree trunks as though they were some sort of protective barrier from whatever was coming towards us.

A figure came scrambling along the path, over a ridge of earth, pulling at the ground with hooked fingers and tumbling forward. It was a man, and he was trying to move faster than his own limbs could manage, sending him faltering against the ground almost as soon as he was able to right himself. He was still yelling, the sound only ceasing when he had exhausted his breath completely and was sucking in new lungfuls of oxygen before bellowing once more.

His madcap scramble turned out to allow him to dive through the small gap in the fence easily, before continuing along the path we had just followed in a whirlwind of legs and arms, his long dark hair flapping across his shoulders. A wide band of dark material was wrapped around his head, just above his eyes. A pair of thin white antlers stuck up from the band, just above either ear. They were small and sharp, and swooped towards the back of his head, but there was no mistaking the shape.

I managed to catch Leon's attention from the far side of the trail. He was clinging to his tree with a look of fear and confusion that I was sure must mirror my own exactly.

"What di-" I began to say but then a long loud howl interrupted me, drowning out the sounds of the fleeing man. I ducked back behind the trunk as the sound of something else crashed up the path beyond the fence.

The figure that appeared was tall and thin, almost skeletal. I felt my eyes pulling wider than they had ever been as I took in the bizarre creature that ran towards the fence in long loping strides. It must have been a head or two taller than Leon, and he was not a short man. Despite being so thin, its chest was thick and barrel shaped. It was covered in spiky black fur, but it moved on its hind legs and swung long arms at its sides.

But the part that sent waves of shock and fear and confusion through me, that flooded my senses in a way that stopped me from reacting or moving, was the thing's head. It was clearly an animal, with a long snout over a mouth that gleamed with long sharp white teeth. Black eyes somehow gleamed despite the dark shadow beneath the trees.

The creature launched itself into the air and jumped over the fence with ease, landing heavily in the path between Leon and myself. I felt my heart swell up in my chest, driving the air from my lungs. My head felt as though it was too heavy for my neck and was about to collapse to the side. Bark stabbed into the palms of my hands as I gripped the tree tighter. I knew, I just knew, that the creature was staring right at me.

Then the man who had run past us screamed again, and the creature made a snuffling noise and sprang forward, resuming the chase.

My body reacted before my mind knew what was happening. My legs shoved against the ground beneath me and flung me backwards, away from the path. I recognised the bolt of fear that shot down my spine when I heard branches snap and crack around me as I tumbled away through the undergrowth. A voice in my head told me that the monster I had just seen, only a few feet away from me, would have heard that noise and now be on my heels. But it was as though the panic and racing heart were disconnected from my mind, as though they were happening to somebody else.

I didn't even try to look behind me, I just ran. I didn't look for a path, or try to aim for any particular direction. Away was the only thing in my mind. My feet thumped into the dirt below and my face was whipped by leaves and twigs. It was a miracle that nothing stabbed into my eyes as I pushed myself to keep going.

My mind must have blanked out for a while, because I came back to myself and realised that I was standing somewhere that I didn't recognise. I panted with my hands on my knees, trying to recover enough oxygen that my brain would start working properly again. I tried to stand up straight and realised that my hands were shaking furiously, and my legs were wobbling and unsteady. The sound of a howl rose from somewhere in the bush behind me. The sky above the treetops over my head was deepening into a smooth dark blue. Night was coming.

"There's nothing in New Zealand that howls," I murmured to myself, speaking aloud in an attempt to feel less alone. It didn't work, instead the way my words vanished into the evening air, skittering like moths, made me feel like the only human who had ever walked beneath these boughs. I had to find Leon.

CHAPTER FIFTY-FOUR

I stood a while longer as blood returned to my limbs. Pins and needles spiked beneath my skin as the feeling returned to my fingers. I slapped at some mosquitoes that were buzzing around my face and shoulders.

Now what do I do, I thought to myself. *Where can I go that is safe?* I turned around, trying to figure out which direction the festival would be, or the lake. Maybe if I could find that fence I could follow it until I get back to the track? But there was no way of knowing where the fence was unless I accidentally ran into it.

Where was Leon? I hadn't seen what he did in my scramble to escape. Had he bolted the other direction through the trees? If so, he was probably as far from the track as I was, but in the opposite direction. Had he tried to follow me? I was terrified at the thought that the creature from the path would be between us. I swallowed, and my throat felt tight and sore. Unless the monster had already caught up to Leon. How would I have known?

I looked up at the trees that loomed around me. Maybe I could climb up and take a look around? I tested my strength on a couple of lower branches. It would be possible, but I didn't know if I'd be able to see much before the branches got too small to hold my weight. Maybe there was a chance I could see Leon from up there?

Just as I was about to resign myself to the climb, I heard a noise from over my shoulder. Any noise should have been enough to give me a heart attack after what I had just seen, but this sounded unusual. It wasn't the breaking brush that might have accompanied the monster if it tracked me down, nor was the sound of howling that I heard before. It wasn't the desired sound of Leon, finding his way to me so that we could plan our escape together. It was a deep thump, a sound that was felt in the soles of my feet more than my ears.

I turned and closed my eyes, trying to isolate the direction that the thudding was coming from. I was amazed to discover that I was able to find the direction without too much trouble. I opened my eyes and started walking towards the sound. *Thank god for the dancing stage,* I told myself.

The bush was difficult to move through. I had careened through it at random, and although I felt as though I had run in a straight line, I knew that there was no way I hadn't been turned and tugged as I went, finding the easier paths in my panic. Now I was trying to stick to a straight path, which led me to the edge of small ravines, or past thick gnarled piles of roots and vine. I kept my attention on the distant music and worked to keep going, no matter what. Darkness seeped down from the night sky overhead, and the hairs on my arms pricked up as the cold wrapped over me.

But bit by bit, the music grew louder. My legs were aching from the awkward journey by the time I realised that I could see lights from the hollow ahead of me. Knowing that there were people ahead, that I might have found a safe place, made tears leak from my eyes.

The lights in the distance grew larger as I kept moving. The darkness of the night was so complete that when they passed behind a tree, I was almost completely blinded. I tried not to let panic take me in those moments, but pressed forward. Soon, the undergrowth grew less, and I was able to walk normally out of the forest.

I could see the dancing stage far away from me. I must have entered the hollow at an end that I had not spent much time at during my days exploring the festival. It was much darker, and there were less people here. But there was a small gathering of people near me and so I headed for them.

The group was standing in a wide circle, and some softer steel drum music was playing from a large square speaker sitting beside them. In the middle of the circle, a tall figure was spinning a long stick that blazed with blossoms of fire at each end. The stick spun in loops, leaving a red trail in my eyes. Sometimes the crowd watching the figure would call out encouragement and celebratory whoops.

As I approached, the figure shifted their grip on the stick and spun it wide, extinguishing the flames. The crowd applauded, and then I saw someone else step forward into the centre. They lowered something at the end of their arms, and I could just make out another person crouched in front of them in the darkness. There was a small spark and then the objects in the standing figures hands lit in a wide fan of flame. They spun the fans with practised ease, sending a surge of heat across the crowd, and then began stepping through a series of graceful poses in time to the music. Even through my wildly racing heart and shattered nerves, I could see it was beautiful.

I stepped up to the back of the crowd.

"Hey, I need help," I said loudly. Most of the crowd didn't hear me, but one or two people nearby turned to see what was going on.

"What's happened?" asked one woman. She stepped closer with concern wrinkling her forehead. She reached out and laid a hand on my shoulder.

"There was–" I paused and licked my lips. What would these people say if I told them what I had seen? Would they believe me? I decided that I had to try anyway. "I saw a monster in the bush."

"What?" The woman laughed nervously and stepped away from me again. Her eyes were even more worried now.

I grimaced. "I know how that sounds, but I'm not making it up, alright? My husband and I were going to swim in the lake at sunset, and then this massive monster came racing up the path chasing after some guy."

"Your husband? Sunset?" The woman looked past me and then turned to meet my eyes again.

"Again, I know it's way past sunset and I'm alone," I realised that I was pleading now. More of the crowd had turned to watch me, and I could make out enough of their faces to know that they were all thinking the same thing that I would have been if I had seen someone wander out of the night talking like this. She's lost touch with the real world.

"Please, I just need to be safe, and I don't think that it's safe out there!"

"I think you've had enough Ashleigh," said a deep voice from around the circle.

CHAPTER FIFTY-FIVE

My heart leapt when I realised that someone recognised me, but immediately fell when I turned and saw who it was. Lochie. The asshole. I shrank away from him as he walked closer.

"No! this bastard wouldn't take no for an answer last night!" I clutched at the woman who had spoken to me, desperately hoping she would help keep him away from me.

Lochie raised his hands in a calming gesture and kept his distance. Others in the crowd were glaring at him.

"Who are you?" snapped the woman, narrowing her eyes at him.

"I'm her husband. She and I-"

"You are not!" I yelled. I could feel my blood draining from my head, and I stumbled in my dizziness.

"-and we took some pills in the bush and she's having a freak-out. I've been trying to find her for hours."

"No!" I screamed as he stepped closer. None of the others were stepping in to stop him so I turned and ran as hard as I could away from him.

"Ash! Come back!" he shouted, but I wasn't listening. My legs were still aching and weak, but I pushed them harder and harder.

I didn't know where to go. Away from the tall bastard with the anger issues meant I was running back to the darkness of the bush, where I had seen the monster chasing that other man. As I reached the trees, I paused to steady myself on a track and glanced back.

A figure was jogging across the grassy slope towards me, alone. Only one figure and I couldn't hope that it was one of the fire dancers coming to help me. Lochie was an entitled prick, and I knew deep in my heart that he was going to keep chasing me to try and avenge his hurt ego from last night.

I wanted to break down on the dirt and let the panic and grief flow out of me, but that would give him time to catch up with me. Instead I gritted my teeth, sucked in deeply, and continued into the forest.

The clouds had thinned and moonlight helped me find a path deeper into the undergrowth. I had to slow down as the path twisted through the trees, and logs threatened to trip me constantly. Sometimes I wondered if the forest itself was trying to catch me and deliver me to the bastard following me. I heard him cracking through the bushes as well, never far enough behind for me to stop.

In my heady panic, my thoughts were racing. My brain was trying to solve the problem while my body ran on automatic. Ideas and words flashed across my mind, in a way that left me barely conscious of them. Why was he so set on chasing me? What sort of creep does that?

An idea struck me so hard it felt like someone had hit me in the stomach. I nearly stopped, before forcing myself to keep moving.

What if he was the monster?

It made a certain horrible sense. Maybe it was a- My own thoughts recoiled from the word that hovered in the back of my mind. I forced myself to think it. Maybe the thing I had seen was a werewolf. It was some unnatural mix of human and animal, a blending of the two, not one or the other. The moon was bright overhead, though hidden in clouds. What if this asshole really was a monster, here to hunt down people and use them as he willed? It would explain his fury, his inability to consider people as people but instead as things that he could use for his own amusement.

Now that I had put the idea to words, what did that mean? Was he the one who had attacked people before? Was he the problem stalking this festival? I remembered how I had discounted the idea that he was the trouble-maker before, because he hadn't looked like the person in the video. But if he really was a mythical monster that changed shape, that wouldn't matter, would it?

I couldn't believe that I was thinking these things. Were-wolves weren't real! They were made up stories, folktales, monsters for horror movies! How in the world could I really be thinking that I had seen one, or that the man following me could be one?

"Ashleigh, we're a long way from the others now. Are you ready to give me what I deserve yet?"

Hearing Lochie's voice from the bush behind me made me gag. Bile burned in the back of my throat.

"I knew you were going to be good when I saw you dancing. I'm looking forward to finding out."

I tripped against a log again and glanced down by my feet. It wasn't a log, it was a thick branch, sticking out from a low bush across the track at ankle height. If I hadn't caught myself, I would have fallen into a particularly rocky dip in the path. I heard Lochie's movement through the undergrowth, not far away.

"I can hear you Ash, I've nearly found you."

Anger welled up in my chest and replaced the terror that had been driving me. Who cares what sort of monster this piece of shit was? He needed dealing with.

I grabbed the low branch I had nearly tripped on and pulled it with all my strength, bending it back towards the bushes to the side of the path. Keeping as tight a hold as I could, I tucked myself in amongst the branches and leaves, hoping that he wouldn't be able to see me clearly until it was too late. Then I waited, clutching onto the thick branch.

My breath sounded like it was rattling in my chest, a rasping noise that was far too loud. Would he hear me? I counted my breaths, trying to slow my breathing and calm my racing heart. My shoulders ached with the effort of pulling the branch.

Lochie stepped out onto the path so suddenly that I nearly let go of the branch too soon, but I managed to quell my surprise and wait until he had moved a few more feet forward. Then I let it go.

"Fuck you," I said as the thick branch whipped through the air and cracked into his ankles. I had timed it well, and it struck both ankles just as he was stepping forward, knocking one leg from under him before the other had found its footing. I saw shock cover his face as he tumbled forward and I flinched as his head struck one of the sharp rocks that stuck up from the track.

CHAPTER FIFTY-SIX

Lochie lay still on the ground and showed no sign of getting up. I counted my breaths again, one hand frantically searching the ground near me for a rock or stick that I might be able to use against him if he got up. In the dim moonlight, deep under the trees, I almost missed the dark pool that spread out from his head.

I stood up slowly.

There was a stone in my belly. Round and hard and cold. It was sucking all the warmth from me, and it drew my attention away from Lochie.

You killed him. The voice was my own, but I shook my head and rubbed my face. My legs were tired. I decided to sit down.

I drew slow shuddering breaths beneath the moonlight as I tried to think clearly, to silence the accusation from my own thoughts. I didn't know for sure if Lochie was dead or just badly injured. I forced myself to watch his body beneath the shadows of the trees. It was almost impossible to see if he was twitching or breathing at all. I considered checking for a pulse, but I couldn't bring myself to come any closer.

He was a monster, I told myself. He was chasing me and he

shouldn't have been. He deserved it. The rock in my stomach was growing hot.

I scrubbed at the tears that were appearing on my cheeks and frowned. I needed to get away from Lochie as soon as I could. I pushed myself back to my feet and started pushing my way back along the trail, hoping that I could find my way back to the dancers.

I stumbled and tripped more on the way back through the bush. My eyes were misted over with tears, no matter how often I told myself off for them, and my mind kept summoning up visions of the surprise that had suffused Lochie's face as he fell. Every breaking stick under my feet recalled the crack of his skull hitting the rock.

I tried to distract myself. I was safe now, at least. It was like a mantra, whirling in my head as though it was carried on an eddying wind. I am okay. I'm okay. I am okay. Each step repeated the phrase. My lips were moving as I mouthed the words to myself.

But was Leon okay? I tried not to think about it. After the monster had rushed between us, I had seen no sign of him. I hadn't heard anything in the bush since then. Thinking of sound made me pause and lift my head. The night bush was quiet, but it was no longer silent. An owl hooted, and insects chirruped. See, I told myself. The forest is coming out of hiding. There can't be any more monsters here. Everything is going to be okay.

It will be okay if I can find Leon.

The rock inside me grew heavier.

Eventually I heard the distant pounding of the basin, and I was able to turn my slow and tired feet in that direction. Shortly after that, I caught glimpses of light through the trees. I wondered if I was approaching the fire dancers again, and what they would think when I came staggering out of the trees. Would they think I was high, like Lochie had claimed? Had they believed him? If they thought he was lying, why hadn't any of them come after us, to help me?

Maybe they had, and they had got lost in the dark and shadow that huddled under the trees.

I didn't have enough energy to plan out what I might say if any of the dancers came over to me. I would just have to hope for the best.

As it turned out, I didn't need to worry. I was further down the hollow than before, and the stage with its pounding music was much closer than the fire dancing circle.

I began to laugh as I hobbled down the hill. Each gust of wind carried me to the edge of sobbing, but I managed to keep myself under control.

Ahead of me dancers spun and bobbed in time with the bass. A thick cloud hung amongst them, mist condensed from the humidity of their bodies, or clinging piles of weed smoke. Neon colour glowed from wristbands, body paint, and sticks clutched in ecstatic hands.

I stood near the edge of the crowd and clutched my sides. Faces pulled into tight grins stared back out of the crowd at me before wheeling away in the throng. Others were blank and their eyes closed, as they leaned back into the melody, their faces turned skyward.

I just needed one familiar face. Any of the people I had met while I was here would do. Hopefully I might find Dai or Daphne dancing here tonight, so that I could collapse into their arms. I dared not hope that I would be able to find Leon in the thick crowd, but just the thought nearly allowed my panicky sobs to break out.

"Ashleigh!" called a voice, barely audible under the music, and a figure detached from the crowd and walked towards me, one arm held up high in greeting. They were tall and strong, but the brilliant lights on the stag behind them hid them in silhouette as they came closer. As they walked further into the moonlight their face became clear

"Finn!" I cried. He would do. I launched myself towards him and collapsed into his arms. As his arms closed around my shoulders, the overwhelming feelings that I had been holding down as I sought safety lurched out of my chest. Huge tearful sobs wracked me and I shuddered as I tried to suck enough air in to replace the wails that were escaping my throat.

"Hey hey hey, it's alright!" I could hear the shock in his voice as he placed a hand on the back of my head and tried to soothe me. His arms felt strong and safe. "What happened?"

I tried to answer him. I lifted my head to look at his face, but the light from the stage behind him made it difficult to find his eyes. My throat was clenching hard and I sniffed. I was unable to get out any words.

Finn's head moved as he looked around and then he moved his arm over my shoulders and started leading me away from the crowd.

"Come on, let's get you somewhere quiet. Then you can take a moment and tell me what's wrong."

CHAPTER FIFTY-SEVEN

I let Finn lead me away from the dancers. As the pounding rhythm receded, my thoughts reassembled themselves. The powerful terror and adrenaline that had soaked through my body at the sight of Lochie, the werewolf, was finally ebbing, like a tide after a storm. Tiredness stabbed deep under my muscles. Walking, even with Finn's support, was difficult. I just wanted to lay down on the grass and sleep.

As my senses returned to my control, I realised that my surroundings were getting much darker. I blinked and looked up. We were beginning to walk back under the edges of the bush.

"What?" I said in surprise.

But Finn shushed me gently and guided me to a log where I could sit down. I lifted one foot onto my knee and started rubbing at my calf muscles, grateful for the chance to finally rest.

"Okay," he said, squatting onto his heels in front of me. "We're quiet. We're alone. Take a breath, and let me know what's wrong."

I wasn't sure where to begin, so at first I just talked about how Leon and I had met Lochie the night before and how he had turned out to be a complete bastard. Finn tutted and his face drew in concern as I described what had happened.

"But I would never have thought that he was literally a monster!" I finished.

"A monster? Like, he was a terrible person?" Finn's head tilted a little in confusion.

"No, a real, honest to god, monster from our nightmares." I continued, explaining how Leon and I had been heading for the lake, when the werewolf had come crashing up the trail, chasing someone I didn't know.

"A what?" Finn looked utterly shocked, so I pressed on quickly, hoping that he would believe me.

"I know, it's ridiculous! But I know what I saw and it was like nothing I had ever seen before!" I described the creature, explaining that I had had a moment to see the thing close up. Finn shook his head, but reached over to touch my knee. I could tell that he was having difficulty believing me, but he didn't try to explain the creature away.

"And you think that whatever it is you saw, you think that it turned into Lochie? Or that Lochie turned into it?" His forehead was creased as he tried to follow my story.

"Yes, it explains so much! He was so controlling and manipulative and entitled and..." My voice trailed off. I didn't know how else I could convince Finn that I was right.

"Wait." Finn licked his lips and cleared his throat. "You said Lochie was all of those things?"

"Yes?"

"What exactly do you mean 'was'? What happened to him?"

"I... I may have hurt him. Badly."

"How?"

"He was chasing me, and I managed to trip him up, and his head hit a rock." My throat was bone dry. It felt good to explain how I had managed to create a simple trap for Lochie as he chased me through the bush. It was like I was unloading that rock that I had felt deep in my guts after I had done it, and passing the big heavy load on to someone else, hopefully someone who could manage the weight.

"Do you think he might be-" I couldn't finish the sentence.

Finn scrubbed his hand through his hair and blew out hard. "So, you are telling me that you might have killed a guy named Lochie, who was absolutely an entitled asshole who was chasing you through the bush, because you thought he was a werewolf?"

I winced at the word 'killed', but I nodded.

"But also you haven't seen your husband since you saw the werewolf?'

I nodded again, less happily this time.

"We should go and check on Lochie immediately, and let someone know to get help. And hopefully we might find your husband at the same time."

I sagged as my muscles relaxed. It was so to be believed and to have someone try to help.

"Yes! Oh god, I would love to find Leon. I hope he's okay."

"Yes, me too," said Finn with a strange tone of voice. He held out a hand and helped me stand. I winced and squeezed my thighs.

"Ugh, my legs are so sore."

"I bet they are, it sounds like you have been through a lot. You wait here while I go and let someone know what happened."

I didn't want to wait alone in the forest, but I agreed that it would be faster if Finn told someone to get help and then returned so we could check on Lochie and look for Leon. The forest felt like a living thing beneath the night sky. The trees breathed overhead and I was sure I heard tiny twigs snapping in every direction. I wondered whether deer were wandering nearby, or if the monster had come back.

Hurry up Finn, I wished inside my head, my breath growing ragged.

Just before I was going to start stumbling back towards the basin and out of the darkness that crowded around me, he reappeared.

"Ash, are you okay?" he grabbed me by my shoulders and hunched over to look into my face.

"Mmm hmm," I replied, though I was shivering. "I think the shock of everything is getting a bit much. It's spooky out here by myself."

"I'm back now. Alright, take me to Lochie."

"Did you find someone?"

"Yes. I know this woman named Siobahn, she has connections all around the festival. She's going to get proper help but she agreed that we should do what we can first."

I was surprised to hear that Finn knew Siobahn. But from what I knew of her, I shouldn't have been. She was clearly an unofficial leader of the Pandaea.

Finn held my hand as I stood up and helped set me moving along a small path in the direction I thought would take me back to where I had left the body of Lochie.

"What if we get lost?" I asked him as the trees loomed overhead, sending the path into darkness.

"I'll stop you before we get too deep into the bush. I can still see some lights from the hollow and hear some of the music."

I strained my ears and relaxed a little when I realised that I could still hear it too.

We walked for nearly ten minutes, following the path around in tight loops that nearly doubled back on each other. I had begun to wonder if I was following the same track that I had found to get back to the hollow, or whether I might have set off along some other deer track, when we rounded a corner and the body of Lochie lay sprawled along the dirt.

"Fuck me," breathed Finn from behind me. I nodded but didn't walk any closer. Finn stepped around me, glancing at my eyes, and then moving closer to the body. He crouched down and placed one hand gingerly on Lochie's back.

From where I stood I could see the dark pool of blood that surrounded Lochie's head, and where the blood was staining the shoulders of his top.

Finn moved his hand down to Lochie's neck and paused. I held my breath. I felt as though any movement or sound that I made would interfere with Finn's check, and I didn't want there to be a chance that he could say I got in the way. I couldn't tell what I wanted him to discover had happened to Lochie.

Finn looked back at me.

"He's really dead."

CHAPTER FIFTY-EIGHT

My stomach clenched hard at Finn's assessment of Lochie's body.

"Is that the branch you tripped him with?" Finn leaned over and touched it. I nodded again though I could barely hear him through the heartbeat that thundered in my head. "It's incredible. You should never have been put into a position like that. But you did an amazing job getting out."

My breath was coming in shallow gasps.

Finn stood up and slapped the dust from his thighs and then looked around into the blackness lurking between the trees around us. "So, this psycho was chasing you and you dealt with him. And your husband was somewhere as well? Leon's out there still?"

"I think so. As far as I know."

Finn looked back at me with an odd expression. "Oh shit," he exclaimed when he saw my face. "Hey, don't panic. You were defending yourself from an attacker. It was bad luck. Siobahn will be here soon, with help."

I nodded, heat pressing at the corners of my eyes.

"Come on, let's find your husband as soon as we can. That will make you feel better."

I nodded again. But despite my agreement, I worried that Lochie might have caught Leon before he found me. Maybe he was already beyond saving. I didn't say that out loud. If I kept the words in my head, then they didn't have to be true.

"Okay, then let's go see if we can find him. Come on, let's start at the last place you saw him."

Finn walked back over to me and we began heading back the way we had come. The rhythmic pounding from the dancing stage in the distance grew louder, but before we broke out into the clear space, we turned away and headed back along the narrow dirt track that wound through the bush towards the lake. Darkness pressed in from either side, leaking from the shadowy undergrowth, but leaving the light and noise of the hollow felt much safer now. I was with Finn. The monster was dead. If I could just find Leon alive and well everything would be okay.

Finn stepped behind me as we followed the track, one hand on the small of my back as we made our way towards the fence where I had last seen my husband. It felt as though I was leading him through the bush, a feeling which was emphasised by the way he asked me about what had happened as we walked.

He asked me about where I had met Lochie, and how I had known that he was bad news. After I explained to him how Lochie had come back to the van with Leon and myself before he became entitled and angry, Finn clucked his tongue in judgement.

"You're right, that's disgusting. Does it worry you to meet guys like that?"

"Not before now. Why, are you worried about whether I'm going to try to kill you next?"

His fingers pressed on my back before he answered.

"I mean, I'd like to think we had a mutually satisfying experience, and you didn't feel pressured by me at any point." I could hear the smile in his voice, so I knew he wasn't really upset or worried.

"We did indeed have a very satisfying experience!" I reached around my side so that I could touch his fingers in reassurance. "And no, you have never made me feel pressured. Thank you for that."

"You're welcome! Of course, I don't know how I would have acted if I had met your husband at the same time. Maybe he just inspires such a tidal wave of erotic sensation that I would have lost control of myself!"

"True, maybe Leon is too sexy for this world." God, where was he?

We turned a corner in the track and saw the dim shape of the chain link fence ahead of us. It was slightly buckled, as usual, with the wire mesh peeled away in one corner, creating the small doorway that people used to access the other side, and the pathway over to the lake.

I paused and Finn nearly bumped into me. He stepped back again quickly. I shivered as I breathed slowly.

"Are you alright?" he asked from over my shoulders.

I nodded. Then I coughed and cleared my throat and then said, "Yes. Yes, I am. It's just that-" I cleared my throat again. "That's where I was standing, and it feels really gross to be back on the spot."

"Where were you standing, exactly?"

"Over here." I walked forward and pointed out the tree that I had hidden myself behind when the monster had come loping up the path. "And Leon would have been just there."

I pointed across the track to a tree on the far side. Finn walked over to the tree and circled it slowly. He lowered his face towards the ground, but I couldn't imagine he would be able to see very much in the darkness.

"So, you were both hiding behind these trees when the werewolf came through?" he asked.

"Yes," I replied. I didn't like the way he kept using the word werewolf though. "Do you have to use that word?"

He straightened up and turned to face me. "What word?"

"Werewolf."

"You don't like me saying that?"

I shook my head.

"But, isn't that what you said you saw?"

"I guess so." I shrugged. "But it seems so ridiculous when you say it out loud. It makes me feel like a fool."

"Oh, does it?" Finn lowered himself back down to the ground by the tree I had pointed out. "I do think that we can tell he was here at least, the branches are snapped and the ferns and things are crushed where he must have been standing." Finn stood up and sucked a deep breath in his nose. "But it's hard to tell which way he might have gone. Do you have any idea, any idea at all?"

"None." The loss of my husband was beginning to sink into my body as I realised that there were fewer and fewer chances that Leon was still alive, still running somewhere out there in the dark. It was like a heavy knife was slowly pushing its way down the back of my ribcage and slicing into my heart.

"Shit, I hope we can find him. He'd be able to back up your story, for one thing."

"You don't believe me?" I was shocked at the thought. Most of my calm had come when I had thought Finn believed me, and was helping me.

"No, no, it's not that! It's just that having more witnesses will help others understand too."

"The fire dancers saw me, when I was looking for help, and they saw Lochie go after me."

"That's right, you did say that."

We both stood in silence, thinking. Finn was standing in the deeper shadow behind the tree, and I had found a patch of moonlight on the track.

CHAPTER FIFTY-NINE

After we stood still by the fence for a moment, Finn moved back up to the path.

"I think he would have headed for the lake."

"Why?"

"Because the werewo- the monster came from that direction. If it kept moving away from there, then it would seem a safer direction to travel."

I understood what he meant, and agreed. At first he led the way through the low gap in the fence, but after holding the wire up for me to get through he urged me to take the lead once more.

"I'll be alright," he said when I asked him about it. "I'll just be watching out behind us."

"But I killed the monster. There's nothing else to worry about."

"I know, I know," he replied cheerfully, patting me reassuringly. "You told me you killed Lochie, I get it."

I frowned but turned to look forwards along the path that led to the lake. I pulled in a deep breath.

"Leon!" I yelled out.

Finn lept as though he had received an electric shock.

"Shhhh! What are you doing!?" He scurried over to me, putting his hands on my shoulders. His eyes looked sharp, a mixture of surprise and anger.

"I'm calling for Leon. Obviously? Is that some sort of problem for you?" I shrugged my way out of his arms. "Lochie isn't going to come after us.

"And you think he was the monster." Finn growled and shook his head. "Even if he was, what the hell makes you think there is only one of them?"

I wanted to throw up. More than one? The idea hadn't occurred to me. Fuck, where was Leon!?

We kept walking along the track towards the lake. My thoughts raced. *He doesn't believe me,* I realised. I had to examine the thought carefully, as though it was a detailed piece of art in my hands. What was it that he didn't believe me about?

I thought about his actions, and his words, and the ways he had reacted to what I had said. At first, I thought that he simply didn't believe me about any of my story. Perhaps he was indulging me as though I had had too much to drink? But Finn had seen the body. He knew that I had done that to Lochie. Or perhaps he thought it had been an accident, and I was only claiming to have been the one who did it? No, from the expression in his eyes when he had crouched over the body and looked at me, I knew Finn believed I had killed the man.

That made it clear what Finn wasn't believing. He didn't believe me that there was a werewolf.

I couldn't blame him. Some woman that he had hooked up with wanders out of the bush, ranting about a werewolf and declaring that she's killed some guy. What was he supposed to think? If I hadn't seen the monster with my own eyes, I would have said that claiming to see one was a sign of insanity or excessive drugs.

But then, why had he stopped me calling out? If there was no werewolf, then there was no other danger out here in the bush.

If I was the only thing out here that had killed someone, why was he trying to keep so quiet?

I became very conscious of his hand on the small of my back. I cast my mind back and realised that he had walked behind me ever since we had entered the bush again. Does he think that I am going to lash out and kill him? No, it couldn't be that. I decided that I would test the theory. I jerked to a stop, as though I was about to spin around and face him.

Finn's fingers left my back and there was a crunch as he stepped away from me.

The bush was silent.

"Are you okay?" he asked eventually.

"Yes. I just thought I saw something."

"Where?"

"Over there." I pointed off to my left. "But it's nothing. I must be getting too tired."

"I'm sure we'll find him soon." Finn didn't move until I resumed walking.

That's it, I'm sure, I told myself. He thinks that I'm dangerous. Does he think that I killed Leon as well? Maybe he thinks I have an accomplice out here somewhere? But then, where does he think we are going?

The slope down to the lake looked much more treacherous in the dim light than it did during the day. The moon was bright, and even though the clouds were thick tonight, they were moving fast. That small mercy was the only reason we were able to see well to carefully make our way down towards the water.

"Is he here?" asked Finn from behind me.

"I don't see him," I said.

"It might take a while. But this seems like a good place to check, in my opinion."

Finn started to walk around the shore to the right, peering under low shrubs and checking the nooks and crannies of the rocky landscape. What did he expect to find, I wondered. Leon's body? Was he hoping to confront me with it?

"What are you doing?" I asked finally. I couldn't figure out what was going on with Finn, and I couldn't handle thinking about it any longer. I just wanted to know.

Finn laughed. It was a mocking, sneering sort of laugh, one that burst out through his nose as though he couldn't stop it.

"I wanted to make sure where he was first," he began, stepping back from me. "Just in case he tried to help. But there's no one out here now. Fuck it."

At first I wasn't sure what I was seeing. I thought that the moon had gone behind a cloud again, and that the shadows it was casting on Finn were tricking my eyes. But then a horrible noise came from his neck, a clunk, and then some part of him jabbed out like a buckling beam and I knew that what I was seeing was real.

Finn's limbs stretched as though they were made of play-dough, becoming skinny and taut, and then swelling as muscle filled in the spaces again. His clothes tore and bunched in strange ways as his legs manoeuvred themselves into an inhuman stance.

The worst thing was his face, though it was thankfully mostly hidden in shadow. Finn's face pulled away from his nose and teeth as they pushed forward from under his skin. Tiny black spikes pierced through the skin in waves, until black fur covered a long snout.

Those eyes that I had danced with, talked with, had sex with; eyes that I had decided would be a comfort until I could find my husband. Those eyes reflected a cold and hungry gleam as I watched him change.

CHAPTER SIXTY

The werewolf stood before me as the moon came out from behind a cloud, revealing its strangeness in full. It was exactly the creature that I had seen pause on the path by the fence.

I felt as though my muscles had frozen solid, and my breath was stuck in my throat. A cold dampness broke out over my skin and the night's chill air would have made me shiver if I was able to move at all.

The tall thin monster swung its head from side to side and its heavy black nostrils snuffled as it smelled the air. It grinned at me, thin furry lips pulling aways from a jaw that was stuffed with dozens of glistening sharp teeth. It lurched forward.

I dove away from it, finally managing to force my muscles into action, and tumbled to the ground. The creature looked amused by my efforts, and it casually stepped after me. I had no idea what to do. It's mouth leaned closer, saliva dripping from the teeth that began to fill my vision.

I dove sideways again, rolling over the dirt and crying out as gravel and stones jabbed into my shoulders and legs. I heard the sickening snap of the jaws behind me.

"Finn, you bastard," I yelled from my position spread out on the bank. "I trusted you! How could you do this?" I was yelling to get the thoughts out of my head more than anything else, and so I was surprised when the werewolf stood straighter and tilted its head at me. The thing slurped its jaws, and its tongue lolled in its mouth, and I realised that it was trying to speak. It shook its head as it found that it was not able to do so, and then made a movement that was obviously a shrug before launching itself at me.

Its body was heavy and hot, and the fur that covered its lanky form was stiff and sharp. It bowled me over and together we tumbled along the ground. It was so large that I was bundled inside its curled figure and panic began to flood my nerves. I lashed out, stretching and punching and crying as I tried to get away from it.

Suddenly, the creature let out a yelp. My eyes snapped open at the sound. My necklace had come free of my top, and the silver cage had clearly bumped into the monster's chest.

At the same moment, the monster flinched away from me. The movement was strong enough that it shoved me, far enough that I was able to find my footing and stand up. I reached to my neck and clutched my silver necklace in my hand, letting the pendant dangle just below my fist. The werewolf snarled.

"Really?" I said. "The necklace hurts?" My disbelief washed over me like a bucket of ice water. I couldn't come to grips with what was happening. It was like I had been caught up in some sort of nightmare.

I swung the necklace a little, enjoying the way it hummed through the air. "Is it because it's silver?" I started laughing, softly at first and then stronger. I wanted to double over and clutch my stomach as I laughed. "How can a simple bloody necklace be a problem for something like you?"

The werewolf snarled. Its lip curled away from its teeth, revealing blood-red gums. The sound was like a chainsaw, deep and throbbing and violent. I shuddered and then quickly lifted the necklace over my head so that I could swing it more freely. I tucked one loop of the chain between my fingers. It felt so small and thin and delicate, like I was holding onto a wisp of spiderweb and yet I was trying to use it to threaten this massive beast confronting me. This was madness!

Maybe that woman had told me the truth, and this necklace really was pure silver. I had always thought that diluting a pure thing meant that it was weakened. But maybe some things were so pure that they drew the taint out of the things around. Maybe pure love could fight back against hate that tried to reduce it. And in the same way, if I was lucky, maybe this pure silver could damage the mingled creature in the water.

"Finn, you piece of shit!"

The werewolf leapt at me.

I turned my head away, squeezing my eyes shut. If this didn't work, I hoped that the bastard would finish me off quickly. I swung the tiny necklace in my hand forward.

I was rewarded by a loud yowl, but then the monster slammed into me again. I was sent flying backward, hooking my fingers desperately at the necklace chain. I was terrified that I might lose it, and it seemed to be the only slight chance I had to keep the creature off me.

I tried to catch myself and pull myself up, but the ground disappeared beneath my feet and I dropped into the icy water of the lake. Just before I splashed under the surface I had a glimpse of the monster scratching at its cheek, as though it had been bitten by a mosquito.

I let the water carry me down, pulling me into the darkness below the surface. Too soon, my feet touched the silty clay of the steep bank. I tried to push myself forward and began stepping up the bank towards the air again. I wasn't sure how long I would be able to hold my breath, especially as I had been caught by surprise. The water currents that slid around me and snuck into my crevices were devastatingly cold.

There was a massive burst of sound above me as the ragged creature dove into the lake, slipping past me in the water. I could barely see anything under here, but I felt it move past me, stretching out towards the deeper water of the lake. As I had hoped, he must have thought I was trying to swim away from him. I pushed off the bank and tried to get my head above the water.

I sucked at the night air greedily, reaching out with my hands for the bank so that I could scramble out of the water, but then I heard a splash from behind me. Finn must have swum to the surface when he didn't find me in the deeper water. I began to turn in the water, trying to lift my hand so I could swing the necklace, and immediately began to sink again.

Before my head slipped under the surface, I saw the monster's massive jaws erupt from the water, and my necklace whipped onto the side of its face. The beast roared and turned its face, meaning that it was unable to get a grip on me as it approached, and the rush of water heaved me further away from its claws.

I touched the thick silty bottom and pushed up again. This time Finn was there, waiting above the water, his eyes shining with fury beneath the moon. He lunged forward again. I was too close to swing the necklace, or to swim aside from his long arms. The necklace didn't seem to be slowing him much anyway, it was an annoyance at best. Without thinking, I rammed my hand forward, with the chain and necklace coiled around it. The werewolf's arms wrapped around me and his teeth glistened before my face. Then my hand disappeared into his throat.

CHAPTER SIXTY-ONE

Immediately the creature spasmed, and I pulled my hand back, letting go of the necklace. His teeth raked long red lines down my arm and the pain made me shriek, letting mouthfuls of water wash into my throat, choking me. I coughed and spluttered as I spun to seek out the shore.

Beside me, the werewolf was reacting in a similar way, clutching at his throat, trying to reach inside his mouth with heavy hands unsuitable for delicate work. Water washed into his mouth as well, and I could see he was fighting to stay afloat.

Bolts of pain shot up my arm from the cuts but I drew strength from the sight of him flailing. His fur was slicked into strange angles and water washed across his face as he kicked and tried to stay above the surface.

I managed to get my feet onto a part of the bank that was shallow enough for me to breathe. I turned and looked out at the surface of the lake, clutching my wounded arm to my chest as I shivered in the cold night air.

Deeper into the lake, the water churned as Finn fought to maintain his footing. The necklace was clearly still stuck deep in his throat. At the reminder of how I had put it there my arm throbbed and a sharp slice of pain shot up my shoulder to the back of my head. I could feel warm blood slowly running down to my elbow. I watched him, gasping, until I was sure that I was not going to fall under the water from my own exhaustion.

But Finn was making no ground. He was not coming closer to the bank. His head dipped beneath the surface more and more often, each time pushing its way back up in a rush of water and rage. Each appearance grew further and further apart, and his movements slower.

Then he slid under the water and did not return.

I stood, watching the water closely. I wanted to turn away, either to find a large stick to try and defend myself with as a club, or to simply run back into the bush and away, fleeing before he could return or something else show up. But instead I stood and watched. I had to be sure.

The night was quiet, and so very still. The ripples that washed against the edge of the lake from his thrashing grew smaller and smaller until they were imperceptible amongst the regular undulations of the still lake. I listened to the trees around me, as the sound of insects chirping began to return. I even heard a mosquito hum past my ear and then vanish.

I took a moment to look closer at my arm. The cuts were long, but shallow. Although they looked dramatic, I would be okay.

I think he's gone, I said to myself. It was hard to believe. I waited longer, still unwilling to trust my senses, but eventually there was nothing else I could do. I clutched my wounded arm closer and turned to follow the track back to the Pandaea. I only hoped that I could find my friends, or my husband. I looked up towards the bush and froze.

Someone was standing at the crest of the hill that overlooked the lake.

The figure began walking down the hill towards me. My instinct was to run, but before I could gather my still cold muscles, the figure lifted a hand and called out.

"Ash? Is that you?" Leon's voice filled my ears with a joy that

I had almost forgotten could exist, after the darkness and fear of the night.

"Leon!" I cried, and I began running up the hill. He ran down to meet me and gathered me into his arms tightly. His head pressed down on the top of mine, and I burrowed my face into his shoulder. The tight strength of his arms crushed me and that strength slowly leaked into me. I began to feel less like my legs were going to collapse underneath me.

As I pulled back, I realised that my face was covered with tears, even as a smile that I couldn't control pulled my lips apart. I could see that Leon's face was the same, and he wiped at his face with one hand before throwing it around me again. I tilted my head back so that he could kiss me.

The feeling of his lips on mine was like coming home. I felt as though I was standing in the place that I was supposed to be. It was warm, and familiar, despite the cold of the night around us. Even though we were stuck in a dark forest, by a quiet lake, at a festival full of strangers, together we were secure and strong and stable. He kissed me until I couldn't take it anymore, and I had to pull away.

"I can't believe that you're okay," I whispered happily.

"I can't believe that I found you!" he answered. His voice caught as he spoke and he had to clear his throat. "I've been running around in that bush for hours, trying to find my way. I was so terrified of what might have happened to you." His fingers dug into my shoulders as he looked over my cut arm.. "And something did. Oh god Ash, what happened?"

"I'm okay, I'm okay."

"I saw that thing, and then I knew you had started running, and I did too, but then I had absolutely no fucking clue where I was and..." his voice trailed off. "I'm so sorry, I didn't mean to abandon you, I just took off and just hoped that you were doing the same."

"It's okay, I did exactly the same thing. I've been looking for you too."

"Did you see where it went?" Leon leaned back a little and glanced around the lake side. The moon was bright enough now that he could see most of the clear space, but the trees still created a black wall surrounding everything else.

"Yeah, actually. In there." I pointed at the lake.

"Shit, we should get out of here!" Leon's eyes widened.

"Absolutely!" I agreed, patting him on the chest. "But we don't have to panic. It's dead."

"Fuck," Leon breathed out slowly. "How?"

"It was a werewolf," I began, and then I had to stop as Leon jerked. His eyes looked at me like I was crazy. "No really!" I continued. "It was! It was that guy I met on the first night, Finn! My silver necklace burnt him, which gave me a chance to get away from him and then I fell in the lake. When he chased me, I rammed the necklace down his throat, and that choked him until he drowned."

Leon was still staring at me.

"You have to believe me," I said. I could feel darkness crowding around my mind again. "If you don't believe then I-" My voice cracked in my throat and I shivered. I couldn't contemplate a world where my own husband didn't believe me.

CHAPTER SIXTY-TWO

"I don't... Let me have a look." Leon stepped closer, placing his hands on my waist and resting his forehead on mine. "Hey. I love you Ash. I believe you. I just..." His voice trailed off. "Let's go check out the lake, huh?" He kissed me gently. Then we both walked down the bank to the water's edge.

We stood together there, examining the shimmering dark surface. Leon squeezed his fingers on my shoulder.

"There's something there!" He pointed out into the lake. He was right, there was something floating in the water, drifting closer to the light dirt of the shallows. "I'm going to make sure it's the creature."

I grabbed his upper arm. "Don't!"

Leon put a hand on mine. "Hey, you said it's dead. I just want to see for myself." He turned to look into my eyes. I felt his presence soothing the fear in my head and leaned forward against him. "It's going to be okay."

He moved carefully and slowly as he approached the rounded shape that was floating closer.

"Do you have something to defend yourself with?" I asked. He paused as he searched for a large stick. He lifted it over his shoulder, like a baseball bat, and I had to laugh. As if a little branch like that was going to be enough to stop Finn if he was luring us closer.

However, the shape in the water didn't move, even when Leon jabbed it with the stick. He waited a long time, bumping it back towards the shallows when it began to slowly drift away. Eventually he looked back at me and said, "I've got to know."

He reached down and grabbed the edge of the shape, then hauled it over to the land. I flinched away from him, my muscles tensing, ready to run for the trees. Water lapped at the edge of the shape.

I was staring down at a strange misshapen version of Finn.

His face and chest were mostly recognisable. There were dark burn marks on his cheeks, and his throat was swollen and puffy. One eye was open, staring unseeing into the sky.

But the rest of his body was a twisted mess of fur and skin. His legs looked like they had been stuffed into sausage skins that were too small, and they puffed up in strange ways. One leg was warped into a zig zag before it ended in a furred paw with large black claws. His arms were similar, misshapen and a mix of fur and claw and human skin.

Leon staggered away from the twisted thing, and made a choking noise.

"This is horrifying," he gasped. He held a hand to his mouth, as though he was worried he might be sick. I could hear his stomach clenching and he leaned over the water of the lake.

"I told you, didn't I?" I said.

"You really did. I'm sorry love, deep down I guess I thought it must have been an escaped animal from a zoo or something, something we couldn't recognise easily in the dark, but..." He shook his head. "You were totally right."

"Now what?"

"I think we get away from here as quickly as we can in case there are any others, and we tell others to get out too."

He took off his shirt and tied it around my arm, pulling it

tight. The thought that there might be more of these things in the forest with us helped us move back through the dark slope and trees, pushing our weary limbs harder than I might have thought possible. We stumbled as we rushed through the inky pathy in the bush.

I was grateful for Leon's arms around me as we moved in a hopping shuffle closer to a jog than a walk. I could feel love and strength flowing into me through him. It staved off the exhaustion that threatened to overwhelm me, the tiredness that pulled at my eyelids and burned my legs. I wanted to curl into a ball and sleep, forgetting everything I had seen, protected by Leon.

The dance hollow, with its noise and lights and mass of dancers felt like another world. It didn't feel real anymore. None of these people had any idea what had just happened in the trees around them. Instead they were dancing and happy and having a great experience. Bastards.

We kept to the outside of the dancers, but there were always others on the grass around our feet. People stood in twos and threes, or lounged on the ground, talking softly or just allowing the music to infuse them. At least two couples were deeply involved in each others' bodies despite the people walking by only a metre or two away.

"Do we just go up and grab people and tell them what happened?" I asked.

"I guess we try to." Leon swallowed and led me forward to the edge of the crowd. A young man with a wide smile was stumbling away from the others and we took the opportunity to talk to him.

"Hey, you need to get out of here!" I called to him, trying to be heard over the pounding music.

"What?" His smile shrank and his forehead creased.

"It's dangerous. There are monsters in the bush!"

He laughed nervously and turned away from us.

"Come on," Leon encouraged me.

Just as we turned back towards the dancers, a figure launched itself out of the crowd and came barrelling towards us. I screamed, and Leon stepped in front of me.

Thankfully, the music was loud enough that my scream was lost in the whoops and ecstasy of the crowd. To my deep relief, the figure barreling towards me turned out to be Daphne. Laughs that were almost sobs punched their way out of my chest as I pulled her into a crushing hug. She returned my enthusiasm and latched onto me like an octopus, her arms wrapping entirely around me. She planted a strong kiss on my cheek.

"Hello gorgeous! Isn't it a fantastic night!"

Her eyes were wide and shining and she was wearing a short white tee shirt with suspenders over her shoulders and tiny black shorts over shiny thigh-high boots. The boots were funny to see, as they were covered in mud. The outfit was not really designed for dancing out in a field.

"We're getting out of here," said Leon before I could muster my thoughts into order enough to respond.

"What? Why?" asked Daphne. She was still smiling and hanging on my shoulders though.

"This place tipped over from worrying into way too dangerous. You were right earlier, we should have left before now."

CHAPTER SIXTY-THREE

The crowd bunched around us, arms in the air as they gyrated to the thumping rhythm. I felt a body brush past me as they spun through the crowd.

"What?" Now Daphne's face grew serious. She gasped as she saw the dark stains on the tee shirt that was tied around my arm. "Holy shit! What happened?"

"I was attacked," I said. "By a-" I paused and pursed my lips. "You're going to think I'm on something, but I'm really not." I put a hand on her shoulder and leaned in closer, willing her to believe me. "I was attacked by a werewolf."

Daphne bit her lower lip to stop a laugh escaping.

"Daphne! I'm really hurt!" I lifted my arm up higher so she could see it more clearly. Dark stains spread on the fabric.

"I'm sorry!" She held up her hands to ward off my criticism, but I could see worry on her face. "I can see that. That looks horrible, we need to get you taken care of. But, a werewolf? Seriously?"

"Meet us at the campsite," said Leon. "We'll explain more there."

"Alright," Daphne nodded. "I'll find Dai as well." She disappeared into the swirling dancers behind us to search for her husband. They stepped apart to allow her in and then closed back around her, like curtains. Eyes stared back at Leon and me, watching us.

"Come on," Leon said. "Let's try and get to the stage."

Together we marched around the side of the dancing crowd, until we were next to the stage. It had been built to lift the DJs and screens and lights up where they could be admired, but there were no steps or ladders on this side. Leon reached out to climb up its rounded bars and onto the stage, when a large man in a leather jacket stepped forward from the shadows. He laid a hand on Leon's shoulder and said "Hey man, you can't just go up there."

I stared at the man. He was dressed so utterly unlike most of the people who were at the Pandaea. His jeans were tight and black, and his jacket bulked out his shoulders. He had a thick spiky beard, and serious eyes.

"Please," I urged him. "Please, we need to get to the microphone and warn everyone!" I reached out to clutch at his arm that still rested on Leon's shoulder.

"Warn everyone? Warn them of what?" The man let go of Leon and turned to face me. A man I hadn't seen was there stepped up to make sure Leon didn't climb up the structure now that he was free.

"There's a monster in the bush!"

"A monster!" The man burst with a short laugh and turned to say something to the other man.

"No really! It was a werewolf and I choked him with my silver necklace!" I grabbed at my throat, before I remembered that I had left my necklace in Finn's throat. The man stepped away from me, his eyes widening. Then he motioned his companion closer and frowned at me.

"I think you two need to come and have a chat with us in the first aid tent."

"They aren't going to help," yelled Leon. "Come on!" He

launched himself away from the security guards and into the dancers.

"Shit!" I cried as I followed him, hoping that the guards wouldn't think that it was worthwhile chasing me. I hoped that they just thought that we were having a bad trip, and would let us go.

As we bounced through the crowd, Leon and I tried to get their attention, yelling "Run! Get out of here! There are monsters here! There's a werewolf in the bush!" at anyone who seemed to notice us, but none of them stopped dancing.

Before I knew it, we burst out of the far side of the crowd. We stumbled for a few steps and then slowed down. Leon put his arm around me to support me as we strode away from the hollow.

"Don't run," he hissed. "We don't want those security guards slowing us down if they see us."

I agreed. We needed to get back to the van and get back home.

"What about warning people though?" I asked.

"They all just thought we were high. We'd have to explain to someone who will listen properly, someone who can get others to pay attention."

"Siobahn was supposed to be coming to help with Lochie."

Leon started to nod and then paused. "What about Lochie?" I realised that he knew that Finn had been the monster that we saw in the bush, but he hadn't heard about how Lochie had chased me, and how I had tripped him into a rock. I drew a shuddery breath and then explained what had happened after I ran from the werewolf, and how it looked as though Lochie might have died from his fall. When I explained that Finn had said he had found Siobahn and asked her to get help we were both silent for a minute.

"Knowing what we know now, surely he didn't actually tell anyone to get help," said Leon.

"I agree. But he said he spoke to Siobahn. How would he

have known who she was, or that I knew her as well? He acted surprised when I said I knew who she was."

"She seems pretty well known here," replied Leon slowly. "Perhaps he just made a guess? Come on, let's try to find her. She might be getting help for Lochie anyway, but she is actually the right person for us to warn regardless."

He drew me back so that we could head to the van, but my hair stood up on the back of my neck.

As we walked away across the grass of the hollow, I turned to look back over my shoulder. There were figures at the edge of the dancing crowd now, still and watching, like statues lining a garden of colourful flowers moving in the wind. Were they watching us? Why had so many people stopped dancing?

I pulled on Leon's arm.

"They're watching us," I whispered.

"Who?"

"There, at the edge of the dancers."

He turned around and looked back. There were still some people standing, but fewer than there had been moments before, and most of them were looking in different directions now or talking to each other.

"Are you sure?" he asked.

"I could have sworn they were watching us," I replied. I wondered whether the shock and stress was affecting my thinking.

"Let's just find Siobahn and get out of here as quickly as we can."

The market was mostly empty as we walked through it. A few people lounged against the empty stalls and food trucks. They watched us wordlessly as we passed by. Again, I felt a chill slide down my spine as I met their unsmiling eyes.

"Leon?" My voice cracked, though I kept it as low as I could. I turned my face toward his shoulder to try and conceal the movement of my mouth. I felt his fingers tighten on my side. It was reassuring to remember how close he was to me.

"Yeah, I feel it too," he murmured. "Don't make eye contact and keep walking."

CHAPTER SIXTY-FOUR

*L*eon and I walked out of the market space and crossed the dark fields that lay between it and the tents. The camping sites were quiet and empty. There was no one sitting outside them tonight, no one walking from one place to another. I wondered how many of the low shelters actually had people inside. Edges of tents caught the breeze and flicked back and forward, providing the only sound in the night except for the distant echo of the dance in the hollow.

I kept pressed close against Leon as we walked along the edge of the campsites, looking for the lane that would lead us back to our van. The wind moaned and the cold air made me shiver.

"Weren't there other people out and about last night? And the night before?" I asked.

"Yeah, I think so," Leon replied.

"Where have they all gone then?"

Leon placed a hand over mine, clearly trying to comfort me. I could feel his back muscles were tight with tension though. "I'm sure they're just dancing with the others," he said. "Or maybe they're asleep," he added, forcing his voice to be cheerful.

"It's not that late," I said. I couldn't believe how hard he was trying to pretend that everything was okay. There was something wrong here, more than just the monster we had left floating in the lake, and I knew that he knew it. Leon didn't say anything else.

As we walked towards the massage tents where Siobahn and her friends had set up their camp, it was clear that no-one was there either. No lights lit the tents and no sounds came from within, not even the soft noise of someone sleeping.

"Shit," said Leon. His face was scrunched up in frustration. "How do we warn Siobahn now?"

"It's okay," I said, thinking through our options as I squeezed his arm. "That's not really a surprise. I can think of three things for us to try. First, we could go back to the hollow and try to find her in the dancers. Second, we could try to warn one of the people by the stage, without trying to get past the guards, to try to get the word out that way. Or we could get packed to go and see if anyone is at that check-in hut that we stopped at when we came in."

Leon's face didn't look any calmer after I had outlined my thoughts for him.

"Do you have any other ideas?" I asked.

He shook his head.

"I think it would be best if we get out of here sooner rather than later," he managed to contribute.

"Okay," I nodded. "We'll pack the van and see if there's someone at the shed. I'm sure we'll find someone before then anyway."

We walked away from the camp and my muscles felt stronger than they had before. A sense of purpose was warming me, and giving me clarity about what I should do next. We were going to get away from all of this, and we were going to warn someone, someone who would listen to us and make sure all the people at the festival would be safe.

As we walked quickly towards our van, I glanced back towards the markets over the tents. At this distance, all I could see were the shadowed shapes of the stalls. But I could also see a couple of figures walking out from the market, heading towards us.

"There's someone coming."

"See, I told you things were normal." Leon made it sound like two people walking after us on this particular dark and silent night was exactly the same as groups of people moving around and engaging in conversation with one another like they had on other nights. It was infuriating.

"They aren't walking," I said. The fear that had been seeping through me clutched at my throat. It was true, the figures were almost jogging but not quite. They certainly weren't out for a stroll in the moonlight. They moved with purpose.

"Shit," said Leon. I could feel his muscles bunching up. "Do you think they found Finn?"

"They might be some of his friends, others like him, coming to make sure we don't get the warning out." My skin prickled with icy cold fear.

"There's a chance they haven't seen us, or they would be sprinting. Do we try to hide?" he asked, turning his eyes to meet mine.

"No, we run."

Together we darted forward along the lane, hunching ourselves over as we moved, hoping that whoever was coming hadn't noticed us in the dark. Before I knew it, Leon was fumbling with the keys outside the van. I couldn't wait to climb inside. All I wanted to do was crawl into the small bed we had built in the back of the van, dive under the thick duvet and pull the edges beneath me, hiding under the covers as though I was a child hiding from monsters under my bed. But these monsters were real, and hiding wasn't going to help. We had to find Siobahn, and then get away.

Leon pulled the door open and encouraged me up into the driver's seat. I began to climb over the seats and he touched my side.

"How's your arm?"

"Really sore. Why?"

"If you can manage, you should drive Ash, you're better than me. "

"Shit." I knew he was right. But I wished I could get into the back anyway. I turned around to see if I could convince him to drive, and saw over his head to the figures that were still getting closer. They were moving faster now. They were definitely jogging, and they were heading straight down the lane towards us, dashing past the rows of dark and empty tents.

"Fuck! Get in!" I hissed at Leon.

He ran around the van to climb in the passenger side. I slammed a hand onto the steering wheel in frustration.

"What's wrong?" he asked as he clambered in.

"You've still got the fucking keys Leon!"

"Shit, sorry!" He dug them out of his pocket and thrust them forward. I snatched them off him and slammed them into the steering column. The engine growled as I turned the ignition, and then I turned on the headlights.

Daphne and Dai were lit up by the twin beams as they ran down the lane towards us, both of them slowing as the lights blasted into their eyes and throwing their arms up over their faces.

"Oh thank fuck for that," I sighed as I realised that it had only been them who I had seen running towards us, and I turned the van off again.

CHAPTER SIXTY-FIVE

I wound down my window and leaned out to talk to our friends.

"Are you guys okay? Why were you running?" It felt as though they were deliberately trying to scare us.

"Daphne said you guys were freaking out and bailing? Is that right?" Dai sounded worried.

"Damn straight it is," I told him.

"I wanted to get to you quickly to check what happened, to maybe see if there was a chance that I could change your mind before you shot through, convince you both to stay." He stepped up next to the window. His normal smile was gone, and his eyes were serious. "But the vibes are seriously fucked up at the moment. What happened?"

"I was attacked." I lifted my wounded arm so that Dai could see that I wasn't kidding around. He blinked and stepped back from the van window, muttering "oh fuck" under his breath. I wasn't going to mention that it had been a werewolf that attacked me, in case he thought I was on something. "We're going to tell Siobahn about it and see if she can make sure everyone else is okay. But then we're getting the hell out of here!"

He nodded. "Yeah that's horrific! Daph and I will leave too."

"There's something weird out there tonight," added Daphne. She was already pulling gear out of their tent and jamming it into the open back door of their car.

"If you guys are going, then we've had our fun." Dai slapped the side of the van and moved to help Daphne with their things. Pots and pans, half inflated airbeds, everything was just shoved into the car with no attempt to save space or pack properly.

"Did you see Siobahn in the market?" Leon asked them, leaning over me to call out the window.

"No, sorry. We weren't really looking for her though," was Dai's muffled response as he jammed an armful of clothes into the footwell of their car.

"Okay, we're going to try and find her as we go to the check-in shed," I explained. "If we don't find her we'll tell whoever's there, and then keep going. See you back in town, yeah?"

"Yeah," replied Daph.

I turned the ignition again. Once the engine started I began rolling the van up the empty lane.

"Do you remember which way is out?" I asked. The festival looked so different in the middle of the night.

"I think it was left here," said Leon, pointing at some wheel tracks that suggested vehicles were using that area as a road. I looked both ways to check I wasn't about to run into another car, and saw a single figure walking towards us from the markets.

"Who's that?" I asked. The figure was only walking, which kept me calm. If it was another monster like Finn, then the figure would have been running. Something about the way they moved seemed familiar to me.

"Is that Siobahn?" asked Leon.

I turned the van towards the figure and the headlights illuminated the woman we knew. She lifted a hand to stop the light from blinding her, and I dipped them then opened the door and jumped out. I jogged ahead of the van to meet her.

"What's going on?" Siobahn asked as I came up to her. The

dipped headlights from the van were bright enough to make her pale skin glow. "Finn told me there had been an accident in the bush and you were involved, but now I find you out here driving around?"

"You mean he really did find you?" I was shocked. I had decided that Finn had completely made up that story to try and get me to lower my guard.

"Yes, but he didn't really tell me what happened. I had to track down my least drunk friends and send them searching through the bush to see if they could find an injured person. I haven't heard from them yet. If someone needs help, better directions would be good." She raised an eyebrow at me.

I felt guilt grip my throat and it was hard to talk.

"I don't think there's much rush." I swallowed thickly. "This guy Lochie was attacking me and I tripped him and he cracked his head on a rock, and I don't think he's-" I couldn't finish the sentence. My chest felt as though it was shrinking.

"Hey, hey," Siobahn stepped closer and put her arms around my shoulders. I felt hot tears pushing their way to the corners of my eyes. "That sounds terrible. But I'm sure it was an accident, or at worst self-defence. We'll get things sorted. Can you show me where it happened?" The weight of her arm was a comforting blanket over my shoulders.

I started to nod and then shook my head. There was no way I was going to re-enter the bush in the darkness of night.

"I can't go back out there," I said. My voice cracked, but I pushed on to explain how Leon and I had seen the werewolf chasing someone through the bush. Her eyes widened, but before she could interrupt me I grabbed her hand and explained that the creature in the bush couldn't have been some wild or escaped animal because I had seen Finn transform into it, and he had tried to kill me. "I jammed my silver locket into his throat and he drowned in the lake." I showed her my bandaged arm as proof. "I think that's what attacked those other people at the festival too."

"That's a pretty crazy story," said Siobahn softly. Her face was slack and I couldn't tell if she thought I had gone off the deep end, or if she might actually take me seriously. Her eyes dug into mine. "You say that you found a pure silver pendant for sale here, at the Pandaea?"

"Please, you have to believe me," I begged. "I know it sounds as though I'm high, but I haven't taken anything at all I swear. This happened to me. If you take your friends to the lake, you'll find Finn's body, and it's clearly not human. But I can't go back out there."

"If my friends and I go?" She tilted her head and narrowed her eyes. "You really aren't going to come and show us?"

"Leon and I are leaving. We wanted to find you, to warn everyone. We realised random people we ran into wouldn't believe us. But I thought there was a chance that you would listen. You know us. You have influence on the people who run the festival. You could get everyone out."

Siobahn sighed. She stepped back a little and rubbed her face.

"I'm so sorry that this happened to you Ashleigh. But you should know that I do believe you."

Relief slid through my veins like icy water. A massive grin stabbed my cheeks. I threw myself forward to hug her. "Oh thank goodness!"

"Yes. I am actually familiar with the creature that you saw."

I froze with my arms around Siobahn. My thoughts were scattering like frightened rabbits.

"You... You're familiar..."

"We know that there are werewolves here."

CHAPTER SIXTY-SIX

I was finding it hard to cope with each new shock that buffeted my senses. It had only been an hour or so since I had been fighting for my life against a monster in a moonlit lake. Now this woman who had welcomed me into her camp was telling me that she knew the monster was here? And she seemed to think there really were more of them! I knew my mouth was hanging open, but I couldn't summon the will to close it.

"I'm sorry." Siobahn was studying me closely, looking at how I reacted. I tried to respond, but I couldn't make words come.

"I know that's bizarre to hear. Let me explain," she said. "We first came out to this valley for our small gathering ages ago and there were probably no more than fifteen or twenty of us. That first year we discovered that something about the place is irresistible to the creatures. There were five of them that year."

"Five?" I choked on the word. Siobahn nodded.

"Luckily there were some amongst us who knew of rituals that allowed us to control the werewolves. There are prayers and invocations of the moon that can keep them from changing, or bind them from harming others. Part of the reason we come back each year is to check how well those rituals are working.

Each year we check that the monsters aren't causing havoc in the real world." Her eyes were wide and serious. Now it felt as though she was the one hoping that she would be believed, not me.

She sighed when I didn't say anything and then carried on.

"Of course, the festival parts of our visit kept getting bigger and more popular, so more and more people would come without any knowledge of what else we were doing here. We have to be careful not to cause a panic."

She grimaced.

"The creatures have been stronger than usual this year."

"Can you kill them?" I had to believe Siobahn when she said that she knew about the werewolves and could control them. She had been so calm when she heard me talking about the monster in the bush. But they had attacked people; so whatever she and her friends were doing, they had to do more!

"Yes, we can. There are less than you might be worried about, but they can be difficult to identify. I was surprised to hear you say that Finn was one, for example. The rituals don't need us to know who they are, but if we can figure it out then we know how to deal with them appropriately. Certainly, if they attack people, we need to react with force. Thank you for trusting me with this."

Siobahn patted my shoulder and turned me around, walking with me back towards my van. Leon was standing next to his open door, watching us.

"Thank you for letting me know it got this bad. It's our fault, we should have taken action before now. But don't worry, we will take care of everything now. You two should get on the road and go home. Take care of yourselves and try to go back to the world out there."

"So, no one else will be hurt?"

"Absolutely not."

"And, none of those monsters will get away from this valley?"

"I promise. That's the whole reason we return here every

year. We don't want the world to have them rampaging through it."

We were nearly at the van. Leon was back inside now, leaning forward to watch us through the windscreen.

"How am I supposed to go back to the world when I know that monsters like that are out there?" I asked. I was imagining something like Finn stalking through the alleys of the city, leaping upon unsuspecting passers-by.

"Try not to worry. I think there is something about this time and this place that makes the transformation possible. I have never heard of any of these monsters turning up out there, even before we started doing the rituals here ." She waved a hand towards the hills that surrounded the valley. "And the world is full of scary things that are more important for you to worry about, like bosses and traffic and war."

We were next to my door and she stopped, turning me to face her. She leaned in to hug me.

"I know that this is a lot, but you've never had to worry about any of this affecting you before you came to the festival, and I swear that you'll never have to worry about it again. Again, my friends and I know what to do with these creatures."

I climbed into the driver's seat. Leon was watching us with a puzzled expression. I wondered what my face looked like. From inside I felt as though the world was upside down.

"It's going to be okay," repeated Siobahn. "Thank you for telling me about this attack."

"Thank goodness she believed you. Do you think she will be able to do something?" my husband asked as I reversed the van away from Siobahn and turned it around.

"Yes. She said that they know about the werewolves and they do something to restrain them, and they know how to deal with them so no-one is hurt."

"What?" Leon looked as though he had been hit in the stomach and the air driven from his lungs.

"I know. We can talk about it while we drive home. For now, I want to get out of this valley."

Soon we saw the small shack that had greeted us on our arrival. Someone was sitting on a chair outside the shack, in the dark.

As we rolled past, heading towards the narrow dirt lane that wound up the hillside, the figure stood and turned to watch us. I held my breath and watched the rear view mirror. The figure watched us until the van turned a corner and I couldn't see him anymore. I let my breath go.

We drove up the winding road in the dark, heading towards sealed roads, streetlights, and civilization. Somewhere ahead of us lay the world we were familiar with, a world with simple expectations, a world where people tried to fit in. It was a world that we had tried to get away from, just for a while. We wanted to let ourselves be who we really were, and the festival has seemed like such a good place to do that.

I thought of Finn, who had been a monster, who hid a beast behind his smile, a beast that attacked innocent people. I was horrified to think of what might have happened to the man who Finn had been chasing when Leon and I saw him.

As I drove I reached over to grip Leon's hand, wincing as my arm pulled against the cuts beneath the makeshift bandage. We were returning to a mundane world with the knowledge that there was something terrible that lay just beneath the surface. I wondered how good Siobahn and her friends were. How well would they protect the others at the festival? Leon squeezed my hand back. Together we would have to figure out how to navigate through the world with this new understanding.

"Looks like Daph and Dai are on the way," said Leon, glancing over his shoulder. "I just saw their car come around the edge of the hill." I saw the glow of headlights wash past the bush beside us as we drove.

"Thank goodness," I said. The sooner we were home, and

able to unpack everything that had happened with our friends, the better.

A cry rose between the dark hills behind our cars.

"Was that a peacock?" asked Leon.

"I hope so."

THE END

You can keep informed of any new writing by A. J Richards by emailing author.ajrichards@gmail.com

ACKNOWLEDGMENTS

After writing my first novel (Crown Your Head With Ivy) that included more spice than my usual attempts, I made some discoveries. One; my style lies more along a horror spectrum than a straightforward romance. Crown Your Head made more than one reader blink in surprise at how it began to turn near the end. This inspired a massive change in cover style, to better communicate the type of story I was telling.

Two; it's fun writing saucy scenes! I got a kick out of trying to find new ways to describe those moments, and thinking of ways to allow those moments to happen that felt like they added to the story. And so, I decided to do it all again.

This time I let myself drift away from trying to meet genre expectations that I wasn't really sure of. I am in more comfortable territory this time around, and I hope that came through as you read it.

As always, I have to mention the incredible support and encouragement of my friend Steff. She's a very successful author, and I would have done absolutely nothing without her prodding and pointing me forward. If you enjoyed this novel in any way, I am sure you would love at least one of her many many books, to be found at www.steffanieholmes.com

I gave this book to Kat to edit, with trepidation. She has been an outstanding editor for all of my writing efforts, but as I drift more and more into horror-style writing she gets less and less keen to read through it! I am hoping that she was comfortable with the balance of sexy and scary in this book.

For festival accuracy, I asked Leanne to give a late draft a go. She is not to blame for anything that doesn't feel right about the Pandaea, I'm just a terrible listener!

Finally, as always, my partner Andy is an inspiration and my stronger supporter. Thank you for helping me get the ending to this right!

ABOUT THE AUTHOR

A. J. Richards lives north of Auckland in New Zealand with their partner, their two daughters, and a small menagerie of household animals. The whole family loves when A. J.'s eldest daughter visits too.

They grew up as a voracious reader of science-fiction and fantasy, often to the annoyance of their unheeded family. Becoming an author was a childhood dream, alongside being a paleontologist, or a rock star.

You can keep informed of any new writing by A. J. Richards by emailing author.ajrichards@gmail.com

www.ingramcontent.com/pod-product-compliance
Lightning Source LLC
Chambersburg PA
CBHW020651120726
47906CB00001B/222